Leah Starr's Revenge

Leah Starr's
Revenge
Vol. 1

A Novel By:

~BoSsWRiTeR~

Founder & President

of

BossWriterPublishing©2012
Tallahassee, Florida.

ISBN-10: 2525371836
ISBN-13: 978-2525371834
BISAC: Mystery/Suspense

ISBN-10: 2-525-37183-6
ISBN-13: 978-2-525-37183-4

Library of Congress Control Number: 2012911513

Printed in the United States of America
Author: Montice "BoSsWRiTeR" Harmon
Cover Design/Graphics: Wilken Tisdale
Associated Editor: Latoya Williams
Editor-in-Chief: Keshia M. Jones
Photography: Joshua Limens

Published by BossWriterPublishing©2012
Tallahassee, Florida 32301-32304
Printed in the United States of America

Prologue:

Leah Starr's Revenge is a riveting story that reads at a pace faster than the pages can be turned. Detective Leah Starr survived intense tragedy when she was just fourteen. A prominent mafia family murdered her parents, leaving Leah devastated and alone. She confronts her most frightening issues in *Leah Starr's Revenge*, right down to the morbid realization that her only way out will be paved with blood.

As Leah matured, her heart grew colder towards the career killers who murdered her parents. Now, her mind is made up that these punks have to pay, and at twenty-one, she has the body, brains, and soul of a woman primed for revenge. With her partner, Life Parker, a mysterious figure on the run, she avenges her parents' deaths by catching every living being who was affiliated with the mafia family.

ONE

My Life

Leah Starr:

I am one of the world's hardest women that have ever walked the face of this earth. According to whom, you ask? Well, I'll let you be the judge of that. However, I am not here to talk about that today. I am enraged and full of pain. My parents were murdered in the middle of one cold summer night. My father was a grounded mobster working for this punk ass mafia, run by Sammy Dresser, the boss man. Before my time, my father pushed millions of drugs into the United States, and took anyone's life if told to do so.

However, as my father got older and wiser, the game became old. He wanted to stop and live a normal life, so we moved away from the city into a little town outside of New Mexico. Everything was going well until one summer night – a night in the year of 1998, to be exact.

My father heard a big bang in the living room of our home. I remember him telling my mother and me to stay inside the room. There was silence when my father walked out, and minutes later, my mother and I heard lots of tussling. My father screamed loudly and my mother grabbed her pistol and went after him. Before leaving the room, she told me to hide in a secret spot that they had prepared if anything went wrong. Now, to this day, my gut tells me my father knew these people would come for him. After my mother left the room, she never returned. I stayed in hiding while these people ransacked the house. After hours of searching, it stopped, and they finally left. I was so afraid. I did not move a muscle. I later cried myself to asleep. When I awoke, I came out of my hiding spot, checking things out. I saw no sign of my parents.

I walked around looking for them, hoping I would find them alive. However, as I searched, I suddenly noticed someone's shadow. I quickly hid behind a wall, blocking my body from being seen. I peeked and there stood a young man who looked only a couple of years older than I was. When he turned his head, I ran. As I ran, I could hear him calling for me to stop. I kept running until two large objects tripped me.

"Oh no!" I screamed, falling over two dead bodies in the hallway-- it was my mother and father. At this time, I was in total shock! I could not breathe.

I could not think. My eyes were wide open. I tried screaming but could not. The shit was so emotional -- my loved ones were lying in front of me, dead. The young man, then, started getting closer to me. He reached down and grabbed my shoulder.

"Get away from me!" I screamed.

"No, I'm not here to hurt you. I'm here to help," he said as he reached out his hand.

I thought to myself, *he must be trying to help, or else this fool would have killed me by now. And why would the killer still be lurking around the crime scene?* I reached out my hand and he grabbed it, pulling me to my feet.

"Are you okay?" he asked in a friendly tone.

"Yes, I'm fine, but my parents aren't," I cried out.

He told me it was alright and then told me his name. I will never forget the look on his face.

"My name is Life Parker," he said as he smiled at me.

Strange, but I felt so safe now. He was around 160 pounds, tall with a muscular build, and with eyes of bolder. He was very attractive and dark-skinned like a Milky Way chocolate bar. He looked a lot older than eighteen years old.

He held me close and walked me next door to a neighbor's house. He called the police and then took off. Before he left, I asked him why he had to go, but he did not tell me. I still wonder from time to time. After he left, police and investigators arrived, asking me all type of questions I did not have the answers to.

1998 was a crazy year for me. Family and Children services quickly placed me into foster care. I went from family to family. It was hard because I did not know any family of my own but my mother and father. The system could not find any of my family members, or at least ones who would be willing to take me in.

My birthday was on May 14, 2001. I was about to graduate from high school; everything was still a shock to me. One day, I got a visit from an old friend.

"Hey, young lady," a voice called for me.

I turned to see who it was, but I was confused. I did not recognize the person calling me, so I kept walking. I thought it was an investigator or one of those fools who killed my parents coming after me.

"Stop, Leah Starr!" he shouted.

"What do you want?" I asked rudely.

"You don't know, I mean, remember me?" he laughed.

"No, I don't. I don't recall ever seeing you."

He walked closer to me and whispered in my ear. "I'm Life Parker."

My heart began to beat faster. I thought for sure I was going to faint.

"Life, where have you been? I've been looking for you."

"Living my life . . . what's been good with you?" he asked me in the sexiest tone.

"Living my life as well. It's been three years since the death of my parents."

An emotional glare came across both of our faces.

"Still no details on who might've had anything to do with it?" he asked.

I stood there shaking my head no. Then, all of a sudden, I noticed an unmarked police car sitting across the street watching us as we spoke.

"Hey, why are the cops scoping us out?"

Life slowly turned his head to see, and when he did, the lights came on and the car sped towards us. Life took off running.

"Life, stop!" I screamed, but he did not stop. When the officers got out of the car, they ran up to me.

"Are you okay, Ms. Starr?"

"I'm fine . . . what's going on?" I asked the officer, confused.

The officer explained that Life Parker was a fugitive on the run for armed robbery and a few murders, including the death of my parents. I could not believe what he was telling me.

"I don't believe he had anything to do with my parents' death . . . it can't be true," I told the officer.

However, they showed me every single detail that tied Life Parker to the death of my parents.

All day and night, I thought hard about what the officer told me. I only had one more week in school and would be starting college the following week. I had too much on my hands, plus the fact the police reported to my foster parents that I connected with my parents' killer. I told them Life Parker saved my life that day.

At this point and time in my life, all I could think about was protecting myself by learning all I needed to know about the law. Soon after graduation, I enrolled in a small tech school for investigation. It only took me two and a half years to complete. I graduated in 2004 and moved to the San Francisco police department and investigated there. At only nineteen years old, I became one of the best in my field. Even though I could not carry a gun just yet, I still did not play the radio. They kept me in the lab most of the time, only until I was ready and old enough to get out there and take on the bad guys face-to-face.

I investigated only five cases during my time there. Oakland Bay had many criminals and I was getting them off the streets case by case. Two years passed and I was ready to take on the streets of San Francisco. I got my first pistol; an all-black Gloc nine. Being twenty-one made a big difference in my life. The department honored me with two medals for my success in closing all cases I was granted. I made good money in investigation; it became a part of my daily routine. However, most of the time, I felt that something was missing, and an old friend brought it to my attention two and a half years after his return.

It was September 10, 2005. I was tired and had had a long day at work. I was working on this puzzling case. After work, I went by Hardees to grab a bite to eat. It was damn near dark. While waiting at the drive-thru, I noticed a familiar face.

"Hey you, come here!" I shouted.

The person stared at me with pure evil in his eyes, as if he wanted to rip my heart out of my chest. My heart dropped into my lap. I never saw so such hatred written across someone's face before. He continued walking, as if he never noticed me. After receiving my food, I circled around the building once more, but saw no sign of him. I thought I was losing it.

Maybe I was, but I know what I saw. I took the long way home. It helped ease my mind and took away the stress. I lived in a small, two-bedroom condominium, and I only paid a grand a month. The neighborhood was quiet and wasn't much crime.

Soon as I got inside, I took a long hot bath, or at least tried. My phone rang as soon as I sat in the tub.

"Hello!" I answered.

Damn, it was my boss. He needed me at the station five minutes earlier than I'd usually arrive.

"Sure, sir. I'll be there."

He bothered me so much. However, I get my way and days off whenever I request them. After my conversation with Lt. Terry, I jumped back in the tub and relaxed.

"Hmm, this here is more like it. Peace."

Everything was right until my doorbell rang, scaring the shit out of me.

"Who in the hell could this be?" I said aloud. "Hold on. I'm coming!"

I shouted as the bell continued to ring.

I got out of the tub, put on my robe, and quickly ran to the front door, hoping whoever it was would not ring my bell again. I looked out the peephole and didn't see anyone standing at the door. Something was wrong. I took three steps away from the front door, quickly grabbing my holster. I pulled my pistol out, making sure it was loaded and ready to fire. I did not have anything on underneath my robe, so I did not go outside.

"Who is it?" I shouted out, but I didn't get a response. I did not worry. I just continued my bath. I was not up for any games at this time of the evening. While resting in my hot bubble bath, I heard a cracking sound outside my window as I bathe. I thought for sure someone was standing outside my window watching me bathe.

For about three minutes, the noise ceased. So, I continued my bath, thinking maybe it was a bird or some type of animal playing around my window. Suddenly, someone knocks on my window. I quickly jumped up, but when I realized I was butt naked, I sat back down.

"Leah, open up," a man shouts..

It sounded like an old man --maybe Lt. Terry? I got up and put on my robe with my pants underneath, grabbing my pistol from the counter.

"Whoever you are, I'll blow your brains out!" I shouted.

"Please, don't shoot me. It's Life."

My heart started racing even more. When he told me who he was, I did not want to let him into my house. Nevertheless, I knew there were questions I needed to ask him, and I wanted answers, too. I told him to meet me at the front door. I was not letting him in through my window. I walked slowly downstairs, thinking hard about the decision I was about to make. Questions came and left my mind.

What if the police was right about Life having something to do with my parents' death? Was he here for something very valuable?

The thoughts flashed in and out of my head. I still had my nine in my hand, just in case he did something stupid. When I opened the door, there he stood, out of breath.

"What do you want?" I asked as I snapped back to reality. "Matter of fact, come in with your hands up," I said, aiming my pistol directly between his eyes. He slowly walked in and noticed my coat.

"Oh, so you're Fed now? Nice career choice, Leah," he said, grinning.

"Cut the bullshit, Life . . . why are you here?" I asked him with my pistol in his face.

Life told me he wanted to help me and explained that he had leads on the mobsters who killed my family. When he mentioned that to me, rage rose from within and came quickly across my face. I got so angry.

"What do you mean, Life? And why should I believe you?" I asked him. He looked at me as if he did not understand my new attitude toward him.

"What's wrong with you, Leah? Besides, do you have a choice?" he asked me, laughing.

"As a matter of fact, I do. I can blow your brains out and become a hero for taking down a fugitive," I said, returning the smile.

"So, I see you're believing the lies they're telling you."

I could not help but to go off on his ass. There must have been some truth to it for him to know the cops told me all there was to know about him being a fugitive.

"You're standing here, in my house, telling me you have leads to my parents' death. Why should I believe you, Life? I don't even know you, and when I ask, you always run away."

"Well, you always catch me at a bad time," Life replied.

"Now you're here and you're not going anywhere. I got questions and I want answers to them!"

Tears fell down my cheeks. I was so upset. If what the cops said about Life was true, he played me hard, and at any given moment, I could easily pull the plug on his games -- and his life. Envy filled my heart. I wanted justice and was going to get it.

"Please trust me, Leah," Life said as he walked towards me. "And put the gun down."

"No, please back away from me and turn around," I told him.

As he did, I placed handcuffs on him and told him to sit on the sofa. I was nervous. I did not know what to believe. I paced back and forth and I could feel Life staring at me.

"Leah, talk to me," Life whispered.

"Shut up, Life. I'm asking all the questions. All I need for you to do is answer them."

He was not going to talk me out of this. I asked him about the day I saw him in our home -- the morning I discovered my parents' dead bodies.

"Leah, I was ordered to kill your parents, but I couldn't. So they did it themselves."

"Don't fucking lie to me!" I shouted in rage, placing my nine to his forehead. He looked me dead in the eyes and told me to believe his every word and to trust him. He then explained to me that he was my only resource to finding those creeps. I held Life in handcuffs for an hour before taking them off. I was not afraid anymore. If he tried me, I was taking him out.

We discussed the people he once worked for, and from that moment forth, I had my mind set on one thing and one thing only: killing everyone of those sons of bitches dead. Someone had to pay, and Life was about to take all nine for them that night. I could taste the blood of the maniacs who took my family away from me.

All night, Life just stared at me. He was even better looking now than before. I guess the saying is true; age makes a difference in people's lives. However, the pain that came along with Life aged him well. My life started on this manhunt for revenge. My mission began with the streets of San Francisco for all the answers I knew were there. Moreover, I was not alone this time; it was now me and my new partner-in-crime, Life Parker.

TWO

Nightmares

The next day, I had to be at the office early, so I did not sleep all night. I was tired and stressed out, but ready for whatever. My boss was Lt. Terry. He was a tall, lanky, African-American in his mid-forties. Talked much shit. However, he was very kind. I loved him. He treated me as his own. He understood me and was there at the time of my parents' death.

I arrived at the station very early. As I parked, Lt. Terry stood outside his unmarked car waiting for me to arrive, smoking a cigar.

"Hey, Leah," he called me.

"Hi Lt. Why so early?"

He did not respond; he just stood there.

"Why am I getting the silent treatment?" I asked. I knew something was not right. "Come on, Lt. What's wrong?"

He turned to the side and handed me a manila envelope.

"What's this?" I asked.

"Just open and read it."

I knew if I wanted answers, I had to open it and read it. I was highly surprised to see records on suspects related to my parents' death.

"Oh, no . . . it can't be."

There were pictures of my father's best friend, Tom Bernard. He tried adopting me once or twice since the death of my parents. It threw me off track. Lt. wanted me to pay Bernard a visit; he was involved in a murder out in Vegas. My job was to take him down, and that would be hard to do -- only because Tom knew I was a cop.

He was like an uncle to me, but I felt, at that moment, very confused about everything. I would politely run in his house and place my nine in his mouth. I really did not care after the fact of knowing Tom knew the foolish punks my father worked for. He could have had something to do with my parents' death. I told Lt. I would get right on it.

Tom stayed in L.A, so I had a long ride ahead of me. Life called me as I was leaving town. He wanted to check in on me to make sure no one had kidnapped me. I wanted to dog his ass out, but told him I was grown and that I would be okay. It is somewhat funny because he did not get mad when I told him I did not need anyone watching me. I told him I would get back at him as soon as I returned.

When I arrived in L.A, I met with Paul Griffin, who was investigating bits and pieces of the case. He was a tall white man who disgusted me with his lip licking; he was no LL Cool J. Paul was about forty or older with a kind spirit and always smiling when he saw me.

"Hey, Ms. Starr. Boy, it's sure nice to see you."

So rude he was, looking at me like I was a piece of meat that he wanted desperately.

"Mr. Griffin, I'm here to review the case on Tom Bernard."

"Well, Ms. Starr, information on him has been turned over to your station in San Francisco," he told me.

"I didn't come all this way for nothing. Plus, he's here in Los Angeles. So, why wouldn't a copy of his files be here?"

"I'm not sure. But I do know you came for a reason," he said, laughing.

"Oh, yeah? What reason might that be?" I asked, looking at the fat fuck.

"Me!" he said cheerfully.

I just looked at him and told him to grow a cock, and that I was not into fat people. I really hurt his feelings.

"Have a nice day, Ms. Starr."

I had to move on to the next step, and that was finding Uncle Tom. I went to one of his hangouts, which was an old bar on West Central. It stayed empty; only familiar people were allowed inside. As I walked in, all eyes were on me. Guys left and right were trying to get with me. Oh yeah -- by the way, your girl is fine. Five-foot-nine with long, black hair, which is all mine, and thick in all the right places. Guys really liked watching me from behind. My eyes are hazel grey, attracting many men with their boldness.

"Damn, baby girl! Give me some time," one guy shouted out at me.

"I just did," I told the ugly guy, walking away from him while his friends laughed.

"What can I do for you, pretty young thing?" a hot bartender with a nice smile said.

"Sweetie, you know nobody supposed to be in here unless invited."

"Kick her ass out!" the ugly guy shouted.

"Shut the hell up, nut face," I replied, pissed off. He jumped up and tried to hit me. I quickly grabbed his hand, body slamming him to the floor.

"Don't fuck with me, hear me?" I screamed, twisting his hand. He shouted as confirmation that he understood.

"Come on, baby . . . let up on him," the bartender asked me. After I let him loose, he told the guy to leave.

"Now, back to you, Ms. Kick Ass. What can I do for you?"

I was somewhat shy; he really got to me with his smile. However, I played it off.

"I'm looking for a friend of mine," I said, looking around the joint.

"What's his name?"

"What make you think it's a he?"

He took a deep breath and looked around.

"Look around, miss lady -- nothing but hard legs in here," he smiled.

I turned my head and cracked a smile. After all the bullshitting around, I told him I was looking for Tom.

"Tommy the Cat?"

"Is that what you all call him?" I asked. I never heard my father call Tom that. Slim told me Tom only came in on Tuesdays and Fridays, but lately, he had not been around.

"Funny, huh?" I asked him, speaking like a true investigator. I had to find more information on this 'Tommy the Cat'. he gave me his info. Victor was his name. He was about six feet, attractive, dark-skinned with a nice smile. Sure, I wanted to get to know him. He was very respectful and nice. Made me wonder what a guy like him was doing in a place like that. Later on, I would find out.

After exchanging information, I left to get a bite to eat at Jack N The Box. I never watched my weight, only because I never gained any. I ate so much fast food, one would think I'd be over two hundred pounds. I drove around town searching for Tom, but had no clue to his whereabouts.

An hour passed and I was tired of driving around searching for him. So I thought I'd take a stroll down memory lane. When I got to my destination, I wondered why I was even there. I got out and walked up to what was once my home. I sat on the steps for a while, thinking of my parents. I became emotional and bad thoughts began to overshadow the good memories that were now a nightmare. It was as if I was dreaming all over again of that night that changed my life forever. I had to get away from this place.

Two years ago, I owned the deeds. I was not sure if I would keep it any longer. All the bad memories I could not handle. I finally got up and left. As soon as I got back into town, I got a room. I needed rest.

Before I fell asleep, everything was perfect. That was until this really awful image of someone coming after my family and me appeared. I tossed and turned all night, dreaming I was running for my life. It was so real. I could feel the rain falling and their footsteps coming towards me. As I got closer to my parents' home, I saw this guy standing ahead of me, reaching out his hand for me to take. I soon realized it was Life. But just before I grabbed his hand, Tom came out of nowhere, grabbing me and snapping my neck.

I woke up in a cold sweat, very nervous and terrified. I got up, poured a cup of cold water, and sat on the end of my bed thinking. I could not put it together. My mind went blank. I got my things together for checkout and went back to the bar.

When I pulled up, Victor was coming out. I was distressed and he could tell. I jumped out and approached him with my Baby Phat jeans hugging my bottle-shaped hips. I could tell he liked what he saw.

He licked his lips and smiled as I walked his way.

"What's wrong, Miss Lady?"

"I really need to talk with Tom."

He seemed as if he knew where to find Tom, but did not want to tell me.

"Please, Victor. I need to know."

I knew he would ask why next. I told him he owed me money and I needed to get it from him. He insisted on giving me the money, but I did a little more convincing. I had to find Tom, no matter what.

"Okay, I'll take you to him. Come ride with me -- your car will be safe here."

I was not sure that was a good idea, and if Tom told Victor I was a cop, I'll have my own shit to drive back in and not be out because I am a fucking cop. I did not think Victor was a bad guy, but a person's personality can be deceiving.

For a minute, I was not sure if Victor knew where to go until we turned into what I thought was a graveyard. It was very dirty and isolated. We drove down a long dirt road that led to a white two-story house. Victor parked and got out.

"He lives here!" Victor shouted, pointing at the house.

"Okay, thanks."

I reloaded my gun before exiting the car when suddenly, Tom came running out the door to greet Victor.

"Hey, my boy," he shouted, hugging and kissing on Victor.

I could tell from the look on Victor's face that he was not with the mushy shit. However, it was what they did.

"Wait a minute . . ." Tom paused for a second, looking at me from a distance. "Leah . . . Leah Starr?"

"Yeah, it's me -- the one and only."

"Come to me, Leah, my child," Tom said, extending his hand out for mine.

I did not want him touching me, but I had to play it cool.

"Hey, Tom," I said with a smile.

He took a step back and I quickly placed my hand on the gun resting on my hip.

"You look just like your mother -- long hair, pretty grey eyes."

Everyone said I look like my mother; she had a medium build, with a nice bottle-shaped frame and a beautiful face. My complexion comes from my father, who was Native Indian and Cuban.

Tom invited me into his home. I thought for sure it would look as bad on the inside as it did on the outside, but Tom had it laid out like a player's pad.

"This is nice, Tom."

"Oh, you should see the others," he grinned, informing me that this was not his only spot. I did not care. I just wanted to know the truth. I wanted to know where I could connect with the head man in charge of Sammy's mafia family. We sat and discussed my concerns, and he told me all I needed to know about who I was dealing with and how dangerous they were. After gathering all I needed from Tom, I warned him about the police and asked him if he had anything to do with my parents' death. He paused and then looked at me with a strange expression.

"How could you ask me a question like that, kid?"

I stared at him, waiting on an answer. "Well, don't keep me waiting."

"No. I did not have anything to do with your parents' murder."

I then noticed Tom kept looking at my neck and wrist.

"What are you looking for?" I asked.

"Oh, nothing. Look, I got to go. I'll talk to you later," he said, leading me to the front door.

I knew Tom was hiding something from me, and I was going to find out one way or another. He denied the murders I asked him about. I had a warrant to lock him up, but I spared him, only because he gave me leads on my parents' death.

I had to get back to San Francisco to see what Life found and to ask him about Tom. I figured he knew something.

Soon as I got into town, I went by the station to drop Tom's files off to Lt. Terry and go meet Life. I was tired, but knew I would not be able to sleep at all. The dreams kept getting worse and worse, and I had to find a way to get them to stop. I figured, the only way was solving this murder case -- bringing justice to my family and peace of mind to myself. I had to catch those guys . . .

THREE

Trust Is Necessary

Thursday, 2005

Trust is necessary, and I knew I had to have it in order to roll with Life. The next morning, I got up and called him. He spent the night at an old motel down on Anderson Street. I told him I would meet him there because we had to discuss some real shit dealing with trust issues.

I arrived at the rundown motel around 7:15 He was standing outside waiting for me. I sat in my car and watched him walk in front of my car. I cracked a smile at him as our eyes met. He walked up to my car and rested his muscular arms in my window.

"Hey, Life Parker,"

"Please, call me Life," he grinned.

"Okay, I really need to have a word with you." He gave me a concerned look. "Sure!"

He jumped in and we went for a ride.

"Now, Life, I've been knowing you for a while now, and one thing I can say I've been foolish on is trusting you."

He laughed at my statement.

"What's so funny?" I asked. I thought for sure I was being very clear.

"No reason. Just listening. Please finish," he requested very humbly.

"Well, I need your help on this case."

"You know I told you I would help. That is the only reason I came to you. Leah, I made you a promise, and I'm going to keep it."

Now, that was what I needed to hear from Life. I knew he had my back. Nevertheless, one thing I have learned along the way in life is that trust comes with tag-a-longs.

"There's just one thing I need from you," Life said.

"Sure, what's that?"

"I want you to help me clear my name."

I made him a promise I would clear his name, but knew now was not a good time to do that.

Later that morning, Life showed me one of the biggest drug spots in San Francisco. I would have not guessed it would be underneath an old family-owned clothing store from the late 1800's. It closed down three years ago after the death of its last owners. Word had it, Stephen Usher got a hold of it and turned it into a drug and whore house.

"How did he get his hands on it?" I asked.

"Not sure, but before his grandparents died, he was very close to them."

Stephen was around my age and very nasty and disrespectful. He treated women like shit and did not see a thing wrong with beating them into a coma. He dated a friend of mine through high school, and now she was a crack head and prostitute.

We arrived at 7:45 and there were people posted all around the store. They looked like trouble, so I grabbed my gun, making sure it was fully loaded.

"Hold on -- they're going to check us before going in. So leave the gun," Life whispered.

I did not want to get caught slipping and end up dead. He convinced me, though, to leave my nine.

"So what now, Life?" I asked.

"You trust me, right?"

I did not say a word. I just turned my head and looked away.

"Wait here, then," he told me.

"Oh, no. You're not going to leave me here," I said as I jumped out the car.

As I walked alongside Life, I noticed the guys grabbing their guns.

"Life, why didn't I bring my gun again?" I asked.

"Guys, we don't want any trouble." Life shouted.

When they realized who he was, they welcomed him. Right then and there, I knew everything was cool. Life chatted with the guys for a second.

"Life," I whispered anxiously as if to say it was time to go inside.

The person next to Life looked at me strangely.

"She's with me; she's okay, man," Life said, taking the person's attention off of me.

I was not sure why we were visiting Stephen. I just knew it had to be for a good reason. When we got inside, the first person I laid eyes on was Stephen, and I was the first person he noticed walking inside.

"Leah!" he shouted.

"Stephen!" I replied.

Life saw that we were old friends. When Stephen walked away, Life asked if we were old lovers. I told him it was nothing, then grinned as if I'd lied.

After standing for about three minutes, Stephen called Life to the back. Life told me to stand in one spot and not go anywhere. That was one thing I had a problem with -- taking orders from a man. Therefore, as he disappeared into Stephen's office, I walked off.

Searching around the old building, I was surprised to see Stephen left the place as his grandparents had it. As I walked further down the hallway, I noticed a sign written in marker that read, "**DO NOT ENTER!**" I was curious, so I walked inside and did a little investigating. I came across some money and two pistols. I knew the money had to be drug money. I wish I could bust his ass for what he once did to my friend, but I can forgive and forget. I noticed a file cabinet and knew it was locked. I was good at picking locks, but before I could even try, I heard two voices coming towards the room, so I quickly hid. The door opened and it was Life and Stephen.

"So Life, what is a girl like Leah doing tagging along with a thug like you?" Stephen grinned while walking towards the cabinet.

"Well, she's helping me."

"With what?"

"She needs some cash and wanted to hit some licks."

Stephen looked at Life in disbelief, but laughed it off.

The two talked about guns, sex, and money. I was getting tired of hearing them go on and on about useless issues. Suddenly, Stephen gave Life a large amount of money, along with a black bag and some files. I sat and watched the two shake hands in agreement and they left. Once they were gone, I searched through the cabinet and found all type of files. Stephen had everything, except what I needed to know. When I was done searching, I saw a gold and platinum pistol 38 magnum and I had to have it. It was brand new, fully-loaded, and ready to shoot. I put it down in my black boots and left the room.

As I walked out, I saw Stephen standing only a couple feet down the hallway. I thought for sure he noticed me, but he did not. I quickly ran three doors down to the restroom, and walked back out into the lobby of the store.

"It took you long enough," Life said as he and Stephen stood waiting for my return.

"I had to use it really bad."

Stephen just stared at me and walked off. He freaked me out. I was ready to pull that thirty-eight out and blow his fucking head off. Life and I left the building. Everyone who was outside was now gone. I found that to be very strange. I told Life that something was funny about the area we were in.

We went back to my place. I had to know what was in those files and what Life was carrying in that black bag.

"What did he give you?" I asked.

"You know damn well what it is, Leah."

I told him I did not know, but Life was no fool; he knew I was in

Stephen's office hiding. I was shocked when he told me he saw me. The only thing I could do was smile. Life opened the bag and showed me guns along with many bullets.

"Ready, huh?" I asked.

"What do you think?"

I cracked another smile. We read files containing information on the mob family my father worked for.

"How could your father trust these people?" Life asked me.

I had no answer. I wanted to ask him the same question, but I guess I would be sounding as if I was being funny. However, loyalty is nothing when you lack respect and dignity for self.

The information threw me off a little; the main man was locked up. I knew I had to pay him a visit and Life thought that would be a wise decision, also. I called the Los Angeles State Prison and set up an appointment to see the motherfucker who had my parents murdered.

Sammy Dresser, the head man in charge and leader of Los Angeles mafia gang was serving life in prison for the murder of his second wife, Loretta Dresser, and best friend, Danny Jock. He caught the two messing around behind his back. Sammy was now in his fifties and rich from all the fraudulent activities he got away with on the streets of San Francisco and L.A. He was convicted in 2002. I had to see him in person and knew it would be hard, being that he was the reason for my parents' death.

I could not believe it, but I got the okay to see him whenever I pleased . . . until death row. They were trying to give his ass the chair, but he kept appealing his cases with high-paid lawyers. Sammy was trying his best to beat the death penalty.

Later that day, I went by the state prison. I was so anxious to see his face. He was someone I had not seen in decades. I did not remember exactly what he looked like, and the pictures on file really threw me off, being that he was now old and looked a lot different.

I was nervous and did not really know why. All I could think of was Sammy telling me all I needed to know about my parents' death. Sammy sat in a room that had only a table and two chairs.

"Sammy Dresser!" I shouted.

He looked up, blinded by the bright light that shined above his face – he could not make out who I was.

"What do you want?" he shouted. I walked over and explained who I was to him.

"I know you don't know me, but soon, you'll know and see my face a lot."

Before I could finish, he told me he knew who I was and mentioned that one day I would come. Tears filled my eyes and I was convinced he killed my parents. But then again, he did not have too. That's why I needed to know who.

"So, you know why I'm here?" I asked him nervously.

"Yes, your parents were killed seven years ago, and now you want answers," he said, grinning.

I ran up to him and grabbed his neck, trying my best to choke him to death.

"Tell me who killed my parents!" I shouted.

He looked me in my eyes fearlessly.

"Leah Starr -- that's your name, right?" he asked me.

"Yes. Leah Starr."

"Mathew and Loran Starr," he said with a nasty grin.

He took a deep breath and explained that my father was a great worker who was always on time doing what he needed to do to take care of our home.

"Your father was honest, truthful, and loyal. However, it all changed the day he left without telling me anything. I told him it would be a mistake. You know the game, Leah -- once a mobster, always a mobster. Either kill or be killed. I gave him a fair chance to leave after hours of convincing me he wanted the best for you all. I told him I would allow him to leave on one condition."

"What was that, Sammy?" I asked.

"Steal me the pink Diamond of Romance," he said with a smile. "I see you don't know what that is."

I shook my head no.

"It's a necklace, with a real diamond, worth millions and millions of dollars."

It all came back to me that my mother wore a pink diamond necklace, but I never knew where she hid it.

"Well, he did just that, and ran away with the necklace," Sammy said, throwing his fist down on the table. I asked him why he was so angry. He explained that the diamond would have saved his marriage; he blamed my father for his wife's adulterous actions.

"She admired that necklace," he said. "I put a search out for your father, not a hit. I swear, I only sent for his return."

"Why should I believe you? There's no coming back for my parents," I said, full of emotion. I could not hold back my tears.

"Stop crying! It's not going to bring them, my wife, or my life back," he shouted.

I did not give a fuck about him or his wife. I just wanted answers.

"Who did you send after my father?"

He told me a cat named Louis, one of his friends. He told me Louis would do anything for him, even to this day. However, he reminded me quickly that he did not tell Louis to kill my father -- only return him with the diamond necklace. I asked Sammy how I could get in touch with Louis, but he just sat there. Sammy had issues; he told me to my face he was behind my parents' death. What could I do to him? He was already locked up and facing the death penalty.

Before I walked out of the room, he asked me about the necklace. He figured I knew where it was. I could not remember, but knew it was underneath that house somewhere. I thought hard, and realized I could use a couple of millions.

My next step was finding Louis; he was my only chance at knowing what took place outside my parents' bedroom that night. I called Life and asked him if he knew anything about Louis. I knew he was still around somewhere, and I felt Sammy would send him after me. Life was not sure of Louis, but knew a couple old cats around the way by that name.

After a discussion with Life, I took off to the station to get leads on all the men named Louis in our area.

"Leah, how far are you on the case?" Lt. Terry asked me.

I was not sure if I should tell him I was not working on Tom's case anymore.

"I need a little more time, Lt."

I did not tell him I stopped. I just needed him to know I was on a slow lead. During some research on the computer, two men named Louis Grant popped up on the screen, both around the ages of forty-five and forty-seven. I was not sure who was the right one, but I had to pay them both a visit. Life waited for me at my place. I knew that if I was going after the killers, I needed someone with me. When we arrived at the first Grant house, my mind was on revenge. I thought of killing him as soon as I asked him the questions no one seemed to have answers to. As we walked towards the front door, rage began to bottle up inside of me. I could not wait to see the guy who did everything for Sammy Dresser.

Life circled around the house while I knocked on the front door, but no one answered. I had my nine and the .38 that I stole from Stephen's store.

"Leah!" Life shouted.

"What is it?" I asked, running towards the backyard to find Life with a dead body lying on the kitchen floor.

"Oh my . . . looks like someone beat us to him."

I felt like someone slapped me in the face. I needed answers. Maybe Louis was not the killer and the real person came and knocked him off before we could get answers. But who knew we were coming? I figured Sammy sent someone to do the job, being that he was the only jerk who knew I would go looking for Louis. I was not sure, but for all I knew, this could've been the wrong Louis.

After the day was through, I sat and thought to myself about how Life was all I had and I needed him more than ever. Somewhere out there, the killer may have still been lurking around, waiting on me to make the wrong move and off my ass. Nevertheless, I would never go out without a fight and that was on my life!

FOUR

Is The Killer Still Out There?

Friday, 2005

On the way back to my place, I thought long and hard about Louis. I really wanted to hear what he had to say. But I was not lucky enough. I had to find a new lead. Louis was not the only person there that night who was withholding information.

Something was on Life's mind; he was quiet and that was not like him. He would have said something to me by now.

"Life, are you okay?"

"We need to take a trip," Life said.

He knew a couple of gang bangers out in Cleveland who would be able to help us out. I wasn't sure with what, but knew Life had an idea and I was down with it. Before I left, I needed to check out this other Louis Grant. My gut told me I needed to pay him a visit, also.

I went over to his place. It was not far from downtown. There were kids everywhere and adults sitting outside drinking and listening to music. In a very ghetto state of mind, all I could think about was if my people would ever make it out with a brighter future.

"Looks like they're having fun," I said to Life.

"Yeah, a good time," he said, laughing.

All the children in the neighborhood ran behind my car like we were there to save them. Life and I got out and walked to Louis Grant's door. Life called his friend Alex over to speak with him. After their conversation ended, Life gave me the okay to knock on the door. A man in his mid-twenties answered.

"Hey, is Louis Grant home?"

"No, he's not."

I knew he was lying by the way he responded, as if he knew I was the police. I told him to let Louis know his girlfriend came looking for him; he quickly changed stance.

"Oh, you're one of his hoes. He told me you were coming by to pick something up from him," he explained. I didn't understand, but this was my way inside, so I played along and walked in. He told me to have a seat and he'd be back in a second.

As I waited, I noticed pictures of this cat with different men. I was not sure if he worked with them or dealt with them on the down low. As I continue scoping these pictures out, I noticed someone I knew.

"Father," I shouted, realizing this was, in fact, *the* Louis.

My heart started racing out of control. I got up and grabbed the picture just before the young man walked back into the living room.

"I thought I told you to have a seat. Just like Louis's hoes -- don't know how to listen."

Before I knew it, he grabbed my hand, pulling me closer to him.

"Please stop," I begged him, giving him a fair chance to step away from me. Playing the innocent role, which made him more forceful, I told him to let go of me, but he would not. Therefore, without a choice, I punched him in his shit. He dropped the brown bag that he was holding and held his mouth. That young punk did not know what he was getting himself into.

"Bitch!" he shouted.

I kicked him in his testicles and he dropped to his knees crying. I grabbed the brown bag and ran out of the house.

"What happened?" Life asked me as I walked towards the car.

"Leah, talk to me." He grabbed me and looked into my eyes.

"Please remove your hands from me," I said, looking evilly into his eyes.

When he released me, I got into my car. Before pulling off, the young man came running out of the house screaming all types of nasty words at me. I wanted to get out and kick his ass, but there were little children standing out watching. I just took off and did not say a word to Life. Minutes later, he apologized to me for not being inside with me. I was not worried about that. I just wanted to find Louis Grant. I thought hard about that and focused more on the fact he was involved with the death of my parents.

"What's in the brown bag?" Life asked me. I was not sure myself, so I gave him the bag to look inside.

"Wow!" he said, pulling out a beautiful diamond necklace. It brought a smile to my face, bringing back old memories.

"That's my mother's necklace," I said. I could not do anything but think that Louis betrayed his partner-in-crime and kept the diamond for himself. Nevertheless, I did not understand why he would still be holding on to it after all this time. I knew Louis killed my mother because she was wearing the diamond necklace the same night she was murdered. I told Life we did not have to look any further for Louis; soon, he would be after us for the diamond. Life thought it would be best if I stayed the night with him, just in case they decided to pay me a visit. I refused his invitation. I wanted them to come looking for me.

Around 12:05 that afternoon, I phoned the prison and asked to speak with Sammy personally to tell him about the heist Louis played on him. He did not take it well, and deep inside, he knew something was not right about Louis. He told me Louis had been acting funny and not coming to see him like he normally would. I thought for sure that after Sammy was locked away, he would try to run what was once Sammy's empire.

He told me to give the diamond to his son. I quickly refused. No way was I giving anything that was left of my parents away to anyone. Suddenly, he hung up. He was highly upset because I refused to give the necklace to his family. I did not give a damn if he was mad. I had something he wanted. Not just that, but I had something Louis wanted, and I knew Sammy would send him after me next.

Later that day, I got word that Sammy was getting out. How, I did not know. But word was deep in the streets of his homecoming. Life was worried Sammy would come for me. I was not scared a bit. Him being free would be a dream come true for me. I wanted someone's blood, so why not that of the mastermind behind the plan that changed my life forever?

Life thought it would be a good idea if I hid the necklace somewhere safe. I had to find a place no one would ever think to look. I did not tell Life because money changes things and I did not need that coming between us. After stashing the necklace in a safe place, I drove around town thinking about everything that was happening. Soon, Louis would come for the diamond and I would be ready.

At 4:09 Lt. Terry phoned me pissed at the fact that I contacted Sammy Dresser. I asked him about Sammy's release, and he assured me it was a lie and Sammy would never see the light of day. I felt a lot safer, but knew something was not right. Lt. told me to get out of town and take a vacation to relieve tension. I wondered why he chose me. I only wanted justice for all, including myself. After I left the station, I did what I would always do when I arrived home -- TV., dinner, and a hot bath.

I was tired and needed rest, so I went to sleep. Life slept downstairs on the sofa. I knew I would be safe if I had someone to watch my back. Those damn dreams continued to control my thoughts. I had to stop them because they were getting worse. I was very nervous and afraid. I heard a crashing sound downstairs. I thought maybe Life was searching for something and could not find it. I slipped on my bedroom shoes and walked downstairs. It was dark and something told me to grab my gun, so I slowly went back upstairs to get it.

I peeped around the corner and saw someone looking through my blinds.

"Put your hands up!" I yelled just before the person took off running out my backdoor. Soon as I started running after him, I was suddenly knocked out cold. I had no idea what was going on.

When I awoke, I whispered Life's name as I saw him sitting across from me tied up. The room was full of clothes; but I could not recall where I was.

I could hear men talking, but could not quite get what they were saying, but I knew I had to get loose. I tried untying the rope around my wrist, but it was too tight. Life began to move, and I got his attention soon after.

"Where are we?" Life asked me in a painful tone.

I wished I knew the answer, but I did not. I looked around trying to figure it out, but had not a clue of my whereabouts. I asked him to untie himself. After trying for about three minutes, he finally broke loose. He ran over and untied me; my head was hurting so much I could barely stand. Life told me to get a grip of myself because we had to escape fast.

We heard someone coming, so we had to hide. While in hiding, I noticed they forgot to take the gun from my ankle. I grabbed it and aimed it at the door.

"What are you doing, Leah -- get somewhere and hide," Life whispered.

I could not hide any longer. I wanted whoever walked through that door to feel the pain I was feeling. The doorknob twisted and my hands poured with sweat and my face was bloody from the impact on the side of my head. I stood directly in front of the door, and soon as it opened, I let three rounds go -- two into the chest and one into the head. One guy hit the floor face first. The person behind him ran for cover. Life jumped up and ran towards the door. I covered his every move, making sure he was not shot. The guy on the outside got up and ran, so I quickly shot him, once in head.

"Who sent you?" I shouted to the punk as he begged for mercy. He was so afraid and speechless.

"Answer me!" I shouted, grabbing him by the shirt.

"Please, don't hurt me," he yelled.

"It's a little too late for mercy."

Life walked up and grabbed him by the neck, choking him. "Tell me who's behind this! Tell me right now," Life shouted.

He looked young -- around eighteen or nineteen. I noticed he had a gun on him, so I grabbed it. He gave in and told us Louis Grant sent them after us, as I expected. Their job was to kidnap and hold us until Louis came for us. Life wanted to stay and wait on Louis. So, we got the young guy's phone and told him to call Louis and tell him to hurry up.

"Hurry up, Louis," the boy said before hanging up.

We waited on Louis's arrival for thirty minutes, but still no sign of him. Life was getting impatient and was ready to leave. I agreed, so we tied the young boy up and took off. As we walked into the hallway, I quickly realized where we were.

"Look, we're in Stephen's store," I shouted.

Life looked around confused to why we were here.

"Why would we be here?" Life asked as we both eyed each other. "That son of a bitch. I'll kill him," he shouted.

Good thing he was not here right now, because I could see the hurt in Life's eyes as he repeatedly stated that Stephen and Louis would pay with their lives. We knew it would not be safe to go back to my place, so we crashed at his. He lived in an old-fashion one-bedroom studio apartment. It was messy, but I did not complain.

"So, Life, where do you think Stephen's at?"

"Probably somewhere causing trouble," Life responded with an evil look on his face. It was motivation for me because I knew he wanted these punks dead like I did.

I wanted Stephen so bad; he had answers to why we ended up in his store. Life was mad because he thought, for a change, he could trust Stephen, but loyalty is not worthy of everyone. Someone had to suffer. I called Lt. Terry and asked him for permission to get some protective wear from the station. He thought that would be a good idea and told me to be safe on my trip out of town. For a minute, I forgot what he had recommended. However, everything I wanted to know was here in town and parts of L.A.

Life and I went by the station and got everything we needed, along with armor. Just when I thought things could not get any worse, I got a call that Sammy Dresser had escaped from prison and that I needed to report to the scene. I dropped Life off and went to the crime scene.

"Return to me safely," Life said as he got out of the car.

"I will. Try to do the same for me, partner."

I met with Lt. at the scene where Sammy had escaped.

"So, the rumors were true. Sammy was getting released," he joked as I exited the car. I laughed along with him, knowing this was a serious matter. We had six dead officers, two injured, and a fugitive on the run.

"Looks to me Sammy was airlifted," I told Lt. He agreed as he walked away.

I figured there was nothing more for me to do but find this old coon. Lt. told me to put this case with the rest and follow up on them hourly.

"Leah, I trust that you will get this maniac before he commits more murders. We need everyone involved with his mafia family behind bars. We need them off the streets NOW," Lt. explained. I could see the worry in his eyes. He knew Sammy was a very bad man who did not deserve freedom, and it would be hell taking him down once he was on the streets. It took the police twenty-eight years to catch him the first time. Deep inside, I knew Lt. wanted me to put an end to Sammy's life, and I was down with that. I would put in extra work to bring him down.

It all came to me as I began searching through old files; maybe Sammy had something to do with Life and me getting kidnapped. In addition, Stephen knew everyone who worked for Sammy; now all I needed to do was find his lame ass and make him spill the beans and pay for what he did.

I wondered where Sammy could be hiding. I left the scene soon as Lt. said I could do so. On the way back to Life's place, I called him. Before I could tell him the bad news, he beat me to it.

"Damn . . . what are we going to do, Life?"

"What else? Find this wacko and put him back where he belongs."

"Why not six feet under?" I asked Life.

"That too. It's whatever you want to do, Leah."

I wanted all those fools dead -- no more playing around. It was my way, now. I had a plan to take them out, one by one. I knew for sure the same idiots who killed my parents were out to kill me now. Therefore, I had to step my game up and do whatever I had to do in order to withstand. Life taught me a lesson about surviving: "Show no mercy and no weakness. Only pain is what you will give." I was ready to bring it full force.

FIVE

Show No Mercy, Only Pain

Saturday 2005

I woke up early and left without notice. I had to find Stephen. Something bothered me all last night. I could not sleep from all the horrible nightmares. All I saw was Stephen's face grinning like the joker he was. I knew for sure he had a home out of state; plus the one in the L.A. area. I paid both homes a visit.

I left Life's crib around 6:45 I had a funny feeling someone was watching me. Soon as I got on the expressway, I noticed a black unmarked car following me. I sped up, trying to ditch the car, but it stayed behind me. I soon came across an exit and quickly got off. As I turned to exit, I slowed to see if this car was really following me. The black unmarked car was coming up on the ramp. I made a turn on Ellison St. and parked at a gas station. Something told me to remain inside the car, but then again, my gut told me to get the hell out. I grabbed my gun and black backpack, which held important information inside, and walked about a mile away from it, just in time to avoid the people in the unmarked car. Soon as the car turned inside the station, it parked next to mine. The car sat there for about three minutes, then backed up and pulled off. I watched them travel down the road and park.

Something did not seem right, so I ran across the street and used the payphone to call Life. All he wanted to know was where I was and to stand still until he arrived.

As much as I wanted these punk bitches myself, Life and I made a promise to take these fools down together. I figured he wanted revenge as much as I did. Moreover, at this moment, I knew Life had my back on everything. I ran back across the street to wait on Life. As soon as I laid eyes on my truck, it went up into flames, exploding.

"Damn," I said. These bastards were not playing around with me. I knew Sammy was behind this. The unmarked car backed up slowly and drove away. I had to make a move on them, so I ran up to a customer at the store and showed him my badge, got into his '97 pickup truck, and took off after them. I eased beside them, and I could tell they did not know I was following them. The person on the passenger side was on the phone with someone. I grabbed my high-tech device out of my black bag, put on my ear gear, and listened in on their conversation. The person was talking to Louis. They thought for sure I was inside my vehicle. Louis was excited that his boys got the job done. However, little did he know I was about to take them out for trying. I got so fucking angry that I ran into the side of their old crown Victoria that was once owned by an officer. The driver blew the horn and sped by me.

"What the hell is going on over there?" Louis asked the passenger.

"Some crazy driver hit our ride."

Louis told them to meet him over at Stephen's place -- just the crowd I needed to see. My cell phone was inside my truck, so I had no way of calling Life. I just knew it was about to go down.

When Life arrived at the Connor store, everything was in flames, including the building. Firefighters made it in time to stop the fire from reaching the gas pumps. When I got back, Life stood watching my truck in flames. He thought for sure I was inside. I parked at the store across the street and walked over where Life stood.

"Hey, you," I said, standing behind him.

I could tell he was relieved from the sound of my voice.

"Fuck! I thought you were . . ." He paused to hug me, and I felt loved. I had not felt that way in a long time. I returned the hug and exhaled. Lt. got word and quickly showed up at the crime scene. He was also relieved to see me after hearing my car had blown up.

"Leah, I want you to be safe . . . far away from here. Please go!" Lt. said, but he already knew I was not going anywhere. I had a fucking job to do and no one was going to stop me.

"No, I'm staying here until Louis and Stephen are in my custody or dead by my hands."

"I want you out of L.A. by tonight, you hear me?"

There was no way I was leaving. I was so close now. I would have had Louis and Stephen by now if I had not returned for Life. At that moment, I had time to go to Stephen's place and act a fool. After talking with Lt. Terry, he gave me one more chance to leave town and return to San Francisco. But I told him no, so he said I had no choice.

"What, you're suspending me?"

He hit me hard with that one, making me give up my gun and badge. Right then and there, I wanted to pistol whip his ass, but he was like a father to me. I just gave him his nine-millimeter and sliver plate and walked off. I got in the car with Life and took off. He mentioned how fucked up it was that

Stephen and Louis tried knocking me off. The first place we went to was Stephen's store.

"Look, Leah, I want you to stay in the car."

There was no way I was about to miss all the action.

"I want to see these bitches cry for mercy when I bring the pain. Not you!"

He said that I would have my time and to trust him, so I waited while he vanished inside. No one was standing outside, which was funny because someone was always ready to greet whoever approached the building. I waited over thirty minutes for Life's return. No one could see the car, so I got out and walked behind the building. I thought it would be safer if I went in through a window. As I climbed through, I could hear voices. It sounded like the guy in the unmarked Crown Victoria, and Stephen. I heard another voice that I didn't quite recognize. I also realized a female was present and recognized her voice, but couldn't put a face with it. The strange thing about it is that they were standing out back, not inside. I snuck to see who it was, and boy, was I correct! I was surprised to see Louis, Stephen, and some strange woman. I could not make out her face just yet. I also noticed Life standing there with a gun to his head by the same asshole I slapped and kicked in the nuts at Louis's place. I got my .38 special ready for fire. I had to do something quickly. This time around, it was my turn to save Life. The woman looked old enough to be someone's grandmother, but a young grandmother. Louis was grabbing her around like one of his tricks. She did not want to be there. I could see the tears and fear in her eyes. I was fixated on her, only because she reminded me so much of my mother; she was beautiful just like her. Suddenly, a phone rang.

"Hello?" Louis answered.

I could not make out who he was talking to, but I could tell it was someone older and very angry. After he hung up, they put handcuffs on the woman and took her inside.

"What do we do with him?" Stephen asked.

Louis shook his head, walked up to Life, and slapped him.

"Traitor! How could you?" he asked Life. It took me to another level. I was not sure what was going on.

"I never knew I owed you anything, Life. Why take from me?" Life just stared him in the eyes.

"I worked for Sammy, not Louis or Stephen," Life told Louis.

That made my heart race. I know I didn't just hear him say that. I did not know if I should save him or kill him along with the rest. Louis told him to get the necklace back or he would kill him, me, and someone I loved. I was confused and upset. I wondered who he was talking about.

I knew for sure he was letting Life go. I ran back to the car and I tried to leave without Life, but he took the keys.

"Shit!" I shouted as I opened the door to exit the car just before spotting Life standing there. He could see I was upset by the look in my eyes.

"Are you okay?"

I could not say a word knowing he had me where he wanted me. He reached to grab me. I pulled out my .38 and shot once. When he fell to the ground, I searched his pockets for the keys. I found them and took off. I was not sure if I hit him or not. But knew I pointed the gun at his chest.

On the way back to his place, I considered that if he wanted me dead or wanted to turn me over to Louis, he would have told them I was outside. I was once again confused about Life. When I arrived at his place, I got all my things together. I could not trust anyone. As I got ready to walk out the front door, I heard a moaning noise. All the lights were out, so I could not see a thing. It sounded like cats were messing around outside. I thought it would be a good idea to go out the back. Soon as I opened the door, I was pushed back into a wooden chair that sat a couple of feet away from my front door. I looked up and Life stood at the door. My pistol had fallen out of my hand and landed across the room. I eyed it, and so did Life. He just stood there with the meanest look on his face I'd ever seen before.

"What do you want from me, Life?" I asked him. I had to know, but he said nothing in return. I tried crawling to my gun, but Life leapt over me and kicked it further.

"Get up!" Life shouted.

I could not. I bumped my leg when I fell, but did not tell him that.

"No! I'm not going anywhere."

"While you tried to kill me, did you forget about our protective gear?" he shouted, showing me his bulletproof vest.

Damn, I felt so stupid. I could only tell him what I heard.

"Me? Why are you trying to kill me? Better yet, why are you still working for Sammy, huh?"

He just looked at me and started laughing.

"What's funny?" I asked.

"You! I thought I told you to wait in the car. Now if your ass would have been caught, I would have had to save you again," he said, grinning.

I forgot Life had on a protective vest -- one of the best in the world.

"Yes, I overheard your conversation and wasn't sure of you anymore."

Life walked closer to me. I thought he was going to kiss me, but instead, he whispered in my ear.

"I'll never hurt you. I was there for you in the beginning of all this bullshit. I'm here now and forever."

I got chill bumps all over. I wanted him so bad. Two months of no loving takes it toll.

After Life and I cleared the air. I left and went to my parents home to clear my thoughts on everything that was going on around me.

"Sir," I shouted, but the man paid me no mind. "Hey sir, please stop. I need to know why you're here?"

"I come here every day. I knew the family who once lived here."

"Where do you stay, sir?"

"I live across the street, back in the woods," he said, taking a good look at me. "Leah Starr?" he asked.

"Yes."

He grabbed me and hugged me tight; I wanted to push away from him, but needed a hug from someone.

"Why are you hugging me, sir?" I asked.

"Please call me Eddie or Ed. I worked with your father when he first moved here. I remember it like it was yesterday."

"The murder?" I asked as he dropped his head.

"My dear, your parents were good as gold. I don't know why anyone would want to harm them."

While Ed and I stood out front, a young guy came out of nowhere and called for him. He was really mean towards him and shouted with sickness. He walked across the street where the guy stood. Something told me deep inside that old man knew something I didn't know. I wanted to ask him more questions, but only when the time was right.

SIX

Dead Bodies

After I checked on the diamond necklace, I grabbed a bite to eat downtown at one of my favorite food stands, *"Mr. Hunts Burgers."* Then stopped by the bank. I needed a new ride. I saw this bad 2005 Lexus -- all black with tinted windows. They only wanted forty-five thousand for it and that was a good deal I had to jump on. We could use this car for undercover missions and Life's old Chevy to do dirty work in. I called Life from the dealership and told him I was on my way back to his place to pick him up.

It was around 1:09 when I returned. He sat outside in a pickup truck.

"Come on, Life," I shouted as I pulled up beside him. He was never the type to rush at anything. He took his time and processed. On the way back to the dealership, I told him that the car was hot. He showed no interest in seeing the car, so I did not say anything else about it.

At 1:24 we arrived at the car lot. I got out, leaving Life inside, only because he refused to come when I asked him.

"What's your problem, Life?"

"This is Sammy's dealership."

I quickly got back in and turned the car on, but Life said it was too late for that. In addition, I had the opportunity to drive away in this car today for free without a down payment. Before I could talk to him, Life punched him directly in the mouth, dragging him into the building. He told me to make sure everyone inside stayed inside and to keep them quit while he took the manager to the back. I wanted to know what was going on. I demanded one of the girls to tie the others. There were not many of them; only three. Two minutes went by, and all of a sudden, I heard screaming coming from the back. All I could do was imagine what was taking place. Minutes later, Life walked from the back with a bag of cash and a pair of car keys with ownership papers.

"Come on, let's go."

Life turned in front of me with his pistol pointed in my direction.

"No," I shouted.

"Don't move."

I thought for sure he was going to shoot me; as I closed my eyes, he let off two shots. I dropped to my knees. When I realized I was not the one who was shot, I opened them.

"Come on, Leah."

I turned and there two bodies lying on the ground. One of them had a gun in hand, and the other a machete. We had to get out of there. I ran towards the Lexus and got inside while Life made a personal call to Sammy. The two talked for three seconds. Life told him to look for his friend, Jacob. He handed me the keys to the Lexus, jumped in his Chevy, and followed me. We did not go back to his place; we drove to San Francisco, where we knew Sammy would not dare step foot.

Coming over the Golden Gate Bridge, I noticed police lights everywhere. Life quickly stopped and pulled over to the side of the bridge. I parked behind him, got out, and ran up to his window. I asked him to get in with me and leave his car parked. He did not think that would be a good idea. He did not want to leave his car, but had no choice. After convincing him, he finally gave in and got into the car with me. As we got closer to the end of the bridge, I noticed Lt Terry.

The wind and rain were heavy. I had to turn on my wipers to see clearer. Lt. did not notice me come up, but I was stopped.

"Yes sir?" I asked the officer kindly as I rolled down my window.

He asked me for my license and registration. I did not have an insurance card, so he asked me to exit the car.

"Sir, do you know who I am?" I asked.

He looked at me and laughed. "Who? Whitney Houston? Or a dark-skinned Aaliyah?" Before I knew it, I was confronting him about his insult. He grabbed me by the arm and tried to restrain me, placing my hand behind my head and slamming me against the hood of my car. I could barely breathe. I quickly resisted his arrest when I regained strength. I kicked him where the sun does not shine, and soon as I did, he curled up like a bitch with cramps. Lt. Terry came running over along with two other officers, pulling their weapons on me.

"What's going on here?" Lt. shouted.

"Just doing what you told me to," I smiled. For some strange reason, Lt did not recognize me.

"Who are you?" he asked, taking a good look at me. After realizing who I was, he grabbed me and placed me in the back of his patrol car.

"We need to talk!" Lt. shouted again.

I asked him about my car and he assured me it'd be delivered to me at the station. Life was still inside. I knew he had warrants and I needed him the most right now and did not need to lose him. Suddenly, my phone rang.

"Hello!"

It was Victor. I realized then that I stood him up. He wanted me back in

L.A. that night. I could not tell him I was sitting in the back seat of my boss's car and that he was the law. I told him I'd see if I could get out later and pay him a visit.

Lt. arrived to the station at 3:25 It was still raining but not as bad as earlier. On my way to the station, Lt. did not say a word to me. I believe he was mad because I did not follow through on the Tom case. He just did not understand my hustle.

"Leah, I'm glad to see you back," he said oddly.

"Sir, are you okay?" I asked, worried.

"Yes, I'm better now knowing you're okay." I knew he was worried about me and could see it all over his face.

"See, I'm getting old, and I understand you're younger and full of energy. However, please slow it down, Leah. Take it easy; life wears you out. Look at me."

I agreed. Lt. worked in investigation for over twenty-eight years; thirty-five in law enforcement. It showed on his face, even though he looked good for a guy in his fifties. I sat listening to his story of surviving San Francisco and how he would die if anything were to happen to me. Lt. did not have any kids, and the moment I walked into his life, he accepted me as his own. I did not understand why, but ever since I met him at the age of fourteen, he made me feel as safe as my father did. Lt. gave me the attention my father left behind and I needed it.

My car arrived soon after I got to the station. Terry talked me to death, but I really enjoyed his conversation. I always learned something from him. He gave me back my gun and silver plate.

"I want you to always remember that I'm here for you, Leah," he said, kissing my forehead.

I got my things and went to my new car. I checked for Life, but there was no sign of him in the back seat. I checked the trunk, and still no Life. As I got inside my car, I noticed a truck backed in at the station -- one I had never seen here before.

"Now, who the hell is this?" I ask myself watching the truck. I sat patiently until a young man jumps out and run towards the front door, placing a package in the mail slot. As the guy ran towards the truck, I began to wonder if that was a bomb or message. I had to find out quickly because Lt. was still inside, along with other officers and workers. I got out quickly, ran to the front door, and reached down to grab the package. I put my ear to it, but there was no sound of a ticking bomb. I laid it down on the front desk and opened it. There was a bloody cloth, along with a letter and pictures of dead bodies. I knew whoever was doing this wasn't playing. They had enough guts to deliver this with surveillance cameras all around the building, along with hundreds of cops on duty. I did not touch the cloth with my hands. I grabbed a pair of gloves and removed blood samples for testing. I called Lt. in to check it out and as he read the letter, he looked at me and repeated the last sentence:

I want my diamond back!

"The crazy man who wrote this wants his jewel back. I'm not sure what he means, but I bet you do."

I smiled as I explained to him Sammy Dresser and Louis Grant wanted my mother's diamond necklace, and were not giving up on them. Another letter I over looked sat inside the box underneath the cloth. I looked at the letter and it was addressed to Lt. Terry from Sammy:

This is Sammy, aka "bad guy". I am writing you because someone you know has something that belongs to me. Tell Leah Starr she better get her fucking mind right and give it up. Tell that bitch and her sidekick, Life Parker, they will pay either way for killing my son and daughter.

Lt.'s eyes bogged in disbelief as he continued reading,

So, stay ready at all times because I am coming full force.

P.S.: Watch your back also, Lt.

Sincerely,

Sammy Dresser.

Lt. stood there with a straight face. I could see he was very worried. I grabbed him and hugged him tight, promising him I would not let anyone harm him. He looked at me, grinned, and promised me the same thing.

I knew he could take on Sammy himself, but age had a toll on both lives and I knew Sammy would not fight alone. Lt. needed help. My next step was finding Life; somehow, I knew someone was following me. First, these fools invade my home and my car, and now insult me on my job.

I got permission to use one of our high tech devices that detected bombs and deactivated them. Lt. Terry and I went to grab dinner to discuss Sammy and Louis. I was going to take them down; if not together, one by one. I still had Life's cell phone, so I called Victor and assured him I would be back in L.A. that night. We discussed a time and place to meet, and called it a date. Minutes into our conversation, an unknown number flashed across the screen. I was not going to answer it at first, but did anyway.

"Hello?" I answered.

"Who is this?" a voice shouted.

"This is Life's sister; who are you?" I asked once more. The girl told me she was Life's baby mama. I knew I had to meet her. I asked where she was located and took down her information. I told her I would be by to see her after she went on about how she needed pampers and baby food for her child, along with some money. It was somewhat funny because Life never mentioned anything about having a baby mother. After I got off the phone with her, I went back to the station to get my car. I thought about Life on the way back. I even called the police station to see if he was booked, and he was not. When I arrived at the station, my car was equipped with a navigation system and other high tech gadgets. I took off to the nearest hotel and got a room. Soon as I was settled in, Lt. called me.

"Bad news . . . looks like all Stephen's workers are dead."

They found over twelve bodies around the store and five more inside the basement. Someone was angry with Stephen's boys, but who? I rushed over to the store to check out the crime scene and was surprised to see how all the bodies were laid out. The officers did not touch any of them. As I inched closer towards the bodies, I noticed a nerve jump in one of the guy's eye. Then his eyeball started moving. I quickly pulled my nine-millimeter out and pointed at each body, but kept my focus on the one in front of me. Lt. Terry walked over and asked me what was wrong. I pointed at the body in front of me and he quickly noticed the same thing and pulled his pistol. As he bent down to check for a pulse and remove the gun from the guy's hand, the guy rose up and punched Lt. in the face. The others got up also; I freaked out and started firing at them, running for cover. One hit me in the chest, but I got him between the eyes.

After our shoot out, all the bad guys were down. There were one body left that did not get up with the rest. Twelve bodies laid lifeless, except one? A few of our guys were injured, but they were okay. This shit blew me away. After I got to my feet, with Lt.'s help, I walked over to the remaining body and placed my pistol to his head.

"Get up, bitch."

He looked at me with an innocent smile. I hit him in the mouth with my pistol.

"Ain't shit funny, asshole," I said as I rolled him over and cuffed his ass. When I got through with him, he would have wished he was murdered along with the rest of his crew.

SEVEN

A Hit Dog Will Holler

Sunday Morning, 2005

After I left the crime scene, I went back to my room. I did not feel like intimidating the kid just yet. In addition, it was past twelve and I needed sex. I called Victor and he surprised me when he told me he was waiting at the borderline for me. I jumped in the shower, put on something sexy, and went to meet him. When I got to the end of the bridge, he was sitting inside a corner store eating a snack, looking sexy as always and edible. Kind of out of my league, but I needed to treat myself to some sexiness. It was nothing major; very simple. I got out the car and walked into the store. Our eyes immediately met and from there, I was ready to get this night started. Every man present, and even the women, stared me down,. I felt as if I were naked. I walked towards him seductively, showing as much cleavage as I could. I was killing those females inside; they wished like hell they were me.

"Damn, Miss Lady," Victor whispered to me as I took a seat next to him.

"I see you came." he said.

"So, what's up, Vic?" I said, blowing into his ear. I was really feeling this guy.

"It's got to be you because you're turning me on," he said, placing his attractive hands on my thigh, which needed attention, along with something else. It turned me on the way he was rubbing my thigh.

"So, Vic, what's next?"

"Are you hungry?" he asked me.

I was, but not for food. Next thing I knew, we were back at my room. It got hot and out of control. He was a real man, taking his time with me. He stripped me down to my panties, spread my legs as wide as they could open, and rubbed and kissed them gently. He took his tongue and played with my lips. I was so ready for him to come inside of me. He took one lip at a time and sucked as if he was sucking a Laffy Taffy resting on the center of his tongue. He rolled his tongue in and out my pussy, there I was speechless. All I could do was moan. It drove me nuts, especially when he played with my clit.

He placed his hands on my mountains and rubbed in motion. He slowly kissed my stomach and licked inside my belly button. He then slipped a finger inside, keeping me wet and ready. I moaned louder. He got on top and kissed me. I loved it, I wanted to do something special, so I told him to lie down. As he did, I kissed on his chest, working my way down to his stomach. I placed my tongue in his belly button, licking in motion. As my ass rose in the air, he grabbed it and squeezed and bounced it up and down. I kissed his manhood, tonguing his balls. His toes curled and I could see it in his eyes that he enjoyed every bit of it.

I started sucking the head of his cock in a circular motion. He moaned and I cracked a smile. I wanted him to get the first one off his chest, then fuck me like a real freak should. After he came, I laid back down and let him do his thing. It was so good. I just loved how he held me and fucked me right. When we were through, he held me tight and told me that was the best fuck of his life. I agreed and knew he was in love with this pussycat.

At 4:35 my phone rang.

"Hello."

"Where are you?" Life asked.

I told him where I was and within fifteen minutes, he was there. Soon as he got to my room, I dogged his ass out.

"Where have you been?"

He started laughing at me. "What?" I asked.

He was making me mad, smiling at me all crazy. I later told him about what happened at Stephens's store. He freaked out.

I left Life at the hotel and went to the station, which was around the corner from the investigation center. When I got inside the building, I went to visit the jerk I arrested to see if he had any leads on Sammy or Stephens's whereabouts. He was sound asleep when I arrived at his cell. I watched him as he rested. He was only a kid and I wondered where his parents were. I told an officer to get him up and bring him to the investigation unit for questioning. I could not wait to talk to him.

When I walked into the room, his eyes grew bigger. I could see he was frightened. I told him to relax and that I have not hurt him yet.

"What do you want from me?" he asked, nervous and scared.

"What do you think I want, partner?" I wanted to bend him over and beat his ass. I was feeling hella good that morning after what took place last night. I was fully energized and ready to beat a bitch to sleep. I lost my cool, grabbed the manila envelope off the table, and threw it in his face. He snapped.

"Bitch, what's wrong with you?"

Big mistake. Next thing he knew, he was flying across the room onto the floor. I walked over to him, placed my foot upon his head, and told him I would kill him if he didn't cooperate. He begged me to let him up and I did.

"Now, tell me everything I need to know, or I'll make sure you get life without parole."

He was only seventeen and believed I could give him that much time. He later told me Sammy and Louis set us up with a surprise. They figured I'd come alone. Sammy and Louis knew what they were doing. He continued to tell me they were there to kidnap me and take me to Sammy, but my team beat me to the crime scene. I thought the set up was smooth, but not smooth enough for Leah Starr. I gave the kid a thumbs up and asked him one more question that I needed to know most importantly.

"Where can I find them, kid?"

"Around Palm Springs." he said.

I knew a couple of cats that stayed that way. So, I thought it would be nice to pay them a visit, and I wasn't going alone. "Hey kid, what's your name?" I asked.

He would not tell the cops who he really was, but told me. "Michael, but my friends call me Mike."

"Well, Mike, we have some business to take care of."

I signed him out of jail on an assignment to help me bust these punks. We left the station at 9:16 and drove to L.A. Mike showed me all the spots Louis hid out at. I had to call Life and put him up on game and let him know where I was located. He tripped when I told him I was not alone and that I had one of Sammy and Louis's workers with me. When I confronted him about his whereabouts, he told me he went back and got his car whenever Lt. and I went to the station. I assured him I was fine. However, Life insisted on coming to L.A. I told him to come, but to call me soon as he arrived.

I wanted so badly to stop by his baby mama's house, but I wanted to be alone. Mike took me to a bar for men who liked strippers. It was not my type of hang out spot, but I had business to take care of. Mike, only seventeen, was not old enough to get in, so I hand cuffed him to the steering wheel.

Soon as I entered, it felt as if someone had sat in my face, the place smelled like fish and ass. I had to get me a drink. I sat at the bar and checked things out. As I did, my phone rang. It was Lt. asking me to do something for him. I told him I was on to something and that it had to wait. He told me soon as I got back into town to stop by his place.

Everyone seemed entertained. I knew what Louis looked like, so I did not need to ask. I did ask the bartender if Louis had been around lately. He was an older cat in his mid-thirties. He talked a lot about how Louis saved his life and how close they were. I was not interested in his conversation about Louis saving lives. I wanted to know where he was so I could take his life, or put him behind bars for life.

"Look, it was nice to know he saved you, but I need him to save me."

"Oh, you need a job?"

This guy was crazy; I had one of the best jobs in San Francisco. However, it would be nice to go undercover to get more information on Louis. In addition, this guy loved to talk; he would tell on himself and on everyone in this building.

"Yes I do -- can you help me?" I asked him in a very sexy tone.

"Sure . . . can you dance?"

"Yes -- one of the best," I assured him.

I really liked dancing. Now, nude? I was not sure about that. I accepted the job and he told me I could start as soon as I showed him I could dance. This was crazy; it was over forty horny men daily, and even more by night. I told him to put on some good dancing music, and I would go on stage and perform. He played "Bedroom Boom," by the Ying Yang Twins. Nice song. I slow danced across the stage. The guys went nuts; even the girls enjoyed and liked how I performed. I was really feeling it until my gun dropped out and everyone's eyes grew wide. I quickly picked it up while the bartender told me to continue. I danced until the song went off; afterwards, he called me over to where he stood and gave me the job. He told me to start whenever I could. I wanted to start that night, but he had a lot of girls booked. Therefore, I told him I'd start tomorrow morning. He told me his name was Todd. I must admit, he was charming and looked good, but talked too damn much for me. He told me before I left that he would tell Louis I was looking for him.

"Sir, that's not necessary." I said. "I want to surprise him." He agreed that Louis would be impressed.

It was close to six when I left the bar. Mike was sound asleep when I returned to the car. I looked at my phone and noticed thirteen missed calls; nobody but Lt. and Life. I called Life and asked him where he was located. I met him at Jack-in-the-Box.

When I parked, Life and I discussed me working at a strip club. He thought it was funny as hell.

"So, now you're a stripper?" he laughed.

"Yup. I shake ass for a living; don't you think I have the body for it?" I asked Life.

He looked at me and smiled. I could tell Life was feeling me on that level. He thought I was hot, but denied the fact I was his type. But I thought he was hot, and I would date someone like him.

My birthday was coming up and I wanted to do something special. Victor called me and asked me out on a second date. I was ready and excited. I finally found me a cute friend I was interested in. When it came to pleasing, he knew just what to do. As we sat at the restaurant, Life noticed something that I did not because I was too busy flirting on the phone with Victor. He tapped me on the shoulder and pointed at Mike. He was having a conversation with some guy we did not know, and was told we were the only ones he spoke to. Life got up and approached the two.

"What is this about?" he asked Mike and the tall, slender guy.

Mike mean-mugged Life. "What it look like? A conversation."

I quickly walked over and joined on the conversation.

"Mike, we had an agreement you were not to talk to anyone but me. Get lost, homie," I said to the fella Mike was talking too.

He gave me the nastiest look, as if he wanted to slap the shit out of me. I grabbed Mike and walked him back over to our table.

"Sit down," I said pushing his body into the chair. "Who is he?" I asked.

He sat there silent, looking away and pretending to ignore me. I then pulled my nine out and sat it on the table.

"What are you going to do with that?" he asked me, looking around.

"I don't care about you looking around; no one is going to save you. I will shoot you and tell the police you tried to escape, pulled out a weapon, and tried to shoot me! Don't play with me, Michael, or you'll get burned."

He told me that the other fella was a friend of his, who also worked for Louis and Sammy. He was explaining that the guy informed him that he was now working for Stephen, someone I wanted badly, and he could provide him the information on their whereabouts. While I gave Mike the third degree, Life stayed behind and pressured the friend.

"So, who you work for and why are you here?"

"I was just getting something to eat and seen a friend of mine. No trouble, man," the friend explained.

I do not think Mike told him I was the police or else he would have run as soon as we walked up. After intimidating the poor guy, Life let him leave without any harm done.

Mike, only seventeen, had no type of guidance and no mother or father. No one cared for him, so I thought I'd give the brother a chance to do right. He was facing serious jail time, so we talked for a while and came to an agreement. I told him to enroll into school and I would see that he only gets probation until he completes classes with good grades – and stays his ass out of trouble.

Soon after we wrapped up, I had some business to take care of and told Life to keep an eye on Mike for me; I was not worried about him escaping because he was now, officially, the police. They would kill him soon as they found out he was released. Suddenly, an unknown number flashed across my screen. I waited, then returned the call to see who it was. It was some chick name Christian and she wanted me to meet her at her place in twenty minutes. I was not sure about that, so I told her I would meet her at a convenience store.

I arrived at 6:20 and waited fifteen minutes before she arrived. I flashed my lights so she would know it was me. She pulled up beside me, got out, and knocked on my window. I unlocked my door and she got inside.

"Hey, my name is Christian -- Life's baby mama."

She looked so young. I greeted her and told her my name. I asked here where her baby was and she told me he was asleep in the back seat of her car. I asked to see him and she allowed me to do so. He was beautiful. She explained that she and Life separated soon after he was convicted. She hated the fact that he'd be gone and she would have to raise their baby alone.

"He gave me ten thousand dollars, but that's been four years ago, and now I'm broke."

"What's the baby's name?" I asked.

"Jeremiah "Life" Parker," she said, smiling at her and Life's creation. I was surprised to know the baby had Life's last name. I see he cared enough to give him his last name.

She had no money to buy baby food or diapers; she barely made it there on an empty tank. She told me the only time she spoke with Life was when she needed something for the baby, only because it was his job. I agreed. I was still confused as to why he didn't he tell me about his child. Now that I think about it, I never knew as much as I thought I knew about Life. I told her I would help as much as I can, but Life had to step up to his responsibility. He looked just like Life -- same nose, ears, and head. I smiled when he opened his eyes. We talked for about an hour; minutes later, it began to rain. Before we parted, I needed to know what she knew about Life working for the mob. She gave me little information and told me she wasn't really sure if it was true, but she had her suspicious moments. Before she left, I gave her three hundred dollars in cash and told her to buy baby food and to make sure she and the baby had a place to stay. I felt as if Life was working for me, anyways; why not give his family what he works so hard for – JUSTICE! She thanked me and told me to make sure Life stayed out of trouble. I could not promise that, but she trusted me enough to open herself up to me about her feelings towards Life.

On my way into town, I thought about that baby and the pathetic look on Christian's face. I called Life to see what he was up to, and he assured me he was okay. My next thought was Victor, so I gave him a call and we met at his bar.

The time was 8:05 and he was fly like always and smelled so good.

"Hey, lil' lady!" he said, smiling as I approached him.

I ran to him and kissed him. It seemed crazy to me, only because I didn't feel like this every day. This guy had me head over heels. We talked and flirted around with each other. Then he asked me a question that still haunts me to this day.

"Do you see yourself spending the rest of your life with me?"

I quickly paused on that question; it showed all over my face. I did not mind taking those steps in my life, but I knew damn well life was not a fairy tale, and it just doesn't end happily ever after.

"I'm not sure," I responded. "Do you see yourself spending the rest of your life with me?" I asked eagerly.

He answered that he could see me as the girl in his life forever. However, I am not that foolish -- not just for anything or anyone. At that point and time, I felt he was a real man and was loyal. Trust was an issue when it came to my heart from past pain and heartache. I was not sure if he could give me what I needed for the rest of my life. And I did not want to make any mistakes. I had a job to do and was determine to do it.

He went on about how he wanted to buy me nice jewels, and I thought that was charming and decent. I made sure he knew those material things were not an issue for me. It was clear I had this young man sprung; I could feel he wanted only my good love and not my heart. However, I could have been wrong.

After dinner, we went back to my place and chilled awhile. Soon after, it went down and was even better than before. I could not deny this man's passion for pleasing a woman.

Life phoned me as soon as we were through. I felt like he was becoming a pest. I made sure I told him when I answered that I would call him in the morning and hung up the phone.

"Who was that, lil' lady?" Victor asks me.

I told him it was just a friend of mine. The next morning, I woke up by myself, and this was always the hardest moment for Victor and me. I rolled over and found a letter he wrote:

"Dear Lady,

I enjoyed our night together and the time we shared holding each other tight. I just want you to know that you're the best thing since fried chicken."

I cracked a smile reading.

I know how much of a blessing it is having you in my life at this moment. I can imagine how it would feel to have you as my own. Only if you accept my offer to be my girl -- my queen. Let's take this thing to the next level. I want you and you want me. Let's make it happen.

Love,

Your one and only,

Victor.

I could smell his cologne on the letter. That letter made my morning. I smiled the whole day thinking about his ass. I had to tell him in person and express my feelings to him face to face. I drove to L.A. and went by his bar. I arrived at 9:10. The place was empty, or at least the parking lot was. While I sat in my car and waited on him to arrive, I noticed some guy standing across the street scoping my vehicle. I made sure my gun was ready and my vision was on him at all times. He stood there for a good five minutes before walking away, and soon after, Victor arrived.

He looked a little lost and confused, so I let down my window so he knew it was me. When he recognized me, his facial expression changed.

"Get out, baby," he shouted.

I was full of smiles. We hugged and we kissed. He then explained that one of his homie's called and told him there was a strange car parked outside his bar. He was glad he did.

"So, did you read my letter?" Victor asked me.

"Yes I did, and I think I'm ready to be your lady -- your queen." I smiled, staring into his eyes. I was ready to be his woman and him my man.

He grabbed my hand and placed a ring on it. For a minute, I was confused and ready to snatch it off. He explained that it was a promise ring with vows of loyalty and trust. I blushed.

"From here on out, I'm yours and you're mine. Anyone who sees you with this ring on, knows you're mine," Victor said just before he kissed me. I was happy I was finally in a relationship. We sat in my ride for a while and talked about each other and all the important things a couple needs to know about each other. Victor and I had a lot in common. His birthday was only a day after mine. I felt important when he asked me all the questions a man needed to know about his woman. We ordered breakfast and ate. Soon after, we made love on the bar. I left him sprung.

Soon as I walked outside, I saw this bitch trying to get inside my car. I ran after her, but knew I would not be able to catch her in my heels. Therefore, I jumped inside my whip and chased her down. She ran in the road, and next thing I knew, she landed on top of my hood. I got out and popped her across the head with my nine.

"Who sent you?" I shouted with my gun aimed at her face.

She looked up at me, and all of a sudden, the scared innocent girl she portrayed called me a dead bitch. Before I knew it, I released one single shot to her right arm. She screamed just before telling me everything I needed to know. And they say a hit dog will holler.

EIGHT

Nothing to Lose

Two months later

I was turning twenty-two and my baby would be turning twenty-six. Victor and I grew closer with time. I continued working at the bar but could never catch Louis. The girls there talked about him all the time, but they'd never seen him around anymore. I felt I wasting my time . . . or was I?

May 3, 2005:

I felt as if Louis knew I was onto him. I was working mornings so I could get a fresh start on everything that took place in the bar. I never told Victor I was dancing in a bar; he did not even know I was an investigator. I can admit that I was hiding secrets from him. But I did not want to lose him. I needed the love he was giving, and I enjoyed the completeness -- being in love with someone.

Mike started school; he hated it, only because a cop followed him all the time. I did not trust him just yet, so I made sure an eye was on him at all times. Life's baby mama and I became real good friends. I helped her get on her feet, a better paying job, and place to stay. Life still didn't know I had dealings with her.

Things grew old in San Francisco and L.A. Lt. Terry called in this new investigator from up north, hoping to catch Tom. I just laughed at the fact that he gave up on me so soon. I wished her luck at finding him, being that she was not from around here. It would be impossible to catch that crook.

I had a talk with Todd about putting me on night shift. My gut told me Louis came then. I told Todd I needed the extra money and that my birthday was coming up and he said it would be cool. Jackpot! I was ready to catch that punk.

After I talked with Todd, I went to my new place. I found a nice crib with three bedrooms and two baths. Victor and Mike stayed with me from time to time. Everything seemed so normal to me, which was weird.

I constantly wondered where Sammy was. I thought for sure he would have come for me by now, or, at least, for Louis. When I arrived home, I had to be alone for just a moment to think about all the madness that was going on around me. I knew these guys could not be that hard to find. I was ready to get on my job and stop them before they took more lives. I had to find more leads. Ever since Mike began school, he had not been able to help me. For now, Life and I were on our own.

I called Life and told him to head over to my place, I had a plan. I explained to him that I wanted to take them on one by one, and Stephen would be my first victim. Then Louis, and finally, Sammy. All this would take place at Chicks, the strip club. He felt the plan would work and wanted in on it. I made a call to Stephen personally, but his personal assistant answered the phone. I had a brief conversation with her, telling her I needed Stephen to meet me at Chicks alone and that jewels and money were involved. I figured she would tell Stephen and he would call and tell Louis. I wanted to get them moving, giving me a better chance at catching them.

I went by the station to speak with Lt. Terry. He acted funny towards me.

"Hey, Lt."

He gave me a strange look.

"What's wrong with you?" I asked.

"You know, I've tried to ignore it. Now, it's driving me crazy."

Damn! I must have struck a nerve; he went off on me. I was not sure what he was considering.

"I don't understand?" I responded.

He grabbed a manila envelope and threw it at me. "What's this, Lt?"

He pointed and told me to read the files inside the envelope. When I opened the envelope, there was a picture of Victor. I quickly closed the envelope and became weary.

"Why won't you read it?" Lt. asked me.

I did not tell him, but I was afraid of what I might discover. I handed the envelope back to him and he refused to accept it. He told me to read it or wish like hell one day I had.

"Now, answer this, Leah -- are you messing around with him?"

From the look on his face, I knew someone had been talking. However, I played it off.

"Me? Oh no, Lt." I laughed.

I know he knew I was lying, but he took my word. I truly believed there was more to why he was upset with me. I did not confront him about it. I just laughed it off. He gave me the files and I really wanted to read them, but my heart kept telling me not too. I placed them inside my bag and left.

I arrived at the club around a little after twelve-thirty. Before I could do anything, I felt I needed back up, and Life was my only option. There was no way Stephen was coming alone, being the coward he was. I needed more guns -- tech nines, to be exact. Even some bombs and knives. Anything that would shed blood. Life told me he knew a couple of friends out on Santa

Barbara Island who could help us out with ammo. Therefore, we made plans to pay them a visit. But I needed to be back in Los Angeles before eight that night.

When I arrived home, I noticed a black Crown Victoria like the one I saw at the convenience store. I got out of my car and walked towards the vehicle, armed with both pistols in my hands. When I got closer, I noticed the car was empty. No sign of anyone. I called a towing truck to get this piece of shit out of my neighborhood and away from my house. Minutes after the towing truck left, Life pulled up.

"You ready, my friend?" he asked, sounding like a Mexican with broken English.

I jumped in and we took off to L.A. We traveled miles outside of San Monica to Santa Barbara, where we would fly onto its island and meet with his friends.

As we flew, I thought about Victor and how safe I felt when I was in his arms, or when he was next to me while I slept at night. He made all my bad dreams go away. I missed his touch and wished I could stop worrying about what was on those files Lt. gave me. Before we landed, I called the station to make sure someone was there to pick Mike up from work. I was not sure if we would be back in time for me to do so.

We arrived on Santa Barbara Island approximately at 3:04 I could barely walk when I exited the plane. Some street thugs who wore tattoos all over their necks and arms greeted us. They took us to an old empty barn.

"Where are we?" I asked Life.

"In hell's nest," he whispered.

I thought it was a set up at first, until one of the guys opened a door located in the center of the barns floor, exposing a long stairway leading to a large room filled with thousands, or maybe millions, of guns. Life told me to get however many guns I could carry.

He did not have to tell me twice. I saw some of the most beautiful weapons. I grabbed what I could, and threw the rest into a duffle bag. Life grabbed all the big guns, choppers, 315's, and tech nines. He also packed some TNT for homemade bombs.

After we gathered all we could, we returned to the plane and packed all the weapons we had inside. Life and the gang bangers discussed personal matters as I sat inside the plane. I thought for a minute that they were arguing, then I realized they were shaking hands in departure.

We had to have over one hundred and eighty rifles. I prayed the plane would not fall as soon as we took flight.

"You sure we're not over weight with these weapons?" I asked Life.

"How about I take these weapons to Cali, then return for you?"

I looked at him crazy.

"It's just a joke, Leah," he said, laughing at the expression on my face.

We must have spent hours searching through those guns. It was 6:33 when we took off, and 8:26 when we got back to San Francisco. I went home and got ready for work and while I did, I could not help but think about that Crown Victoria that sat outside my crib. I wondered if the owner had picked it up yet. Besides that, I was ready to go in for work.

I could not wait to see Stephen's face. I could see his blood all over the place. My heart was blazing with rage for him, Louis, and Sammy Dresser. After getting dressed, I walked downstairs to find guns laying out all over my living room floor.

"Life, what are you doing?" I asked.

"I'm loading them."

I told him to hurry and put them away. I then got my things and left for work. Life followed me with all those guns neatly hidden in his trunk. Soon as we arrived at the club, I parked on the side where all the reserved guests were to enter and watched for about thirty minutes before going inside. Stephen was not sure whom he was meeting, but I had an idea he knew it would be me and would not come alone. Minutes more into watching the scene, my phone rang.

"What's up, Mike?"

"I'll be getting off work early tonight. I need you to come get me at 9:30."

"Okay, but stay inside until I get there."

"Ten-four."

I was hoping I would have caught Stephen before 9:30 I remembered that I told an officer to pick Mike up from work before I left, so if I need more time, I knew I had it.

Life parked behind me just in case someone tried to snatch me from behind. I noticed a limo pulling in with "Life or Death: You Choose" written on the front plate. I just knew it had to be Stephen. Tonight, that title would become reality. Stephen stepped out of the limo and stood there as if he was the main attraction. And from the looks of it, everyone gave him that affection, as if he were some lord. It made my fucking stomach ill. Two females, who looked like hookers, escorted him in. Soon as he walked inside, I gave Life the signal that I was entering the building.

I noticed Stephen standing in the hallway checking out the scene and observing the audience. I went inside the dressing room and got dressed. I could hear the other females ranting and raving about Stephen, as if he were the sexist motherfucker on earth.

"Don't you think so, new girl?" one girl asked me.

"I don't think he's all that hot," I answered.

She got upset and told me it was not what I thought. She asked me the fucking question! I was not worried about her; the bitch did not want to see me one on one. And I would have beaten the shit out of her anyway. Only one chick named Spirit, a very nice girl who loved to talk, spoke to me. This was my opportunity to ask all I could about Louis.

"How do you know Louis?" she asked me, over excited.

I told her he was an idol around here, and every girl wanted to either meet him or have a one-night stand with him. She agreed and whispered in my ear that he was her boyfriend. Jackpot! All I needed was someone close to Louis and I knew he would be mine. Spirit would be my lead to catching him.

I saw Stephen talking with some person he was trying to escape from. I guess the person was a drunk, or maybe Stephen owed him some money. I watched him walk upstairs to the V.I.P section. I had to get up there, but before going, I needed to disguise myself. I put on a colored wig and made sure I covered my face with makeup.

Before I could get to Stephen's booth, Todd ran up and told me it was my turn to go on stage. I danced to R. Kelly's single, "Wind for Me". As I did, I could see Stephen watching me from V.I.P, and Life sitting far back watching me also. I felt so sexy and attractive. I closed my eyes and pictured myself dancing for Victor. As I fantasized, another girl came out behind me and started dancing on my ass. I turned around and it was Spirit.

"What are you doing?" I asked her.

"Dancing with you. Believe me, I hate this as much as you do," she replied.

That made me feel a lot better. For a second, I thought she was enjoying it, and at that time, I was not into girls. When the song was finished, I walked out to where Life sat and gave him a lap dance.

"I see you're good at this."

"Yeah, I've always loved dancing."

He was really enjoying the lap dance; I could see it in his eyes as he watched my hips and admired my breasts.

Todd walked over and interrupted. He informed me Stephen wanted me to come sit with him in V.I.P. Life whispered that he would be watching my every move, showing me his nine. Somehow, he managed to sneak it inside.

Soon as I reached the top step, Stephen looked me directly in the eyes. However, he did not recognize me. It had to be the makeup I was wearing. My face felt like it weighed a thousand pounds. Stephen pointed me out and asked me to dance and I did.

Minutes after I started dancing, he left for the restroom. However, before leaving, he asked me to follow him. As I did, his phone rang.

"Hey brother, where are you?" he answered. I was not sure who he was talking to.

"Get the door, bitch," he shouted.

I looked at him and he stared me in my face. I quickly turned my head away because he looked as if he knew who I was.

"Okay, daddy," I answered.

It made me sick to think of calling him daddy. He went straight to the stall and took a leak. He told whoever he was talking to that he would meet them at Vic's bar tonight. I thought that was strange; he was hanging around my boyfriend's bar. The only person I could think of was Tom, who hung out at Victor's bar all the time.

"So, how long have you've been here?" Stephen asked me. I had to change my voice, so I deepened it up a bit.

"For bout two months."

"You know, you look just like this bitch I know named Leah -- do you know her?" he asked, walking towards me. I told him I did not know who she was.

"Well, tonight, your name is Leah. I've always wanted to fuck her when she was best friends with one of my ex-girlfriends." he laughed.

I wanted to throw up all over his trifling ass. As he pulled me closer, I quickly pushed him away. He drew back to hit me, and I drew my gun underneath his chin. He started laughing as if it were a joke.

"What's this?" he asked.

"What does it look like, bitch? Now put your fucking hands up."

"This has to be a joke," he repeated as he laughed. I told him it was reality and tonight he had to decide between life and death, which he really had no choice.

"I hope this is part of Todd's program. If not, you're one dead bitch," he grinned.

I pulled off the wig to show him I was dead ass serious. "Leah Starr! I knew it was you!" he shouted in disbelief as I handcuffed him. "What do you want from me?" he asked.

"Answers," I replied.

It was 9:23 and I had to go get Mike. On the way out, I called Life and told him to meet me out back. I made Stephen lay in the trunk.

"Let me out of here right now!" Stephen shouted.

Poor boy was so used to giving orders, but did not know how to take them. I opened the trunk and pistol-whipped his ass -- giving him a taste of his own medicine. After Life finally decided to show, I told him to take Stephen back to his crib and wait for me there.

When I got to Mike's job, something seemed strange. He was nowhere to be found. My phone rang minutes after my arrival.

"Mike, where are you?" I whispered. He didn't say a word. "Talk to me, Mike."

All of a sudden, someone snatched the phone.

"Bitch, if you want Mike back, you better give up the diamond . . . and I want fifty million upfront in advance."

This guy was crazy. I told him not to hurt the kid. He explained that he was the Louis I had been looking for.

"This is Louis, and I killed your father by Sammy's command. Also, I know Life is working with you to catch me. If you were a smart girl, you would watch whom you trust. And forget about Lt. Terry. I've waited over twenty years to knock him off -- just waited for the right time to do it." He laughed loudly in my ear before hanging up.

I called the station for Lt, but they told me he took off early. I told the operator to send a unit over to his residence as soon as possible. I tried calling the house, but no one answered. I called a second time and the phone was busy. That was not like Terry. He always had an open line for calls to get through.

My heart raced as I rushed out to his home in San Francisco. By the time I made it there, police cars were everywhere. I got out and ran up to the front door. My heart dropped when I saw yellow tape wrapped around the house. Lt. Terry was injured, but still alive. I rushed by his side as they put him inside the ambulance.

Soon as we arrived at the hospital, I waited until I was able to see him. Minutes later, a doctor came out and said Lt. wanted to speak with me. I thought then that everything was going to be all right until I walked into his room and saw the look on his face. I knew God was calling him home. He called me to his bedside and held my hand.

"Leah, I needed to speak with you this one last time before leaving."

I told him not to talk that way, and that everything was going to be okay.

"No, Leah, it isn't. I want you to know I love you very much. The best child any man could ever want."

He squeezed my hand and pulled me closer to him. He told me that I'd be able to find a tape of everything that took place in his home and to watch it and go from there. My heart was broken all over again. All I could do was cry. At that moment, I had **nothing to lose**...

NINE

Hit List

May 4, 2005

All night, I cried. My best friend and the only father figure I had was gone. Highly upset, I knew I was in no position to investigate Stephen. I would have snapped and killed him. Life did not know anything about what happened and I did not give him a chance to ask me anything.

Whenever Victor stopped by, I went into another room and locked myself inside. I was badly torn and didn't feel like talking to anyone at all. I ordered the station not to touch a thing in Lt.'s home. I wanted to investigate his case and they respected the fact that he and I were close.

I was sleep by midnight. Victor knocked on my bedroom door all night, but I did not answer. He eventually gave up and went to bed.

The next morning when I opened my door, he was lying there. I couldn't do anything but smile; quickly, it melted away when I realized I was mourning. I woke him up with a kiss.

"Good morning, baby," he spoke.

"Sleep well?"

"No, I did not sleep well."

He was a little upset about me closing myself out and not explaining what was bothering me. I did not want anyone feeling sorry for me or trying to understand my feelings.

"I had a long night and needed some time alone. Nothing personal." "Just remember -- I'm always here for you, Leah."

I felt the need to open myself up to Victor, but my heart told me to hold back my feelings until I knew it was real. I could not play the fool and let anyone hurt me.

After I got dressed, I walked out to check the mailbox and noticed that same black Crown Victoria I called to have removed from my property. My mind went blank and all I could see was blood covering my eyes as Stephen, Louis, Sammy, and Lt's faces flashed in my head. I went back inside and grabbed one of the bombs Life left behind. I was enraged and ready for destruction. I walked up to the vehicle and knocked on the window. Two men sat inside watching me as I stood there.

I bent down and pulled the pin, rolled the bomb underneath the car, and turned and walked away.

"Have a nice trip to hell, sons of bitches!" I shouted.

Victor stood at the front door watching, wondering what was going on. I could hear the guys laughing as I walked away. By the time I got to my mailbox, the car exploded. I grabbed my mail and went back inside as if nothing ever happened.

"What the hell was that about, Leah?" Victor asked me.

"Boom! That's what just happened," I said dropping the pin into his hand.

He thought how I took control over the situation was sexy. He later told me he noticed the same car parked outside one morning before leaving, but it was always empty when he looked inside. I needed to get to work, and the first place I stopped by was the station to get money for Mike's ransom. After I was finished, I took off to Lt.'s place to collect evidence.

When I arrived, the place was torn to pieces. Terry had a security system set up in his office. Whoever did this was searching for something that was not worth killing him for. I am sure they did not get anything important. Terry would have told me.

When I finally found the video system, I ran it back and watched. What I witnessed brought tears to my eyes; they treated him so bad and enjoyed every bit of it. I noticed four of them. She looked familiar. The rest had their backs turned away from the camera, as if they knew it was there. The funny thing about it was that I knew Lt. did not allow anyone at his home after nine. I figured it had to be someone he trusted out of the four. That really threw me off. I zoomed in on the four and realized I'd seen her before. I noticed a shiny piece of metal that looked like an I.D. badge, and it dawned on me. Why would they attack Lt. Terry? I could not figure it out. Before I left, I grabbed the tape and called the station to come and clean the house.

At 10:25 I arrived at Life's apartment. I walked in, went straight to Stephen and punched him in the jaw.

"What's that for?" he shouted.

I told him it was for everything -- making everyone's life a living hell, for looking at me, for breathing the same air as me.

"Look, I want to know where Sammy is, and I want to know now!"

He hesitated to speak, so I punched him in his mouth this time. He started screaming for help, which only made the situation worse, and me madder.

"Shut the fuck up. I haven't given you a reason to scream like a bitch," I shouted before repeating the question, threatening to make the situation worse for him.

He was so afraid. I could tell. I cocked my nine, aimed it at his forehead, and counted.

"Five . . . four . . . three . . . two . . ."

"Okay, okay. I'll tell you!" he shouted.

"I'm listening."

"He's out of state," Stephen grinned.

I quickly pulled the trigger, shooting a piece of his ear off, sending a loud shockwave through his sensory nerves. He screamed intensely.

"Don't play with me, Stephen. I'll make you pay," I told him, placing the gun beside the opposite ear. He acted as if he did not hear me, so I shot the other ear completely off. He screamed so loud, Life had to come and cover his mouth.

"If you're going to kill him, do it now. Don't play with him," Life whispered.

"I'm a woman of my word, and he will suffer."

I grabbed Stephen by the hair, pulling it out. I realized he could not hear me anymore. It brought a tear to my eye. I could not believe the animal I was becoming. As I walked towards the window, Stephen whispered something.

"What is it?" I asked.

"He's in Palm Dale. He has a spot there," he said.

"Write the address down," I said, handing him a piece of paper with a pen.

He pointed to his jacket and told me to get his cell phone. Great, just the information I needed to contact Sammy and Louis. After I gathered all the information I needed, I aimed my pistol at his head, but before I could pull the trigger, he went into shock, shaking out of control.

"What are we going to do?" asked Life.

I figured there was only one thing left, and that was taking him out. I shot him twice in the head. He didn't feel a thing.

Life cleaned up the mess and got rid of the body. As I contemplated my next plan, Stephen's phone rang. It was Louis leaving a message telling Stephen where they were hiding Mike. Bingo. I needed that lead.

I've always been the type to keep things to myself, so I did not inform anyone about anything. However, I did call the station and ask them about the new investigator Lt. hired weeks ago. Something was not right about this chick, and as I expected she had been missing in action for three days now. I thought it was funny that my birthday was only three days away, and I had to spend it on a killing spree.

This was only the beginning, and I was not bullshitting around anymore. I had the station run a background check on her and nothing came up. There was nothing about her being permitted to be an officer. How did this get past Lt.? I had to dig in deeper on her, but first, I needed to add her to my hit list.

I called Louis and he said he wanted to meet in downtown L.A. Park to make exchanges. He threatened me to be there at 3:00 on the dot or Mike would die. Louis did not know what I looked like, so it would be hard for him to identify me -- unless someone pointed me out. Life called to tell me he got word of Louis and Sammy eating downtown L.A. and said he was heading that way now.

"Where are they?" I asked myself as Life pulled up. I got out, ran over where he parked, and got inside. "So, which restaurant are they eating at?" I asked.

He pointed at a small table outside a restaurant, and there sat Louis and Sammy.

"What are we waiting for?" I asked impatiently.

"There's innocent people out here. Let's wait and follow them. Looks to me they drove together."

He was right about the innocent people. Then again, what about the innocent people I had lost? I wanted Sammy and Louis so bad.

We sat there and watched the two eat and laugh as if they were not wanted. It just made me sick, and I refused to let them get away this time.

"I'm an investigator, Life. Let me go up there and shoot the shit out of both of them."

He was not letting me out of that vehicle. But I saw a woman sitting only three feet away from Life's car reading the San Francisco Times. I got out and snatched the paper from her. Life just looked at me.

"What? She was sitting too close, anyway." I replied.

The woman stood up and starting talking shit. I pulled out my pistol and sat it on my lap so she could see it. She got the picture and walked her ass away.

Lt. Terry was all over the front page. His story was two pages long. It announced his death and life achievements. I tore out his article and placed it inside my jacket. My heart was hurting looking at Lt's picture, realizing the fucks that killed him were sitting across the street from me enjoying a hot meal. I told Life I couldn't wait any longer and jumped out, running towards Sammy and Louis. A car came out of nowhere and charged towards me. I shot at the windshield, hitting the driver twice in the chest. Sammy and Louis noticed the commotion and got up from their table. A whole heap of guys came running from the parking lot towards me as I ran after Sammy and Louis. Life jumped out of his car with his automatic, shooting them down to their knees. I ran as fast as I could, but before I could reach Sammy or Louis, they jumped inside a truck parked on the side of the restaurant building. I shot at the truck multiple times, but they still got away.

"Damn!" I shouted.

I was so disappointed in myself. I could hear Louis laughing and shouting as they pulled.

"You better have my money by three."

I was not upset. I knew I would see them again soon.

When I returned to Life's car, my phone rang and it was Louis talking mad shit. He explained to me there had been a change of plans, and told me to wait later that night to meet him. That way, we both would not know what to expect. I did, and that was his fucking head. I just listened to him talk shit and brag about how they got away unharmed. I warned him.

"Louis, you've made a mistake. You killed my parents, and now, my best friend. Believe me when I say you will pay." He just laughed and mocked me.

I thought about Mike. He was a good kid caught up with the wrong people. However, my heart was starting not to give a fuck. I wanted payback for my parents, and now Lt. Terry. I did not care about anything else. Louis did not give me a time. I made my mind up to show before dark.

I went home and took a hot bath, trying my best to ease my mind. I put on a little music to help. It made a big difference. As I lay in the tub, I could hear footsteps coming up the stairs. I just laid back and continued relaxing. I had a machine gun with me, so I was good. I grabbed the remote and turned the music down just to be sure. The footsteps got closer towards the door.

"Knock, knock. Baby are you in there?"

It was Victor. A smile appeared on my face as I answered. "Yes,"

He walked in and sat on the edge of the tub. "I'll rub your back if you want me to."

"I'd love for you too." I said, blushing as he looked into my eyes passionately.

As he rubbed my back, I closed my eyes and pictured myself far away from everything. Suddenly, he sort of fell in and touched my gun.

"Leah, what's that?" he asked, pulling the gun up out of the water. I told him to be careful because it could go off.

"Damn, where did you get this? What's going on, Leah?" he asked me seriously.

I did not want to lie. I figured I had done that enough. I told him it was for my protection.

"Protection from who?"

"No one," I said, looking into his eyes.

I could not tell him why I really needed the gun. He was no longer worried and asked me if I wanted to go out and celebrate our birthdays together. I was not up for fun, but what the hell.

I finished bathing and put on something sexy for him. I needed something to take my mind off murdering a bitch. And Victor made that possible . . .

TEN

A Man's Worth

After dinner, we went back home and made passionate love. Afterwards, something told me to ask him if he'd ever been in trouble, so I did.

"Victor, I have a question."

"What is it?" he asked in the sexiest tone.

"Have you ever been arrested?"

He explained he had been arrested only on dope charges and that was it. For some strange reason, I felt he was not being honest with me, and it was about time that I found out.

Soon as he fell asleep, I pulled the manila envelope out and begin reading. As I read his history, I saw the dope charges on him, along with gang related crimes. I wondered why he never discussed his past with me. I guess the same reason I never volunteered to share mine. I was impressed to discover his achievements inside also. He completed high school and attended collage at one of Cali's finest schools. This guy was worth keeping, and had ambitions for a brighter future.

I sat in bed and watched him sleep. I wanted more nights like this, but I had to take care of issues that were more important. As I continued reading his files, I discovered the second part was not so lovely. Victor had connections to Sammy's mob family. Scary. I read on and saw he was charged with murder in 1998 and was under investigation for the murder of,

"My father!" I whispered loudly.

I placed my hand over my mouth and cried. I could not believe this shit was happening to me. Was I sleeping with the enemy? As I continued reading, I found out the charges were later dropped because he had an alibi.

I wondered if he knew I was Mathew Starr's daughter. I saw why Terry wanted me to read those files. I was so terrified. What scared me the most was when I looked over where he rested, he was staring me directly in the eyes. It really freaked me the fuck out. He stared at me for a minute before turning over and going back to sleep.

An hour later, Louis called me and said he was ready to meet in Central Park. So, I got dressed and left out. Life was already on his way there. I could not get Victor off my mind, convincing myself that this had to be a dream. I was so in love with him and could not see myself hurting him. It brought me to tears wondering if the man I love murdered my family.

When I arrived at the park, I noticed Mike sitting on a bench alone. I knew something was fishy about this scene. I also noticed Life standing afar. I did not see Louis anywhere; just this tall guy standing a couple of feet away from Mike. I knew he was packing heat by the way he crossed his arms over his chest. No one saw me, not even Life. I had to think of something quick. I walked back to my car and popped the trunk. I had all types of wigs, makeup kits, and outfits from working at the strip club. When I was all dressed, I called Life and told him the plan. He thought my plan was nuts, but worth a try.

I walked around to where Mike was and sat beside him. I could see the gunman was interested in me, so I winked at him and he cracked a smile in return. I got up and walked over towards him.

"Come closer," he asked me.

I flirted a little. He pulled his hand out of his coat. I knew I had him.

"Come . . . let's go somewhere," I whispered in his ear, trying to convince him to leave with me. But he kept telling me he had to wait on a drop off. I saw no way to get him out of the park. I told him we could do it right there, and he grinned and told me I was a naughty girl. I took off my earrings and placed them inside my jacket.

Suddenly, his phone rang. I tried my best to listen to his conversation. But instead, he walked away. I whispered to Mike and told him to run over where Life stood.

The guy turned and realized Mike was gone. He ran over to where I stood, grabbing my arm.

"Where is the boy? Where did he go? Did you see him?"

I played crazy and acted as if I did not know what he was saying. He raised his hand up to slap me, but I ducked just in time, bending low enough to hit him in his balls and upper handing him in the nose. He tried reaching for his gun, but he was too slow. I pulled my knife out and slit his throat.

As I ran towards my car, I heard gunshots. My heart dropped. I did not know who was shot or who pulled the trigger. I ran as fast as I could to see what happen and discovered a body on the ground.

"Oh my goodness!" I shouted as Life lay lifeless on the ground. He had been shot, and there was no sign of Mike or my car. I started panicking, looking around for help, but there was no one in sight. "Damn it!" I shouted.

Louis played me. He had the money, my diamonds, and Mike. In addition, he shot Life. I walked over to Life's body and just stared. Tears fell as I realized another close friend was taken away from me. I had to get away, so I jumped inside Life's Chevy and took off.

On my way home, I felt a sharp pain in my stomach. I had to vomit. I quickly pulled over, climbed to the passenger side, got out, and threw up. It must have been something I ate. I felt a lot better after releasing the vomit. I climbed back inside the car and took off. I was so worried and confused, thinking about how Louis had won once again. I drove top speed swirling from lane to lane. I was heated and enraged.

When I arrived home, I noticed an unmarked patrol car parked only a couple of houses down from mine. I got out of the car and walked towards my door. An unknown figure walked up behind me.

"Leah Starr?"

I could not yet make out who it was, but I could tell it was a woman. I placed my hand on my weapon.

"It's you!" I replied.

"Yes -- the one and only."

I quickly drew my pistol and pulled the trigger. Nevertheless, she moved just in time. She ran towards me and kicked me backwards onto the hood of Life's car. My gun fell out of my hand and vanished. When I finally laid eyes on it, she quickly jumped on top of me, pulling my hair and trying her best to keep me from reaching my gun. I bowed her in the face, pushing her away from me.

"Bitch, you're going to die . . . just like Terry," she shouted.

She rose to her feet and so did I. I backed up a couple of steps to give her room. She pulled out a knife and aimed it at me.

"I'm going to cut you up like I did your boss," she shouted.

"That's all you got?" I yelled as I smiled.

She put her knife away, pulled out a 357, and aimed it at me. I smiled again.

"What's so funny, Lear Starr?"

I told her to fight me like a woman and put away the gun. She started laughing at me and turned her back away. I walked up and tried grabbing her, but she swung and hit me in the face with her pistol.

"You ugly bitch," I shouted.

She placed her gun inside her holster. "Come on, Starr. Fight me."

"What do you choose, life or death?"

I pushed her into my flowerbed, jumped on top of her, and beat the shit out of her. She screamed for me to stop, but there was no way I was letting up on her now. All I could think about was Lt. Terry and how he suffered when they tortured him. She placed her hands over her face, trying her best to block my blows; it was not helping much at all. She tried reaching for her gun, but I grabbed it and threw it underneath the car. After I beat her half to death, I cuffed her, and dragged her inside my house.

"You must be crazy to think I'll talk. Kill me," she shouted.

"Oh, you will talk. And answer every question I ask you."

She looked at me and laughed. "I told you to kill me."

I wanted to, but I couldn't just then. I had other plans. I walked into my kitchen and boiled some hot water. While I waited for it to heat up, I walked back inside the living room where she sat tied up.

"What the fuck you looking at?" she screamed.

I shook my head. If only she knew how she was about to suffer as Lt. did before he died. I only wanted to know one thing: why?

"Why did you set Terry up?"

She sat there as if I were talking to someone else. I walked closer to her, reached into my pocket, and pulled out a lighter. Her eyes got bigger. I could tell she was nervous.

"Now talk."

I put the lighter closer to her chest and she screamed. At this time, my patience was running thin, and I wanted her to feel the pain I had been feeling for the past seven years. I grabbed her by the hair and lit the lighter. It burned quickly. She then said something under her breath.

"What did you say?" I asked her, lighting the lighter again.

She said to me pain was her best friend. I figured she'll be able to handle what I had in store for her next. I asked her one last time was she going to talk, and she said no and tried spitting on me. What a mistake.

I walked into the kitchen and put on my gloves. I returned to the living room holding a hot pot of boiling water. She looked behind her as if there were somewhere to go. I placed the pot beside her feet and tried taking her shoes off. She tried to fight it, but I soon got them completely off.

"What are you going to do?" she asked me.

I grabbed her feet and placed them inside the pot. She screamed so loud, it sounded as if someone was opera singing. My ears rang badly, but that did not stop me.

The skin on her feet began to roll off; chunks of meat fell into the pot. It was so disgusting. She soon went into shock and started shaking. the pot was full of blood and skin. This bitch was done. I sat there and watched her die a painful death.

Life was not around this time to clean up my dirt, so I had to do it myself. I cleaned up and got rid of her body. These mother-fuckers had to pay for the pain they were causing me. I went through her car and found identification. Her real name was Nicole Lorton, and she was thirty-two years old and lived in Oakland.

She lied to Terry about who she really was, only to get close enough to kill him. I was fired and ready to chop someone's head off. It was time for war. The fucked up part was that the diamond did not belong to any of us. However, they had taken too many things away from me. They took my family, my two best friends, and my jewel. Now, I was riding solo. And not stop getting what I want.

ELEVEN

A Man's Worth

PT. 2

I left the house and drove around town looking for my ride. But there was no sign of it. Something told me to go to Oakland City and look around.

This was the worst birthday I had ever had . . . or was it? It was not over just yet. I had only an hour to celebrate, so I thought I'd pay Victor a visit before creeping off.

When I arrived, his homies were standing outside. I had on a hoodie and blue jeans. They did not recognize me because I was not in my Lexus, and I looked rundown. Usually, I was dressed for success, but today was not my fucking day. When I went inside, I noticed a familiar face. As I got closer, I realized it was Tom. I sat next to him and we talked.

I asked him about Sammy and the last time they had seen each other. He said it had been over two weeks since he had heard from Sammy. Since his escape from prison, that would explain the roadblock held that night on the Golden Gate Bridge when Life and I returned to San Francisco.

Tom had input on everything, I was starting to wonder about him. He started asking me weird questions about jewelry. I noticed also that he was looking at my neck and wrist.

Victor walked out, noticing the two of us talking, and came over with a Jack Daniels for me. He kissed me on the forehead and smiled gently. I just stared at him and cracked a slight smile. I was confused, but knew he had me where he wanted me. The thought of this man made my panties wet. He was worth a try, but then again, it came to me unexpectedly that this man may have had something to do with my parents' murder. It would break my heart, and how I would destroy his, if this was true.

Tom excused himself, leaving Victor and me alone to talk. Victor could see something was bothering me; it was all over my face. As we sat there staring at each other, a tear fell down my cheek.

"Baby what's wrong?" he asked, wiping the tear away.

I could not tell him. I did not know how he would react or where our relationship would go. But I asked him a real emotional question.

"Have you ever lost someone close to you?"

He smiled and shook his head to affirm he had. I asked him who, and he looked away as an emotional memory resurfaced. I rubbed his back, trying to comfort him. He took a deep breath and explained that his family was murdered. I asked him what happened and he explained his father, like mine, was a part of a mob and was killed. I quickly hugged him and gave him a long kiss. I told him I had somewhere to be and that I would be late coming home. He did not ask me why or where I was going; he just informed me he would be late also.

Spirit told me she lived in Oakland City, so I drove out that way. I wanted to pay her a visit. She claimed she and Louis were in a relationship. I did not know exactly where she stayed, so I asked around and no one seemed to know her. I stopped by a corner store where hookers hung out and asked some of them where I could find her. A guy name Eddie knew Spirit and told me she tricked with him a couple of times. It did not take long for me to get her address and number from him.

I thought it would be safe to call first. When I told her who I was, she asked me why I had not been back to work. I told her I had to see about my sick grandmother. When I told her I was in her city, she invited me over and said only she and a female friend were at the house.

I felt good vibes when I arrived. She stood outside and waited for my arrival. I was not sure if Louis knew what I looked like. But I was prepared for anything.

Spirit approached me with a hug and a kiss on the cheek. She introduced me to her friend, and we sat and talked about the job and Louis, of course. Before I knew it, time flew by, and I was ready to go.

Before I left, she received a phone call. I tried to listen in on her conversation, but had no luck. I wished I had my earpiece. I knew it was a man because she could not stop laughing. When he hung up, she told me it was Louis, canceling his arrival.

"Damn!" I said to myself. She heard me.

"Excuse me?" she asked.

I told her I remembered I had to meet my boyfriend at 1:30, and it was past time. So I left. I had to go home; something was not right.

When I arrived, I noticed a light on and no sign of Victor's car. I parked on the side of the road and walked up to my house. I always take the backdoor when I feel something is out of place in my house. When I got inside, everything looked normal, but as I climbed the stairs, I noticed my bedroom door was halfway open. I know I closed it before leaving.

When I reached the top of the stairs, I already had my nine ready to fire. I slowly pushed my door open with my foot. No sign of anyone, but someone had been in my house searching through my things. My files were everywhere and Victor's stash was gone. I picked up all the papers, placed them on top of my dresser, and looked around the room.

As I walked closer to my bed, I noticed a letter. It was from Victor.

TWELVE

Untold Secrets Discovered

May 7, 2005

Three days after my birthday, I was sick. I could not eat or sleep. I was really stressing out, especially when I read Victor's letter. He was upset. I thought I had lost Victor, the only man I loved. I cried. I was upset, but it did not last long.

I knew for sure Victor knew I was a cop, and maybe the daughter of the family he had killed. I tried calling him, but he would not answer any of my calls. I even tried going to his bar, but no sign of Victor. My twenty-second birthday was shit. I never wanted to remember that day again.

I could not find Victor all of a sudden. While I sat thinking to myself, my phone rang. My caller I.D. read C. Fuller. I had no idea who that was. After another two minutes, my phone rang again.

"Who the hell is this?" I shouted.

"Hey Leah -- this is Christian. How are you?"

Something was not right, but I played along.

"I'm fine -- a little sick, but I'll be okay," I replied.

"Well, I was wondering if you could come over?" she whispered. I knew someone was there with her and was not an invited guest.

"Who's with you, Christian?" I whispered.

"Just come . . . bye!" she whispered loudly before hanging up. I jumped up, got dressed, and took off to her place.

When I arrived, there was a blue pickup truck sitting outside Christian's apartment. I got out and ran to the front door. I could hear shouting inside. I knocked on the door twice, taking two steps back with my hand on my pistol. Everything got quiet. I knocked again.

"What do you want?" a guy asked me, swinging the door wide open.

"I'm here to see Christian," I said.

The guy looked so familiar. I had seen him somewhere; just could not put a name with his face or remember where I saw him.

"Do I know you?" he asked, staring at me. I looked at him and shook my head no. I was not trying to be friendly at all.

"I know now. You're Victor's girl."

"Okay, you did look familiar," I said smiling. "It's nice seeing you again. How is Victor?"

"He's fine."

He told me he'd let Christian know I've been by, and to have a nice night.

I began to feel tension. Before he closed the door, I noticed Christian standing in the kitchen with her child. I pushed the door back open and pulled out my pistol.

"Get your hands up!" I shouted.

"What did I do?" he shouted, looking at me confused. I told him to fall to his knees and place his hands behind his head. I cuffed him. Christian was very upset. She ran up behind him and punched him in the face.

"You fucking loser. I hate you!" she screamed.

"Now you have nuts. Victor's dating an undercover hoe cop," he said, laughing.

I kicked him in his ass, making him fall forward.

"You're a cop, Leah?" Christian asked me.

I explained that I was an investigator, seeking justice for my family's death.

"What are you going to do to me?" he shouted.

I had a plan. I made him walk outside towards the dumpster and told him to get inside and close the lid. We walked away and could hear him shouting from inside.

"That's why Victor left you. You're a cop; plus he killed your bitch ass father!"

I almost choked on my spit. I turned around and walked back towards the dumpster.

"What did you say?" I asked.

"You heard me. Victor told me everything," he said laughing. I stood there dazed and confused. I wanted to know more.

"Where is he?"

"I'm not telling you. That would make me a snitch, now wouldn't it?"

He did not know what he was getting himself into. I pulled my pistol out and aimed it at his forehead.

"I'll kill you."

"Oh, now you threaten me. That's against the law, especially for a cop,"

"Tell me now, bastard."

He licked his lips and stuck his tongue out at me. "I heard it was good."

Christian shouted for me to shoot him, but I did not pay her any attention. I aimed the gun at his feet and pulled the trigger. He curled up and cried like a baby.

Christian and I looked at each other laughing. "This isn't funny, you bitches." he shouted.

I aimed at the other foot and shot it. He cried out that his feet were bleeding.

"No kidding. We do see that much, asshole." Christian told him.

"Now, where is Victor?" I asked him once more, pointing at his legs. He fell to his face and asked me not to shoot him.

"Well?" I asked.

"Okay I'll tell you. Just don't shoot me again," he begged. "He's with boss man."

"Boss man?" I asked.

"Sammy. Victor still does business with him."

My heart nearly shot through my shirt. No fucking way Victor was still working for Sammy Dresser. I asked the guy where I could find them. He told me the two worked in Victor's bar. Since he knew so much about Sammy's whereabouts, I got all the information I needed. When I asked him about Louis, he claimed he knew nothing.

After I got all I needed, I let him go. For goodness sake, his feet were swollen badly. Christian thought I should have killed him; she told me he was a dangerous man who knew people that would come back and kill her, the baby, and me. I told her not to fear and that I would not let anything happen to her or her child.

I went straight to Vic's bar. I had to see him and maybe get lucky enough to catch Sammy. When I walked in, I was surprised to see Victor sitting at the bar talking to one of his employees. I walked over and sat beside him. I was nervous at first. I overheard him talking about being faithful and how women were deceitful. I wanted to say something but held my peace.

The guy he was talking to asked him about me and he explained he was mad at me and never wanted to see me again.

Could it be that serious? Next thing I knew, one of the guys at the bar asked me what I was drinking, and I told him Victor's blood if he did not tell me the truth.

"What are you doing here?" Victor asked after overhearing what I told the bartender. I slapped him in the face.

"What are you doing here?" he asked again, holding his bottom lip.

"You bastard. Is it true?" I shouted.

He looked at me crazy. After realizing it was over, I wanted to kill him. However, passion for love burned within me. He grabbed my arm and pulled me into his office.

"Sit down!" he demanded. But I refused. He picked me up and threw me into his office chair.

"Now, I like you a lot. But you lied to me; plus, you went behind my back."

I did not understand what he was saying. What did I do behind his back?

"What did I lie about, Victor?"

"About your life and trust for me."

"What do you mean I didn't trust you? You lied to me about very important things. I really care for you, Victor, but now . . . "

An evil look came across my face.

"Now what, Leah?"

I could not tell him I wanted to kill him. I felt my love was turning into hate. He told me I could have told him I was a cop and about my family. When he mentioned my family, it ticked me off.

"So, is it true?" I screamed as rage filled my eyes.

"Is what true -- me killing your father?"

"Yes, and my mother."

"No, it's not. And your mother isn't dead."

He was confusing the hell out of me.

"Wait . . . my mother was lying beside my father dead."

He said my mother was not dead and the last time he saw her was last Wednesday. I could not believe him. I screamed and called him a liar and a murderer. I reached for my gun and aimed it at Victor.

"It's like that now?" he asked me, taking slow steps backwards.

"You must pay for what you've done." I cried out.

I did not want to do it, but felt I had to. I wanted all the bad dreams to stop.

"Leah, I didn't kill no one. I promise . . . trust me."

Something deep inside told me not to do it. I was enraged, confused, and trigger-happy.

"Well, if you didn't kill them . . ."

He cut me short and corrected my saying 'them' instead of 'him'.

"No, my mother is dead, too. Stop playing mind games with me, Victor. I'm not bullshitting around. I'm serious."

When he walked up to me, I quickly told him to back off. He told me to trust him and I was not sure if I could at that time. However, the love was still there. I knew, as I loved him, I could hate him with the snap of a finger.

"Just trust me, baby," he said, holding out his hand for me to hold.

"Do you know who did it?"

"All I know is Sammy's partners, Louis and Stephen, had something to do with it. It was over some necklace; that's all I know."

"Will you help me find them?"

I pretended as if I trusted him, but did not. He agreed to help me out, but did not want either one of us harmed. I was not worried about dying or about dying alone. My enemies would sure enough lay six feet under before I did.

I did not want Victor involved if he did not have anything to do with my parents' death. However, if he did, he would die along with his crew.

While he sat next to me talking about us, I focused my thoughts on Sammy and that bitch, Louis. I later found out Victor's friend, Lloyd Williams, was a twenty-eight-year-old mob leader. He said Lloyd may come back and retaliate. I was ready for pistol play and the opportunity to blow his head off this go round. Victor gave me insight on how to take Sammy and Louis down.

I found out the truth about Christian, Victor, and my parents. Trust was necessary and required being careful. I knew things would not be the same between Victor and me. I could not just let him get away like that. I had to keep a close eye on him. We both paid attention to each other a lot more. There were no more secrets; he knew everything about me now. I felt there was still something missing -- something I still did not know about him. I was going to figure it out, though.

When I arrived home, I laid in my bed and thought about my childhood and how close my mother and I were. I could still see her smile and feel her warm hugs. My mother was a good woman and I knew she would not live without me. That part bothered me the most and left me confused.

I could not sleep. After I daydreamed about Victor, I thought about Life. I had not heard anything about his death. Someone would have discovered his body by now. Something was strange. Christian did not mention anything about his death.

That made me wonder. I had to find out if Life was dead.

THIRTEEN

Deaths Playground

My mind went blank. I had to find myself. So, I went to the station to do a little research. I was surprised to see there were no reports on Life's capture, or the findings of his body. I drove back to the park to the spot where I last saw his body.

There was no evidence that police had been there. This was really freaking me out. I called his cell phone and it rang, but no answer. Since I was there, I thought I'd take a walk through the park and shoot a couple breezes. I needed to clear my mind and concentrate. Five minutes into walking, I got a call.

A cop from the station gave me a heads up on Sammy's whereabouts. Since his escape, reports had come in that he had been living in Baldwin Hills. When I called Victor, he told me both Sammy and Louis had someone spying on his shop. I told him to be careful and keep his heat on him at all times. Then, I went by Chicks to see Todd.

"Hey, Leah," all the girls shouted as I entered the building. I greeted them back and walked up to Spirit.

"Have you seen Todd?"

"He's in the hospital," Spirit said.

"For what?"

"He got beat really bad by my man and a couple of other guys. You have not heard about Stephen? Someone did a number on him."

I cracked a smile on the behalf of Stephen. "What's so funny?" Spirit asked me.

"Nothing. You mentioned your boyfriend. You do mean Louis and his crew, right?"

"Yeah -- they beat him only because none of the security was working the night Stephen was kidnapped. Stephen was Louis's moneymaker." She explained that Louis invested millions of dollars into Stephen's business. That made a lot of sense, and opened new leads.

"My Louis never meant to hurt anyone. He just wanted to make money like I do, and I'm not mad at him," she laughed.

I wanted to knock her ass out, but I kept my cool.

"So, where is Louis? I never got a chance to meet him."

"He's here now. I'll go get him. He likes meeting beautiful girls like you," Spirit said, giggling.

I hated that shit so much. She had the most nagging laugh I had ever heard. I was not sure if Louis would know it was me. I did not care; I was ready to shoot him.

"He's busy. He'll meet you later," she said with an attitude, as if Louis made her mad. "He was on his way out when I approached him about meeting you. He slapped me and told me to come back out here and make his money."

"Why do you take that from him?"

"I'm tired of this shit. He tells me he'll kill me if I try to leave."

I thought to myself that she was going to be the one who brought him to me. She asked me to go out with her tomorrow night. I told her I would go only if I got the chance to meet Louis. She agreed, and we had a date.

After I left the club, I got another call from Louis. I was not sure if he knew I was inside. He told me if I wanted Mike alive, I had to hurry up and save him. He told me I could find Mike located at the park where we made the transaction.

I told Louis before hanging up to give up what was due and to give me what I deserve. He asked me what I meant, and I said I was referring to his life and my necklace. He told me I would never catch him alive and hung up the phone. Before I took off, I called the ambulance and sent them straight to Mike.

When I arrived to the park, the ambulance was taking Mike to the hospital. I sat inside the car, and I felt as if Louis was somewhere watching, waiting for me. Victor called me and told me where Louis's crew was hanging out and warned me that Louis would be near. He also told me Louis and Sammy knew we dated. Lloyd Williams told them everything. Now I feared they would come after Victor and kill him also.

By now, Sammy and Louis knew I would not stop at getting what I wanted. When I pulled up to my house, I noticed three cars outside. I knew something was fishy. I drove by slowly, peeping out the scene. I saw four heads in each car; these guys were deep.

I had to think fast. I drove down the street and parked at an empty resident. I made sure I put my hoodie over my head and grabbed my backpack.

All the houses had fences, so I had no choice but to jog down the walkway. As I got closer, I reached into my backpack and pulled out three bombs and held them until I got close to the cars.

Once I was close, I rolled all three bombs underneath the cars and ran as fast as I could. Minutes later, the cars were upside down and burnt to pieces.

I did not want to enter the house just yet. There was no telling what waited inside. I knew cops would show soon, so I left and went to the hospital to see Mike.

I did not know how badly Mike was hurt. I signed in and spoke with a nurse. She told me Mike was beaten and tortured badly. I wanted to see him but they made me wait.

Two hours had passed and still no one had seen Mike. I got up and walked around the hospital. As I walked from door to door, I finally came across Mike's name. I looked around to see if anyone noticed me before going inside. I was clear, but Mike was not.

"Put your hands up!" I shouted as a man stood over Mike. He was not a doctor, but he was dressed in patient's gown.

"Don't shoot me," he begged.

His voice sent chills through my body. "Who are you?" I asked him.

He turned, and to my surprise, it was Life. I nearly fainted.

"Oh my goodness . . . Life!"

I walked over to him and hugged him tight and kissed him.

"My bad," I said, apologizing. "I'm just happy to see you." I cried.

I asked him how he got into the hospital without being caught. He told me he used fake identification. He was shot twice in the leg and once in the arm.

"What's with all the tears? I'm very much alive," he smiled.

"I see! But I've been through so much since you've been out of my life," I said, holding his hand tight.

Mike lay motionless, unconscious, and badly battered. I did not recognize him because his face was swollen. Life told me he was sorry for not being more careful with Mike. I knew Life meant well, realizing we all fail at some point and time. I told him not to blame himself. I knew part of it was my fault for putting us in so much danger. I told Life the plan Victor and I came up with and we went on from there. It gave me strength to have Life back by my side.

The next day, Life was set free. I was so excited he was in good shape; he limped a little, but was set to go. I let him take the wheel.

"So, what's the 411 on Sammy and Louis?"

I gave him a heads up about Spirit, Louis's trick. Tonight, we were going out and I was meeting Louis face-to-face, pretending to be one of his groupies.

"So, how is your relationship with Vic?"

I really did not want to answer that question. However, I knew I needed someone I could talk to about it.

"Right now bumpy. Trust issues."

"With you?" Life asked.

"Not just me, but with him also; did you ever know Victor before I did?"

I had to ask Life. The two once worked for the same guy: Sammy Dresser. Somehow, they ran across each other before.

"I've seen him around. But friendship wise, no."

I knew I could trust Life, but became confused because he was still alive. Why would he make me believe he was dead, or call me to let me know he was okay? I never asked. I was just glad that he was alive and safe.

We left the hospital, grabbed a bite to eat, and talked more on tonight's plan. I was so ready to meet Louis.

I went to Beverly Hills to get a nice fit, and treated myself to manicure and pedicure. I also got my hair done It was my time and I deserved it. The only relaxation I had gotten was hot baths, and they're always interrupted by someone or something.

As I sat thinking about Victor, I wanted so badly to sleep with him. However, something told me not to. We both needed to earn trust back in each other. He knew about me, but still I did not know what I needed to know about him.

Soon as I left downtown L.A., I got a call from Victor. He told me someone shot up his bar. Bullets were everywhere, but no one was hurt. I knew we had to take these guys out. Victor told me he was waiting at my house. However, I needed to see Life before going home. I had a very important question to ask him.

As I drove, I noticed a yellow Mustang following me. I drove ten miles over the legal speed limit. The car was still on my tail. I slowed to see what the person had in mind. As the car drove beside me, I noticed three guys inside. One showed me his pistol. I gave him the finger and drove faster. As I picked up speed, the car caught up and drove next to me once again. One of the guys tried taking pictures of me. However, I drove off before he could.

I knew then Louis was behind this and wanted these guys to get a clear I.D. on me. I had to make an exit and lose these cowards. The window of the Mustang rolled down and the driver pointed his pistol at me. I smashed on the breaks and pulled my pistol, shooting the driver in the head from the rear window. The car automatically lost control, hitting a truck from behind, and flipping upside down into a ditch. I rear ended a car in front of me and was pissed.

"Damn it!" I shouted, hitting the dashboard.

The first person I thought about was Life. He was going to kill me about his Chevy. It was damaged badly. I did not know how I was going to tell him. I had to call 911 because of the accident.

The three guys remained inside the car. One crawled out screaming for help, and the guy I rear-ended ran over to help him. I reached inside Life's glove compartment to get the registration and noticed a pack of cigarettes. I grabbed one out of the pack and fired it up. I had never smoked a day in my life until that day.

The police arrived, loaded the two dead bodies, and took one to jail. Polices and investigators asked me all kinds of questions about the guys in the Mustang. I did not have time to waste with them. I had questions I needed to be answered and no one seemed to have the fucking answers. I told them to get out of my face and let me handle my business.

Life's car was towed to the junkyard to be repaired. I did not want him to see the damage I had caused to his car. I had an officer take me to a car lot. I needed a car quickly -- something nice.

I spotted a burnt orange 2006 two-door Mustang with tinted windows and 20-inch low-profile wheels. I put a down-payment on it and drove off.

It was 6:33 when I arrived at Life's place. He was standing outside feeding a stray dog.

"Where is my car?" he asked me, as if I traded his in for a new one. I smiled as I exited the car. "That smile tells me my car is gone," he said.

"Not quite. It's getting fixed."

"What happen to it?" he shouted.

I explained how three assholes tried taking me off the road. I told him he'd get it back tomorrow. He stood there looking at my car.

"Is it fast?" he asked, as if he wanted to take it for a drive.

"Sure . . . want to drive it?"

I almost lost my mind when Life got behind the wheel. He took it up to 100 mph. I must admit -- I enjoyed the rush.

"I like this car, Leah. How much was it?"

"Not much. I only put three grand down on it."

"So, are you ready for tonight?" Life asked.

"Sure. I haven't been more motivated in my life."

Life sat there staring at me, saying I looked nice with my hair all done up. I told him he should consider a makeover.

"That's why you're going to be fat. We just ate like three hours ago," he said, laughing.

I did not think it was funny at all. I was not going to be fat. I just needed something to take the place of my stress. He did not understand, and I didn't expect him to.

We arrived at my place because Life didn't want anything to pop off. Plus, he did not have any transportation. As soon as I got in, I took a shower.

"What should I do?" I asked myself. This whole situation was becoming a game to me. I had to play my cards right or get burned. While in the shower, my cell phone went off. I jumped out and answered it.

"Hello?"

"Hey, I'm ready when you are." It was Spirit.

She was ready to go out, but had a problem. She explained Louis did not want her going out. I could hear him in the background talking shit. She said Louis would not let her out of his sight. I told her to come anyway. However, she was afraid only because he had been drinking.

Jackpot! The same mistake Stephen made, Louis was now making. I needed to get Spirit out of her apartment. However, she said she was not at her place; she was at Louis's house. Suddenly, I heard a struggle.

"Hello?" I shouted.

No answer. I heard Spirit screaming for Louis to let her go. He was trying to grab the phone.

"Hello . . . who is this?" he shouted. I did not say a word.

"I know you're still there. Punk, if I catch you, I'm going to kill you," he shouted before hanging up. He thought I was a guy. Now I knew for a fact Spirit was telling the truth about her relationship with Louis.

This bastard had Spirit so afraid of him. I needed to get her out of his house. I did not know where he stayed since he moved away from his last spot. I tried calling the number back but it was busy. I also called her cell, but no answer. I got dressed and told Life what took place. I had to get back in touch with Spirit; she was my only lead to Louis.

Life and I drove around for a good thirty minutes. It was now 8:45 and most of the clubs were opening. Life told me to go to the Housetop, the most popular club in L.A. where everyone met up and partied. We sat in the parking lot and watched the scene.

"You think Sammy or Louis will be here tonight?"

I was dazed and fascinated by the life of those partygoers. "Leah!" Life shouted.

"Yeah," I answered, coming back to reality.

"Did you hear me?"

"No . . . what was it?"

"Do you think they'll be here tonight?" I was not sure. But I hoped so.

My phone suddenly rang. Lucky me; it was Spirit. I told her to meet me at the Housetop. I made sure she knew I was already outside waiting for her to arrive. Life and I got out and sat on the hood of the car. Minutes after, Spirit pulled up in a Taurus and parked beside me.

"Hey, Leah,"

"What's up?"

She told me she had a long day and needed a break. I could tell. She looked stressed out.

We finally decided to go inside. But Life wanted to stay behind.

"Come on, Life."

"Oh no, this life isn't for me. You two go ahead."

I knew I could not convince Life enough to get him inside, so I gave up. For a twenty-six year old, he acted like an old man.

When we got inside the club, it was packed and hot. I went straight to the bar and got a drink.

"Leah, your friend is nice looking," Spirit said.

"Who? Life?" I asked, as if I was confused as to whom she was talking about.

"Yes. He is hot. A little weird, but sexy,"

I smiled and noticed Spirit staring at me. "What, Spirit?"

"I know you're doing him," she giggled.

"No! He is my ace. That's it."

"Come on, let's dance!" Spirit shouted, grabbing my hand and leading me to the dance floor.

I danced and enjoyed myself, but remained aware of my surroundings. Guys walked up to Spirit and me, asking to dance. However, we denied them. First, I was not in there looking for a man. I had man problems already and didn't need anymore.

Spirit finally gave in and soon drifted off with some strange guy, leaving me all alone on the dance floor. I went back to the bar, took a seat, and scoped the scene.

"You were getting down out there," Life said, laughing as he walked up beside me.

"Yeah, I was trying to enjoy myself."

I was ready to go. But I had to find Spirit.

"Where could she be?" I said, getting impatient.

I signaled Life to be on lookout for Spirit and let me know when he saw her. I was hot and needed air, so I hit the front door.

When I walked out, I noticed a group of guys standing out front. They looked familiar, but I could not recall where I have seen them before.

As I walked by, one of the guys tried tripping me with his foot. I stopped and looked the guy right in his eyes.

"What, bitch!" he shouted.

I did not want to mess my plans up, so just cracked a smile and walked away.

"Don't walk away from me, bitch!" he shouted.

I stopped in my tracks, closed my eyes, and took a deep breath. I could hear the other guys laughing. I turned around and walked back to where they were.

"Hey, I don't mean to bother. But why are you calling me names like you know me?" I asked as respectfully as I could.

"Because you're a whore," he responded, getting in my face. "A black bitch who fucks everything, but don't want to fuck me," he said laughing with his friends.

It all came back to me. Fred was the same asshole who tried to holler at me back at Victor's bar -- how sad. Now he wanted to pick.

"You're so sweet, but bitter. I like that." I said, flirting and laughing in his face.

"Oh, yeah?"

"Yes. I love a man in control."

"Now that's what I'm talking about," he smiled.

I played on his emotions. He really thought I wanted him. I rubbed his chest, letting him know I was into him. I pulled him close and whispered in his ear.

"Now cut the bullshit. I know you want me, so let's make it happen."

I was tipsy, but not enough to fuck him; not this lame ass piece of shit. Soon as we made our way towards his car, Spirit came out shouting.

"Leah, where are you going?"

Little did she know I was about to give Fred something he'd never forget. However, I had another plan, I ran over to Spirit and told her I was ready to meet Louis. As we walked toward our cars, Spirit grabbed my arm.

"Leah, I don't think that'll be a good idea," she whispered to me.

"Why not," I asked.

"Because I know he's going to trip when I get there. He already didn't want me going out tonight," she said in a weary tone.

"Well, he can't be that upset with you," I smiled.

She walked away from me to her car. If only she knew how badly I wanted his ass to pay. It was no way I was letting her talk me out of this.

10:05 I followed Spirit from the club. I was so anxious and ready to meet Louis. I made sure my makeup was right and I did not look like a cop at all. It took twenty minutes to get to Louis's house.

Nevada? I was not sure where we were going, but I followed. I noticed a blue pickup truck following me. It had to be Life.

We arrived in this suburban neighbor hood. Damn, Louis was celebrating and enjoying his life while others he had hurt suffered. I continued driving by as Spirit parked. She got out of her car waving me down to stop.

I parked four houses down and walked up to Louis's house. A lot of people stood outside, mostly girls, and a couple of guys. No familiar faces. I also noticed two of Louis's crew standing afar.

When we entered the house, I saw Louis sitting off to himself drinking. I whispered to Spirit to take him to the back away from all those people so he would not make a fool out of her. She agreed and went over to him.

He acted an ass, snatching her up by the arm. When she tried helping him up from falling, he snatched his arm away from her. I quickly took a seat and watched their every move. When they moved, I moved.

When they got inside one of the rooms, I could hear the two fuss. Minutes later, Spirit walked out and got me.

"Come on; he wants to meet you." I got anxious and excited.

"It's about time." I whispered as we walked into the room.

"Hmm . . . you look familiar. Who are you?"

I did not know if I should say something or not. He might just recognize my voice and know who I am off rip.

"I'm Lisa. A big fan," I said smiling.

Raged filled my eyes. I wanted to pull out and kill him on the spot. "Come closer," he demanded.

I walked closer, but kept my hand close to my pistol. When I got next to him, he grabbed my wrist really tight, and I had a flashback to the night my parents were killed and lost control of myself.

"Let me go!" I shouted, pulling my pistol out and shooting him once in the chest. Spirit hid behind a chair and covered her mouth, surprised to see me shoot someone. I pointed the gun at her, and demanded her to place a chair against the door so no one could enter.

He was still alive. I walked over to him and shot him in the shoulder.

"Bastard," I said, staring into his eyes without any mercy.

Spirit shouted, "You're in big trouble. Now you have to die."

I heard running; someone was coming. Gunshots came from everywhere and the door swung wide open. Life came through the window, shooting five of the guys dead. Louis fell onto the floor and started crawling towards the door. I shot as many as six people. I did not quite understand where they were coming from. Soon, my gun ran out of bullets, and I had no choice but to use my knife. I jumped up and sliced three guys' necks as they entered the room. One guy was seven feet tall. I jumped on him, stabbing him in the neck multiple times. I stuck one in the eye and gutted the other. Blood was everywhere.

I looked around for Louis but saw no sign of him. My heart started beating fast as I searched for him. When I ran downstairs, I saw Life holding on to Louis, keeping him from escaping through the front door. I was relieved and excited we had that son of a bitch now, and we were going to make him suffer.

FOURTEEN

You'll Never Catch Him Alive

That is what Louis told me. That I would never catch Sammy Dresser alive; I would have proven him wrong, but he had to die and only had a little time to live. Life put him inside the trunk of my car and we took off to his place. My crib was hot, and I knew Louis's crew would soon come after me.

"Stop holding me. Kill me right now," Louis shouted.

I told him to shut the hell up. I needed time to talk things over with Life.

"So . . . " Life asked.

"I'm not sure. I need a plan. I was wondering if they found the necklace."

"Well, there's only one way to find out," Life said pulling out his pocketknife.

"I have a very important question to ask you, and I'm going to ask you once," Life told Louis.

Louis just lay there without saying a word.

"Oh, so now you don't hear me?" Life shouted, sticking Louis in the back.

"Okay, what the fuck is it?" Louis shouted. Life turned and smiled at me.

"Where is the pink diamond necklace?" Louis gave Life a dirty look.

"5, 4, 3, 2 . . ."

"Okay. They're with Leah." Life looked at me.

"Stop lying, Louis. You stole my car," I shouted, punching him in the face.

"What is that suppose to mean? I did not steal your car, and I don't know where that necklace is."

"Then why did you keep Mike -- why did you let him go?" I asked upset and wary. He was really pissing me off.

"Because the kid was no use anymore. I only wanted the money."

He explained his boys worked for him and did whatever he asked. I wanted names and where they could be located. He later told me they hung out at Victors bar.

"So, you did not take my car?"

"No, I did not. What for?" he asked.

Life told him the diamonds were inside. Louis started laughing,

"What's so funny?" I asked.

"Nothing -- all I can say is fool, fool, fool. There's no way you'll get the necklace or money back."

I raised my gun towards his face.

"You think I'm something to play with, don't you?" I asked with intentions to pop a cap in his ass.

"I was just saying. They are not giving you anything. Your car may be stripped down and all the parts could have been sold. The boys don't work for free," he said, cracking a smile.

"Boys, huh? Sound to me like you know who has my car."

"Well I do, but why would I tell you?"

I quickly grabbed his collar. "Who has my car?" I shouted.

"Sammy! He got some guys from Eagle Wood to steal your car. I'm not sure if he used our main connect."

Life called me over where he stood. "What's up, Life?"

"I think I know where to find your car and your necklace. But it won't be easy getting them back."

I did not care. I wanted my property back. I wanted to kill Louis, but

Life assured me he would come in handy later. I spared his life once more, but warned Life -- one false move or statement and I was going to take him out.

Before leaving the house, we tied Louis up and placed him inside a closet full of Life's old dirty boots. No comfort for him at all.

We took off to L.A. I wanted to know what I was dealing with -- hard cold killers or some pussy punks like Sammy and Louis who like to run instead of facing their fears and fighting it out.

As we drove through the hood, thugs crowded the streets looking at my ride. I dared anyone to try anything. I was one-hundred percent ready to blow someone's head off. I did not know the area that well.

"That's where Sammy's crew hangs out at. And a lot of his tricks."

Life knew these guys personally. He parked and walked over to my side and posted by the car.

"Listen carefully; no false move or we're dead."

"These guys can't be all that bad." I whispered.

Minutes later, an unmarked car drove by. The gang of guys standing outside let lose thousands of bullets into the car. When the car wrecked two guys ran and jumped inside and took off.

"Where are they going?" I asked Life.

"Taking the car to a chop shop."

That explained the dead bodies that had been popping up on the Westside, along with their cars disappearing. Now I knew who was doing the robbing and killing.

"I'll be back," Life said. I quickly stopped him.

"No, they'll kill you. Don't go."

"Do not worry about me. I used to work with these guys. They know me," he smiled with his face inches away from mine, as if he wanted to kiss me.

Before he took off, I gave him protection gear. I did not want to lose him again. He told me not to worry and that I had never lost him, and never would.

He stood afar talking to someone. I could see the guy was happy to see him and walked with him inside the shop. I could not see anything and became a little concern. While I sat watching for his return, my phone rang, scaring the shit out of me. It was Spirit. I took a deep breath before answering.

"Hello."

All I could hear was screaming.

"Where is Louis? I can't believe you played me, Leah."

I told her that he was still alive, but not for long. She threatened to call the police on me if I did not let him go. If only she knew I was a fucking cop. I told her to go on ahead, call them, and make sure she told them my full name. She called me a bitch and hung up the phone. I did not care. I did not give a damn about anyone but me, Life, and Victor.

I began to worry about Life. Twenty minutes went by, and still no sign of him. I wanted to get out, but did not want anyone to identify me. A limo pulled up and my gut told me Sammy was inside. However, I was not sure because a Tahoe pulled up behind the limo. I grabbed my cell and called Life.

"Life, get out of there. I think Sammy just pulled up outside along with some guys dressed in all black."

Life told me he saw my Lexus and the guys were about to tear it apart. I knew if they did that, they would find the necklace. I had to stop that from happening, and I needed to make a move soon. I told Life to make a deal with them and to hold off until tomorrow. I had to have that necklace.

Before I could say another word, Life told me he had to go because Sammy just walked inside. All the men with him walked inside with him, except two of them, they stood outside with weapons.

All I could do was hope and pray Life made it out alive. I got out of the car and walked the opposite way to avoid the two guys who stood outside the building. My nerves were getting bad, my hands were shaking, and I had to piss.

I turned around and ran up to the two guys and starting speaking Spanish. I noticed one of the guys was Puerto Rican. "Please. I need to use the restroom," I said in Spanish.

"Get away. No restrooms," the other guy shouted.

I did not think he knew Spanish, but he did. I begged and begged, but still no success at getting inside.

"If you do not get away, I'll shoot you in the bladder and you'll piss all over yourself," the guy shouted.

"Come on, let her in. Maybe she'll suck something,"

He had me fucked up. However, I played along with them. "Come on, baby; we want to see you piss."

Sick bastards. I wanted to kill them. Soon as I got inside, they followed me.

"Crazy, but interesting. I always wanted two guys at once," I replied.

I told them to put their guns down and come play.

"Come on, baby; let me go first," one asked.

I told him to wait his turn. When one came closer, I kicked him in the balls, grabbed the other one's dick, and snatched it out of socket. Both dropped to their knees.

"How does it feel?" I shouted.

One grabbed me around my neck and tried choking me. I reached for my knife and tried cutting his wrist, but the other guy grabbed my arm. I punched him in the face and he instantly let go. I quickly went to work on him with my knife.

"Who are you and what did we do?" one of the guys shouted.

"First of all, you disrespected me. Then you tried me like some hoe." "I'm sorry. I just wanted to have a little fun with you."

"We just did," I said walking out of the restroom.

I walked down the hall by a conference room. Everyone stood at attention to Sammy, as if he was some damn king. I watched through the door window. I was trying to locate Life, but no sign of him. I noticed a door next to the conference room loaded with stolen cars. My Lexus had to be somewhere in that room. Therefore, I crawled so no one would see me and went inside.

It had to be over a hundred cars inside. Some tore down, most still well put together. I ran from car to car searching for mine. Bingo!

I noticed a rack full of tags and saw mine. Someone came running down the hallway. I was not sure who. I just noticed a body running by. I had to find somewhere to hide quickly, fast, and in a hurry.

Whoever ran by looked inside and noticed me. He walked in and looked around for three minutes. I stayed still until he left the room.

I got up and continued searching until I found my car. When I did, I jumped inside and wired it on. I was nervous. I could hear Sammy giving his speech. The shed was closed, so I had to open it in order to get out. I slowly opened the shed enough to get the car through it, got back inside, and backed my car out.

I began searching for the necklace, but could not find it. I phoned Life and told him to exit the building right then. I was going to blow the place up with Sammy and his army inside.

I noticed the black Tahoe going to the back and Life coming out front. I told him to get inside my Mustang and drive it behind me. I drove in front of the building and tossed two bombs out of the window in front of the door, sending the building up in flames.

"Yes! I got him," I shouted.

"Now he's dead. Did you get the necklace?" Life asked me. I did not answer. I was too upset.

"Hello!" Life shouted.

"No. It was not inside the car where I hid it."

"Are you sure?"

"Yes I'm sure. I believe those bastards found it."

That necklace was the only thing I had left of my parents. Now I had no memory of them; nothing but the fucking house I do not even live in. I could not wait to get back to Life's place so I could kill Louis. I owed him that much.

I followed Life but he was not going home. I flashed him down to see where he was taking us.

"Where are you going? We need to get back to your crib."

"We need to check on Mike. He's awake now. I called the hospital minutes ago."

When he mentioned Mike, my anger went away. Mike did need someone right then.

When we arrived, I was tired and stressed. Soon as I hit the door, my phone rang. Life told me not to answer, but it was Victor. I had to answer it.

"Yes, Victor?"

"Where are you?" he asked concern.

"I'm at the hospital. Why, what's up?"

"I need you right now. It's very important."

I told him it had to wait. Soon as I was through, I would be home. "Leah, honey, it's me," a female voice said.

"Me who?" I asked.

"Your mother . . ."

FIFTEEN

Mother Is That You?

When I got that call, it blew my mind. It could not be true, but I felt this connection over the phone. If my mother was still alive, why in the hell would she hide from me all these years? I had to know.

Victor told me I could find them at an old rundown restaurant. For many years, rumors spread that drugs were run out of this shack. Cops never caught on or had any evidence the rumors were true. My father used to hang out there when I younger. I knew the owner really well, and so did my mother.

It was late. However, the news I got from Victor had me wide awake. I told Victor I was on my way and told Life I had something to take care of before leaving the hospital.

When I walked inside the building, there stood a woman who looked just like my mother.

"Leah, dear," she said, holding out her arms towards me. I did not know what to do.

"Mother, is that really you?"

My heart stopped beating for a minute as I gazed into her eyes. My knees became weak, but I gained enough strength to leap into her arms.

"Mother, it's you," I whispered in her ear.

The place was empty. No one was there but my mother, Victor, and me. As we parted, I asked her why, after all this time. She explained that Sammy kept her in captivity for years, knowing she was his only way to the necklace, and a replacement for his wife. I still did not comprehend. I was lost and confused. I know I witnessed two dead bodies lying in front of me.

"Honey, I'm here now. But I can't get away from Sammy."

"What do you mean? You can leave now, he's dead," I explained to her.

She shook her head, telling me we were not free.

"Baby, he's very much alive."

"No, he is not. I blew a building up with him inside. He's dead."

"Are you sure, sweetie? Because from the looks of it, I'm very much alive."

It was Sammy.

"Get her!" he shouted.

"Get off of me!" I shouted as three guys grabbed me.

"Smart, but not smart enough. I left the building just in time. Now, I have a question."

"What do you want from me, Sammy?" I shouted.

"Come on, don't play stupid. Even though you are for trying to take me out. Crazy, crazy, crazy mistake."

I knew what he wanted, but played as if I didn't know. "The pink diamond; you have the necklace, Sammy."

"Cut the bullshit. I have no necklace. You have it bitch, and I want it now," he shouted, enraged and furious.

When it all came back to me, I realized I'd been set up. "Victor . . . mother. Why?"

Victor looked at me and asked me what I was talking about. "You have played a dirty game," I shouted in tears.

I looked at my mother and shook my head.

"Baby, I have to make it out of here alive," Victor told me.

"Oh yeah, what about me, Victor?" I asked.

"Life is not what it always seems. We have to get it how we live."

I could not believe he was telling me this. I counted to ten, holding back my tears.

"Loren! You and your pitiful daughter will die if I do not get my jewel back. Now talk to her, damn it!" Sammy shouted to her.

"Please, honey," Loren said, touching my face. I moved away.

"Do not touch me ever again!" I screamed.

"Baby, it does not have to be this way. The jewel belongs to him -- give it back," she begged me.

"I do not have them. Moreover, it's my necklace. Remember, you gave it to me."

"Fuck it! Maybe if we beat that ass a little, she'll talk," Sammy shouted, telling his boys to beat me.

Victor stepped up and told Sammy that would not be necessary. "So, you're in love with her?" Sammy asked Victor.

"No, sir," he said hesitantly. "I never loved her."

A tear rolled down my cheek. I noticed how sorry he was for saying it. However, if he only knew how sorry he would be once I got my hands on him.

"I wish I would have killed you when I had the chance," I told Victor.

One of the guys came from the side and sucker-punched me. I fell to the floor and the rest of the guys walked up and started kicking me all over. Sammy stood there laughing.

"Stop them, Sammy. They're going to kill her," Loren shouted.

"I do not care. You will be next if you do not get the hell away from me. Now move!" he shouted, pushing her to the floor.

"Stop," Sammy shouted.

"Why, boss?" one of the guys asked.

"Because I said so. Now, Victor, it's your turn."

"What? No!" Victor shouted.

"Why not? You said you didn't love her, so . . . "

"No, sir, not at all. I could care less."

I knew he was lying. It was written all over his face. "Well, prove me wrong, playboy."

Victor took a long stare at Sammy before walking towards me, bending down and whispering something to me.

"I'm so sorry. Please forgive me."

"It'll be a cold day in Hell before I forgive you!" I shouted. His face went from emotional to rage. He pushed me down off my knees and began punching me. I could not take it anymore and fought back, getting the best of him until someone walked behind me and knocked me out cold. When I awoke, I was tied to a chair in chains.

"Untie me now!" I screamed.

I was inside a empty room. Dark and cold, I sat all alone. I began to pray aloud, hoping God would save me. I later realized I still had my jacket on, and that made it easier to get loose. I struggled a little, but tried my best.

Suddenly, my phone rang. I knew it was Life checking up on me.

"Damn it." I shouted trying to get lose.

I needed Life so bad at that moment. I kept struggling to get lose.

All of a sudden, I heard footsteps. Someone was standing outside the door picking the lock, trying to get inside. I finally broke free, but I could barely run. My legs were hurting and my stomach was cramping bad. I hid behind the stairway just in time before the door opened.

I could not see who it was. I just waited patiently for them to come closer so I could knock them the fuck out. I could tell it was a guy by his figure.

When he walked towards the stairs, I grabbed his ankles, sending him to the floor.

"Fuck!" he shouted.

I ran around the stairway to see who it was but it was so dark. I quickly ran towards the chair I was tied up to pick it up. Before I could hit him with it, he kicked me backwards. I landed on my back, but quickly got back on my feet with a .38 special aimed in my face.

"Don't shoot!" I shouted.

"Leah, is that you?"

"Life, is that you?"

When he said yes, I was so happy I cried. I thought for sure I was one dead bitch. How did he know I was there?

SIXTEEN

Another Tough Lost

That question puzzled my mind. How did he know where I was? My trust was burning out, even with Life. Whenever we exited the building, I realized where I was. It was one of Sammy's hideouts. Life walked me to my car. Soon as we were inside the car, I had to know.

"Life, how did you know I was here?"

He remained silent, as if he did not hear me speak. "Life, how did you know?" I repeated myself.

"Victor called me and told me I could find you here."

I smiled.

"Son of a bitch," I mumbled under my breath.

"The question is how did he know?" Life asked me.

I just looked away. I had nothing to say. I began to have flashbacks of my mother and father lying dead in front of me. Then, pictures of this woman claiming to be Loren Starr -- how was it possible? Then, it came to me. I never heard second shots. My mother was never murdered.

"What's on your mind?" Life asked.

"Nothing, just take me home. Shit!" I screamed. A sharp pain arose in my stomach.

"Are you okay?" Life asked.

I thought I was until I noticed blood running down my legs.

"Take me to the hospital. Hurry."

This was crazy. I did not know what was happening to me. I was so afraid. I woke up in the hospital. I did not remember how I got into bed and no one was around to tell me. A nurse walked in minutes later to assist me.

"Sweetie, you're awake," she said smiling.

I quickly asked her what was wrong with me. She looked at me as if she did not want to tell me.

"Ma'am, what's wrong with me? Why was I bleeding?"

What she was about to tell me, I will never forget.

"Please tell me," I begged her.

She walked over towards me and sat next to me, holding my hand.

"Well, Miss Starr, you had a miscarriage."

I quickly went into a panic attack. "No! I lost a child?" I asked sobbing.

"Yes ma'am. I'm sorry."

I could not think straight. I asked the nurse to give me some privacy. I lay there crying my heart out, wondering what it would have been like being a mother. Now I would never know -- all because of Sammy Dresser.

I was so upset. I pulled the IV out of my arm and ran out of the room. The nurses tried stopping me, but I fought back and broke free. I did not know cops were there. They stopped me and tried restraining me. Doctors shot me with medication to calm me down. I passed out. I was a nut in rage.

I woke up in a mental institution, tied down to a bed. It did not make my situation any better. I went even crazier.

Months passed, and they still had me in lockdown. I cried each day I was there. I was so weak and full of emotions. A big ass crybaby. However, things began to change as my heart grew calm, but colder and colder.

I got a visitor. I did not know who it was, so I denied the visit. The person kept sending messages back to me, so I finally accepted.

Cuffed and escorted by three officers, I was considered dangerous. Only because I beat the shit out of six officers and four other patients. When I walked inside the visitation room, I noticed this white chick waiting on me to be seated.

"Hey, Leah Starr. I've heard a lot about you."

"And . . ." I replied.

"And I am impressed with your ability to take on these tough guys. But even more impressed with your connections with Life Parker and Sammy Dresser."

"So, what do you want from me?" I asked her with a nasty attitude. I was not about to rat on Life or allowing anyone justice for Sammy's capture.

"First of all, Leah, I don't need the smart lip. Second of all, my name is Carla Spencer."

"And?" I shouted.

"I've been an investigator for LAPD for twenty years," she explained. "So you're Elaine Spencer's . . ."

"Sister!" she replied.

She looked just like Elaine, Sammy's wife, whom he killed six year prior to my father's death. She wanted justice and my help. However, I had my own issues to handle and wanted Sammy all to myself.

"So, will you help me?" she asked me with her fingers crossed.

"I don't know. Can you get me out of here?" I asked.

"I'm not sure. You're considered a threat to society."

"Society? I don't think so. Sammy Dresser was a fucking major threat."

She shook her head as if there is nothing she could do.

"If there's a problem, I can't help you. Sorry."

I got up and called for an officer to take me back to my room. "Wait! I'll see what I can do."

I needed out. When I went back to my room, I wrote down all I needed to do when I was released -- kill Sammy, Louis, Victor and my so-called mother. That's if the bitch was not already dead by the time I got my hands on her.

Throughout this fucked up journey, I have been joking around. It was time to grow up and become less naive. Soon as I got a chance to make a phone call, I called Life to see if Louis was still alive. He assured me he was and I told him to take good care of that bitch because I was heading home to take his head off. He also told me Mike was home and he was doing well. I wanted to speak with him, but he was still in school.

I was now a new and improve woman -- ready to take the world by storm. After sitting for hours waiting on Carla to return for me, I gave up. Two days passed and still no sign of return for me. She fooled the fuck out of me.

The six o'clock news came on, and to my surprise, Sammy's picture popped up on the front screen. He was wanted for murder and escape and the reward was for one million dollars, dead or alive. One million was a lot of money and I wouldn't mind having it. I noticed that Carla put the ad out on Sammy. That told me she would not be back. She wanted the world to help her now.

I sat waiting patiently for my release. I was not crazy -- just raged the fuck out. Days passed, then months. When a year passed, it was time to escape.

My birthday in that crazy house was boring. They threw a birthday party, as if I was a fucking child. Something told me to nut up, but I had a good feeling, and did not understand why. However, I knew I was going home soon. While everyone rejoiced, I sat watching. I was now twenty-two years old and my life was on hold, locked inside a crazy house. Suddenly, I got a visit. It was Carla. A year passed and now this hoe wanted to return.

"What the hell do you want?" I shouted.

"I told you about your mouth," she replied.

"Bitch, you don't run shit here. So don't ever in your life tell me to watch my mouth or I'll . . ."

I stopped. I could not finish. "Or you'll what?"

"Do it and you'll find out?"

"I see you're not ready to get out. I guess another year would complete you."

"Hey! So you're here to get me out?"

"I was, but threats won't get you anywhere."

"I do not make threats." I replied.

"Come on, don't fuck me over or you'll be right back in here. You know you're certified crazy."

I wanted to knock her ass out. I just mugged the shit off and called her a bitch under my breath.

"What was that?" she asked

"Oh, nothing," I said smiling.

It felt so good to be free and to smell fresh air freely and not through a fence.

"Am I still an investigator?"

"I'm not sure. Are you?" she asked me.

To my understanding, I was. Another issue bothered me about Life. Why was she asking me about him?

"Why did you ask me about a guy name Life Parker?"

She explained that Life had something to do with her sister getting kidnapped and brought to Sammy. I wondered how she knew for sure it was him.

We drove for hours and finally ended up in Nevada. "Why are we here?" I asked.

It had been a minute since I'd been to Nevada. I explained to Carla I worked on a murder case back in '04. She told me Sammy was in Nevada gambling with some friends. We road around to all the clubs, but no sign of Sammy;

In my jacket was my old cell phone. I was not sure if it worked, so I tried it.

"That should be off, shouldn't it?" Carla asked me. However, it was not.

"Hey friend. Where are you? Hello!" I shouted when I did not get a response.

"Leah, is that you?" Life asked surprised to hear from me.

"Yeah. I'm out now."

"Where are you?" he asked. I told him I was in Nevada. When I did, Carla grabbed the phone and hung it up. I wanted to punch her in her shit.

"Tell no one where we are. Who was that, anyway?"

She tried looking at my received calls, but I grabbed my phone back from her. "Give it here. Now!" she demanded.

"I told you I was not you're fucking child, and you don't run a damn thing here, bitch." I then punched her in the face. She swerved to the side of the road.

"I will kill you," she shouted.

I just sat there and stared in her eyes.

"Do it!" I replied.

"Oh, you don't want that. I don't play games," she told me.

I got out of the car and began walking. She pulled up beside me and demanded me to get back inside.

"Get in, Leah!"

I kept on walking as if I did not hear her. She stopped the car and got out.

"Freeze or I'll shoot." I turned around and walked back towards her.

"You better shoot me now, or you'll regret the day you didn't," I smiled saying.

"Real funny -- you're not that bad." she grinned.

"Try me."

She thought I was bullshitting, but I was not.

"I'll see about you later," I said, walking away.

When I got out of her sight, I called Life and asked him to come and get me. However, before I took another long ride, I needed a bite to eat. I walked over to a McDonalds. When I finished eating, Life, called me.

"Where are you?" I answered. He told me he was around the corner so I waited. He pulled up in his Chevy.

"Get in," he tells me.

"How did you get the car back?"

"I went and got it. Anymore questions." "No..."

On the way to San Francisco, there were no words between Life and me. I liked it that way. All I could think about was killing Sammy, his crew, and the ones he loved dearly. I truly believed he loved no one. The man was a wild animal. I couldn't believe a meek man like my father would ever work for someone like him. However, maybe there was another side of my father I never knew, and I was becoming that part of him.

Approaching the driveway, I noticed a young man washing my Mustang.

"Who is that, Life?" I asked curious.

"Why don't you get out and see."

I got out and walked over towards the young guy. "Who are you?" I asked as his back was facing me.

"It's me -- Mike. It's good to see you." He grabbed me and gave me a hug.

Wow, Mike got a lot bigger and grown. He had hair on his face now and was handsome. It blew my mind. A year passed and he turned into a prince. I was amazed. I walked along side my car looking on the inside.

"So, how long have you been driving it?" I asked Mike.

"For about a year. After I finished high school, I got my license and begin driving it." He glanced at me with a smile. I returned a soft smile.

"Who's been paying on it?" I turned and asked Life. He pointed at Mike.

"Hmm, learning responsibilities, huh?"

"Yeah, I got to know how one day."

I told him since he had been paying the bill, he could have it. I still had my Lexus. It was like new. Life did not drive it, but kept it tuned up.

I was out and ready to begin my search for Sammy, and so was Life and Mike.

"Life, all bullshit aside, I'm ready to take on Sammy."

"It's about time. I was starting to think you were playing around with him," Life said laughing.

"Where is Louis?" I asked.

"Oh, he's in the basement still." Mike said, making me smile.

"Is he in good shape?" I asked Life.

"He's like a pet dog. I feed him, but let him wash his own ass."

We all laughed. However, my laugh quickly turned to a frown. I opened the door to find Louis sound asleep in the basement. He was comfortable and relaxed.

"He's living well," I whispered to Life and Mike.

Suddenly, I hit him across the head with a steel pole I found in the basement.

"Ouch!" Louis screamed, rubbing his head. "Leah Starr!" he shouted, looking up at me.

"Yes, it's me, bitch. Back to make your life a living hell."

SEVENTEEN

Every Dog Has His Day

My father always told me that we all would pay for our dirty deeds. As a child, I used to pretend I was the President of the United States of America, ruling and controlling everyone's decisions. Now that I was grown, my life involved justice for all. I never thought the day would come when I would be avenging my father's death or doing what he soon regretted.

Those who hurt me had to feel what I was feeling. Life was right about me playing around, and now I was suffering. However, I had always been the type to learn from my mistakes. Now that I was wiser and ready, I would do what I had to do. What didn't kill me shall made me stronger.

I sat and mapped out a plan of how I was going about taking Sammy out finally. The streets were screaming for help and needed me back. Banks were being robbed, bodies were coming up missing. I knew Sammy was behind all this madness.

I tried my hardest not to think about my unborn child. I did not even tell Life about my pregnancy, or anyone. It was too hard to talk about. Tears filled my eyes as I thought about my life and how it was ruin by one asshole. I realized there was no changing or going back to what has already been done.

Days out of the mental institute, I discovered my investigation licenses were suspended for two years. I did not care; that was not going to stop me now.

Carla Spencer called me a couple of times to see what I had come across. I told that bitch nothing and not to worry about Sammy. She did not know but she was on my hit list.

I met up with some salesmen downtown about selling my parents' home. I figured if I was not planning on staying there, why keep it? I did not stay in the house I had. I needed to change locations for my safety.

I awoke, and drove downtown to sign over my ownership rights. While pulling up, I noticed a black Tahoe like the one Sammy rode in. I wondered what he'd be doing in San Francisco. It didn't matter. I wanted his mother fucking ass. I followed the Tahoe as soon as it pulled off. I called the guys I were to meet and told them I would be a little late. I lied and said I had car issues.

As I drove behind the Tahoe, I saw two heads. I tried to make out who they were, but could not at the time. The truck pulled over and I made contact with the driver, but it was not Sammy. I did not think he was brave enough to show his face in my town with a price tag for one million on his head. I would have blown up everyone inside that Tahoe to pieces.

I entered the coffee shop and there sat two handsome guys. One was medium built with corn rolls, and the other was short with a low fade.

I quickly walked into the restroom and made sure I was top notch and my hair was legit. At first, I wore it down before putting it into a ponytail. I did not wear makeup at all. I was too cute to age my skin. I put on some lip-gloss, pushed up my bra, and proceeded.

When I walked back into the diner, the guys were gone. I looked around and noticed the two walking towards their cars. I hurried and ran outside after them.

"Hey!" I shouted getting their attention. They looked at me as if they witnessed an angel for the first time in their lives. Who could blame them, I have that effect on men. They walked over towards me and introduced themselves.

"Sorry about that. I'm Traven Poet. Nice to meet you," one replied with a smile and a kiss on my hand.

He was such a gentlemen. He had beautiful eyes. He looked as if he just smoked twenty blunts.

"Excuse me, partner. My name is Lance Tucker. It's a pleasure to meet you," he said, bowing his head as if I was a queen.

These guys had taste. We went inside and negotiated business on the house. While we discussed the pricing, all I could think about was sex. It had been over a year since I laid up or been out on a date with anyone. I could have taken on the both of those guys and still respect myself.

As we talked, I paid close attention to their actions and looked at their hands. Lance was wearing a wedding band. He noticed me looking and covered his hand. I mugged him and turned my attention towards Traven. I had no respect for men who cheated on their wives.

"So, how much would I get for the house?" I asked.

Lance said thirty thousand, but I knew better. Traven disagreed also. My parents paid over one hundred thousand dollars for that house.

"So, how much?" I asked once again.

"Hmm . . . four bedrooms, upstairs, and basement. You'll get about seventy or eighty thousand," Traven told me.

"Now that's more like it," I said smiling.

Lance was getting jealous because Traven was making the sell very interesting and I pretty much had nothing to say to him.

"I would love to see the house, inside and out," Traven explained.

"Sure, that's no problem. When can we arrange that?"

Lance interrupted and told me they would call me whenever they figured out a date. He then got up and walked away. Just what I wanted -- Traven and me alone.

"So, Traven."

He quickly corrected me, telling me to call him Tray. He smiled and placed his paperwork inside his briefcase.

"Looks like you need a bigger briefcase," I said laughing while he struggled getting the papers in order.

"Yeah, I have to put in a request for a new one," he grinned.

"So. Tray, when will I see you again?"

He handed me his business card. "Anytime! But make sure your man doesn't find out."

"Okay, I'll call you. But there's one problem," I said.

"What's that?" he asked.

I whispered, "I don't have a man."

"That's even better. No man, no problems. You know I would love to take you out sometime."

That made my day to hear him say that. As he walked away I watched, sipping my coffee.

My next move was back to Life's crib. Louis and I had unfinished business to tend to.

I called the station and Lt. Paul Griffin said he had something for me.

"Ms. Starr, how are you?"

"I'm fine. Are those mine?" I asked.

He held paychecks I had not received. All that time I was locked away. He explained they never took me off of payroll.

Lt. Paul worked on the force for thirty-five years. He was a vet and it showed. He and Lt. Terry started around the same time and fought together on some of San Francisco's top cases, like the Zodiac killings.

He walked over, gave me my checks, and placed his hand on my shoulder.

"You have been one of our best detectives. Now what's going on?" he asked, squeezing my shoulder tightly.

"Sir, I don't know. I have been trying to capture Sammy Dresser and his crew. Plus get justice for my father's death."

He took a long look at me and told me my job was to save and protect the streets from criminals like Sammy, not dwell on the past and try to make it better. I looked him in the eyes and told him we all deserve justice. And the only way we can get that is to kill. I wanted justice so bad I could taste it.

When we were done talking, I left. I headed to my house, hoping it was still there. As I parked in the driveway, a neighbor walked over.

"Hey, Miss Starr," Mrs. Thomas said.

"Ma'am."

"Some guys came to your house cleaning and searching around for things. I called the cops, but before they could catch them they got away," she explained.

Mrs. Thomas was very noisy and that was a good thing. Eyes in the neighborhood that watched every movement. When I checked my mailbox, it was full of mail. Mostly bills I had not paid. I had to visit the bank.

"Hey, Leah, we haven't seen you around in a long time," a security man greeted me as I walked inside of the bank. I smiled in response.

"What can I do for you, Miss Starr?"

"I'm here to deposit these checks," I said handing them to her. "No problem. Give me a second."

As she typed in my information, I took a trip to the restroom. On my way there, I noticed a familiar face. As I came closer, I realized it was Victor going into the men's restroom. I followed him inside.

As he walked towards the toilet to piss, I walked up behind him, and waited until he finished. When he turned around, I quickly reached after his cock and cut it off. He screamed so loud, I had to grabbed his mouth and placed my knife at his throat.

"Shut up, bitch," I demanded.

I could see he was surprised to see me. I jumped up and locked the restroom door.

I walked back over to him and watched him cry like a baby.

"Why, Leah?"

I looked at him and kicked his leg, screaming.

"Why! You betrayed me. Not just that, but you lied. Then set me up. You'll never be able to fuck or ever have kids." I said laughing. "Payback's a bitch huh?"

He remained silent. I walked over and bent down in his face.

"Isn't it, fuck face? You did me wrong and now it's my turn." I got up and paced back and forth. I tried so hard not to cry. I thought about the baby and thought he should know.

"I'm sorry, Leah," he sobbed.

"Yeah, right Victor. That's what they all say when they're suffering."

I walked back towards him and grabbed my stomach.

"Victor!" I whispered.

"Yes," he answered.

"I was carrying your child. Your baby, Victor, and you allowed Sammy to hurt me, and you know what?" I said bending down as he held his bloody cock in his hand.

"What's that, Leah?" he asked in pain.

"I lost the baby. He or she is gone. Dead, Victor."

He shouted for help. I told him no one could hear his cry, or care about his heartless ass.

"You wouldn't kill me here. Not in public."

"You must not know me. Then again, you don't know me. I will get away with it. Remember, you were accused of killing my mother and father."

"But she isn't dead." he said.

"Not yet. However, she will be when I get my hands on her. I do not have a mother; she's dead."

He began shaking. I did not want him to die just yet, but suffer a little while longer, or maybe for the rest of his life. He tried getting up but I pushed him back down.

"Stay down, bastard. I want you to deliver a message to Sammy."

I told Victor to tell Sammy and my mother that I was coming like a bat out of hell with no limits.

Before I walked out the door, I turned around and took off the promise ring he'd given me and tossed it to him.

"Promise broken. Bye, Victor," I said, exiting the restroom.

"You're back just in time. Your checks are deposited," said the bank teller. After getting my receipt, I noticed my balance was outstanding. I asked her how I ended up with over one hundred thousand dollars in the bank. She explained that over eighty thousand dollars of my parents' insurance money was deposited into my account. I did not complain at all; shit, I was rich.

I needed to see Louis -- we had business to take care of. Therefore, I went straight to Life's crib. He mentioned a woman came by looking for me. Strange, but I paid it no mind. I needed a little time to myself. Victor brought back memories, a lot of which I wanted to forget. I had to get my mind together before I did anything else, and I had to clear it up.

I considered whether or not I should go back to L.A and blow every drug hole up or stick with plan one and use Louis. I think that would work for me; that way, I could kill both him and Sammy at once. A dog had to pay, and Victor paid a horrible price.

EIGHTEEN

Plan A: The Set Up

After I got my mind together, I went down into the basement to speak with Louis.

"What do you want, Leah?" Louis shouted.

I had a couple of options for him to consider. He did not have much of a choice.

"Sounds nice, but what's the catch?" he asked.

"There is no catch. All you have to do is locate Sammy and lead us to him."

"He's not going to buy it. Not at all."

"Why not, smart guy?"

"Because I've been away for over a year now, and with me popping up out of the blue, he'll kill me."

Louis was afraid of Sammy. I could see the fear in his eyes.

"You're shaking. Are you afraid?"

"Hell, no. I'm not afraid of anything." he replied.

"You better be. You know this is a dirty game you are getting yourself into. So, get ready. Are you ready Louis?" I asked looking into his eyes.

"I should be asking you that, Miss Starr. Taking down Sammy isn't going to be easy," he explains.

All that bullshit might have scared him, but it sounded good to me. I had to see it to believe it. I explained to Louis that he had no choice. I needed him to work with me or die, and I meant it. His time was running out.

After we finish talking, I called Life into the basement.

"So, do you think this is going to work?" Life asked.

"Why wouldn't it?"

"Well, Sammy's no fool. I know this for sure, and Louis we cannot trust. He's Sammy's friend."

I did not have the patience to wait. I told Life I did not have time. We needed to act fast on our plan before it was too late.

"You have to be patient. The time will come," Life told me.

While I sat thinking to myself, my phone rang. I jumped up and answered.

"Hello!" It was Christian.

"Hey, Leah. What are you doing?"

"Nothing. How are you, Christian?"

"I've been great. Look, I have something for you -- when will I see you again?" she asked.

I explained I was busy and would be by sometime tomorrow to see her

"Where have you been? I've been looking for you."

"I've been out of town on vacation."

"Sure -- just don't forget about me. Bye, Leah." she shouted before hanging up.

"Bye, Christian.

"When I hung up and turned around, there Life stood.

"What's up, Life?"

He did not say a word. He just stared at me strange. He asked who was on the phone and I told him it was a coworker from the station named Christina.

On my way out the door, I called Lt. Paul Griffin. I needed the files on Sammy to continue the case.

"Hey, Lt."

"How are you, Leah? Have you found any new leads on Sammy Dresser?"

I explained I only knew what the streets were saying and ran into a couple of Sammy's friends. I figured Lt. Paul knew a lot about Sammy Dresser, and I wanted to get it out of him. I always heard about the cops and knew Lt. Paul had some type of relationship with Sammy once upon a time in his life.

"So Lt,, what all do you know about Sammy Dresser?" I asked, twirling my fingers on his desk.

"Well, what do you want to know?" he asked me, taking a deep breath.

"I would like to know everything."

Lt. explained the beginning of Sammy's troubled past, which later led to the creation of his mafia family.

Before I left the station, I read some of the files I was given and discovered the files I were reading were from the FBI. TOP SECRET! I found the information useful and very much needed.

I was getting sleepy. I walked inside the station kitchen and got a cup of coffee along with a donut to eat. Minutes later, Lt. walked in.

"So you're still here," he asked, rubbing his eyes yawning. I could see sheep jumping over his eyelids.

"Yeah, trying to puzzle things together. I have a question, if it's okay to ask," I smiled.

"Sure. What is it?"

"Why haven't you giving this information to anyone? It's good enough to capture Sammy."

He looked at me as if I told the world. "Lt., are you okay?" I asked.

He stood there dazed. He came back to reality, snapping from whatever he was imagining.

"Just a flashback," he replied at ease.

"So, Lt.," I asked, refreshing his memory for my reason of questioning.

"I forgot I had the files I retrieved. Plus, the information there are leads I discovered years ago from my own investigation," he explained tense as he played with his fingertips. I could see he was hiding something from me.

"Are you okay, Lt. Paul? You're not telling me something I need to know."

"Sammy is behind YOU!" I grabbed my gun and quickly turned. But no one was there.

He started laughing, pointing at me as if I was a fucking joke.

"Get it together Leah. He's not that brave to step front in my building." He continued laughing like an ass. The joke was on me, so I laughed along with his old dried up ass. I felt he was still not telling me enough. However, the files I now had would open new ideas to catching and killing Sammy Dresser. I could not wait.

"Speak!" I answered. I heard someone laughing.

"You're very brave. I thought you'd be dead by now. But I see you're alive and cutting off dicks," he laughed outrageously.

I knew it was Sammy.

"So, I see you got my message as I expected. Where are you?" I asked, demanding his location.

"Don't worry about that. The question is where you are with my diamond?"

I told him I had the diamond, but he had to pay. He laughed and made a joke out of what I was saying.

"Your mother. That's what you want?" he asked.

I told him he could keep that trick. As far as I was concerned, my mother was still dead.

"Oh, yeah, poor Victor told her what you said. She was heartbroken by your cruel words. You should learn some respect. It's not her fault. It's your fathers'."

I told him to watch his mouth. There was no luck in getting him to shut the fuck up. I told him to man up and say all that shit in my face and not run this time.

Lt. stood there and tried his best to recognize the voice on the other end of my phone. I am sure he knew in fact who it was.

I told Sammy I wanted three million dollars or the necklace would be sold for money. His whole attitude changed quickly.

"Three million is too much. The necklace is only worth $1.5 million," he explained to me as if I cared.

"I know how much it is worth. Remember it's my diamond necklace and you are buying it for three million. No other options are available."

He took a deep breath and laughed.

"I don't see shit funny, Sammy."

"Am I making you upset?"

I realized Sammy had to be on drugs. The man I visited in prison was nothing like this. Was this really Sammy Dresser? I did not know what to believe. The ones I had trusted stabbed me in the back and left me for dead. I told him when he got the money to call me back to discuss business.

"Sammy?" Lt. Paul asked.

I nodded yes grabbing my things to leave. "What did he want?"

"He wanted my diamond necklace."

I told Lt. I would see him later. I explained I needed to rest.

I arrived to Life's place, took a shower, and went to sleep.

"Get up, sleepy head. I made you something to eat." Mike woke me up with breakfast in bed. It smelled really good. I never had breakfast in bed before.

"Where's Life?" I asked Mike.

"He said he was headed to a friend's house. I think her name is Christian; do you know her?"

I jumped up quickly and tried grabbing my cell phone. However, before I could dial a number, Christian was calling.

"Damn. Should I answer?" I shouted.

"I don't know. Should you?" Mike replied.

"Here, answer it and tell them it's the wrong number," I said throwing the phone to Mike.

"Hello."

He handed the phone to me. "Here it's Life."

My heart dropped. I did not want to answer, but fuck it. I had to face him anyway.

"Hello." I answered with confidence.

"Leah, why did you lie to me? You told me she was . . ."

He paused a minute before continuing.

"You don't have to explain anything to me," he shouted before hanging up.

Life was upset. However, he would get over it. I had been hurt too many times to let this bullshit get me down. I finished my meal and got a hot bath before starting my day.

After I got out of the tub, I received a call from someone special. Tray, he asked me out for lunch. I told him I would meet him around twelve at a Italian palace in Union Square circle. Every star in Hollywood ate there and networked with the finest in taste.

Around 11:30 I went by a jewel shop and had a necklace made identical to the one Sammy wanted so badly. I kept a photo of the original necklace so it would not be hard to identify. The jeweler told me he would have a copy made by that afternoon.

I arrived at Union Square around 12:00. He greeted me with flowers and candy.

"How nice, thanks a lot," I said with a smile on my face. I gave him a kiss on the cheek and thanked him once more.

"So, do you have new resources on my home?" I asked.

He quickly pulled out paperwork and handed it to me. "Here, read these papers."

I read them and discovered the value of my parents' home was $93.879. I was shocked to know that much value was inside that house. He asked me if I wanted to go through with it or think on it. I told him I would handle that later. I wanted to enjoy him first.

We sat and he talked about us doing things together. I hadn't known him that long and was not looking for a relationship. But I enjoyed the moment while it lasted.

"So, Leah, what do you plan on doing with the money?" he asked, gazing into my eyes.

I was feeling him hard, but tried my best to hold back. That's how I got fucked up with Victor. I saw something in Tray. However, I couldn't do him, not just yet.

"Well, I want to start my own business in investigation. Oh, yeah, that's what I do for a living, by the way."

I wanted to tell him the truth from the start. I did not want to keep anything hidden from him and hoped he felt the same inside.

"That's not a problem, is it?" I asked.

"No, good money." he smiled.

"Do you go out much?"

"Well, with my job, I never get have time to party. In addition, I am working on a big case right now. The Sammy Dresser case."

"I heard about that nut taking over the streets. I don't allow my kids to ride the public bus because of his foolishness."

When he mentioned children, I began to wonder if he was married. I never asked him was he single. What a crazy mistake. "Do you have a girlfriend?" I had to ask. He looked at me funny.

"Why you ask me that?" he asked me, playing in his cup of coffee.

"Just asking. It's better to know now, than find out later. Now, do you!" I shouted noticing my temper change.

"Sorry, I have no girlfriend. I do have an ex-wife. We have two lovely kids together."

I smiled because I loved kids, and someday wanted some of my own.

"How old are they?" I asked. "Seven and four. Two boys."

He explained he had joint custody. Baby mama became a hot mess that he could not handle any more.

"So, what are your boys' names?" I asked, sucking the cream from my coffee off my fingertips.

"Travian and Alexander Poet. They are sports fans."

I asked him what sports was their favorite, and he told me basketball. I thought that was cute because I loved basketball as well. Tray told me they loved the L.A Lakers. Kobe Bryant was their favorite. My favorite team was the Boston Cavaliers. Lebron James was my favorite player. It was his first year in the NBA, and he was on fire. The kid got game.

"That's great. Maybe after we take care of business we can plan a trip to a game. I would love to meet you're boys."

We sat face-to-face smiling at each other. While gazing into each other's eyes, my phone rang. The screen read anonymous, it had to be Sammy or one of his boys.

"Speak!"

"Where are you?"

"The question is where are you? I'm doing what I do each day and that's taking assholes like you off the streets," I said calmly as I got up from the table.

Tray whispered, "Who is it?" I walked away without a reply and continued my conversation with Sammy.

Sammy explained he had the $3 million in cash. He told me where he wanted to meet. However, I quickly corrected him and told him I would be making the arrangements this go round. There was no way he was setting me up for the kill this time. I lost my car, and almost lost a friends' in the process.

We arranged to meet at the Golden Gate Bridge. I told him to be there at 3:00, or I was going to the jewel shop to pawn the diamond and leave the country. I needed those fake jewels. I called to see if I could have them by three. They told me they could, but I would be charged for the rush. I didn't care. I needed them now.

After the conversation ended, I turned my attention back to Tray.

"Here you go," I said, signing the papers and pushing them back in his direction.

"It's done; hey, I'll take you on that offer. While you were handling business on the phone, I called my kids. They would love to go to a basketball game," he explained. I told him we had a deal and held out my hand and we shook on it.

I was so glad and anxious to see Sammy Dresser. I knew there was a catch to whatever Sammy had going on. I phoned Life and told him to meet me at the stadium. There we could act out plan A.

NINETEEN

Golden Gate Park: The Trade!

It was show time. Life and I gathered guns. We had to get things right. We went to the park and set up bombs in all the locations we thought Sammy would be, first closing down the park so no one but the right people got hurt. If this plan did not succeed, we always had plan B.

When I got the necklace from the shop, I was amazed to see how identical they were to the original jewels.

Life arrived and Mike was with him. He wanted a piece of the action. At first, I disagreed, but he was grown and suffered from Sammy as well. Why not get a piece of the action, or at least watch Sammy die. I sat alone in my ride waiting on the clock to strike three.

"Where are you? I'm about to leave." I shouted, answering the phone.

He begged me not to leave. While speaking with him, a black limo pulled up and parked. I sat patiently waiting for him to exit the car. I did not know if I wanted to kill him or go through with this plan. I stayed inside my seat and hit Life up on his walkie-talkie. He told me to lay low and not to blow my cover.

While I waited, a woman stepped out of the Limo. I tried my best to get a good look at her. Life buzzed me and told me it was my mother. I kept an close eye on her.

"Where are you? I have things to do?" Sammy shouted.

I told him to have the money dropped off at the nearest bench, and I would do the same with the jewel. His window rolled down and he handed Loren two briefcases. She walked over, dropped the two briefcases, and stood next to them by the bench. I popped my trunk and out jumped Louis.

"Go and get my money," I shouted. I told him to check to see if it was real before walking away.

Louis had on a hoodie to cover his identity so Sammy would not recognize him. When he approached the bench, I noticed Loren telling him something. We had Louis wired but only Life could hear their conversation.

He grabbed only one briefcase and left the other one behind. I asked Life what they were discussing and he told me Loren told Louis to get one at a time, and to bring the jewel with him the next time he returned.

Louis handed me the briefcase, and I gave him the jewel. He walked back over and gave them to Loren. She took off quickly as Louis checked the briefcase.

Suddenly, the second briefcase exploded.

"Fuck!" I shouted, watching Louis and the money go up into flames. Life and Mike started letting off shots at the limo. I sat back and watched with my nine in my lap. It was like July 4th. Smoke was everywhere. Life came over the walkie-talkie and told me to leave. He assured me the limo was in pieces. Was Sammy dead? Deep inside, something told me different. As I pulled off, Loren ran out in front of my car, "Please stop. Help me!" she screamed in distress, running around to my window.

I sat there for a minute and stared directly in her eyes before driving off. It was no way I was about to let her inside my car. While I was driving my phone rang. My heart dropped.

"Hello," I whispered.

It was silence; all I could hear was heavy breathing.

All of a sudden, I heard a loud laugh over the phone. I knew it was Sammy. Just when I thought the punk was dead, he popped up.

"What do you want?" I asked.

"You're a very smart girl. We both won. You got your money, or most of it," he said laughing. "I tried to kill you, you tried killing me, and it did not work. So, what now? Do we continue trying or let bygones be bygones? It's your choice."

I knew I would have to move on to Plan B. Soon, he would find out the diamond wasn't real and be after me once again. I told him I had a job to do and that was to take him out. He had to pay.

"Oh, is that so? How are you and your mother getting along?" he asked grinning.

"She's a little worn out. I don't need her anymore."

This man was fucking nuts, and I had to end this finally.

"I guess I'll see you around," he told me before ending the call.

As I drove, I opened the briefcase and looked at the money. It had to be over a million dollars.

When I got to Life's crib, it was all over the news.

Every time I turned the television on, it was there. Louis's body was discovered and identified.

"It was a pleasure taking him out," Life said, walking into the living room.

I told him to hold his nuts on that one.

"Sammy isn't dead." "How do you know that?"

I snapped and shouted,

"How do you know if he is?

"Calm down -- you're not going to dog me in my own shit."

I got up and packed my things. I didn't have to be there. So, I left.

"Where are you going, Leah?" Mike asked me.

I did not say a word to him. While I packed, Mike told me I had a guest.

"What do you want? I thought I left you at the park," I shouted.

It was Loren standing at the bedroom door looking pitiful.

"You did. However, Life was generous to give me a ride. Leah, I have nowhere to go," she said, grabbing my hands.

I quickly snatched my hand away from hers. "Don't ever touch me again. You're not my mother." I grabbed my bags and walked towards the front door. Before I could open it, Loren stood in my way.

"Get out of my way, woman!" I shouted.

"I'm your mother. You will respect me," she screamed. I pushed her out of my way and told her to make wise decisions and let me be. She walked up and placed her arms around me tightly.

"Let me go, mother. If you loved me or cared anything about me, you would have fought for me." I broke down in tears. I was torn; not only on the inside, but also now on the outside. She tried wiping my tears. But I pushed her hand away from me.

"I had no choice. I tried, Leah. Lord knows I tried," she said pulling at her hair and sobbing like a mad woman.

"I don't need a mother. The mother I knew years ago wouldn't have left me all alone."

She fell to her knees and begged me not to walk out on her. I had no pity for anyone at that moment in my life. My heart was not weak. Not even for my own mother. I was heartless.

I walked out the house, but before I did, I grabbed my money.

"Where are you going, Leah?" Life yelled.

"Out of your house. I have my own place."

"Can I come?" asked Mike.

I told him things were about to get very dangerous. He would be safer there with Life. I felt I was in no shape to protect him.

"Fuck the world!" I shouted.

I headed to my place and it looked so peaceful when I arrived. Everything was how I left it.

I had over one hundred thousand dollars in the bank, plus the money from Sammy. When I got comfortable, I poured the money out and began counting it. While I counted, I thought about my next plan. It had to be on point. No mistakes whatsoever.

The files also indicated that Sammy had an estate out in San Diego he bought back in 2001. That would be location number one. Location number two would be his shopping market in Oakland -- a spot where he dealt all his drugs and dirt.

The whole investigation was becoming interesting to me. By five o'clock, I counted $369,876.

Lt. Paul called at 5:21.

"Leah, did you have anything to do with the Golden Gate incident?"

"No, why?" I asked.

He explained Carla Spencer came by the office looking for me and mentioned something about Sammy having something to do with the Golden Gate incident. He also told me Carla mentioned I was the mastermind behind the operation. Correct, but how did she know that? Nosey bitch.

After convincing Lt. Paul, I was clear. He asked me to join him for his 60th birthday party in two days. I told him I would love too and would see him soon. I continued counting and was surprised to have counted $1.5 million of cold cash.

"Son of a bitch!" I shouted.

He said the jewel were worth this much, and that has what he gave me. I had to find a safe place to put the money. I could not take it to the bank; they would know something was not right with me having all this money. Therefore, I found a safe spot and hid it.

It was relaxing time for me. I turned on some music, and ran a tub full of hot bubbles. As I laid back and relaxed, I thought about Tray. I never dated a man with kids. This could be fun.

I thought about the danger I could cause Tray and his family if Sammy knew anything about them. I could not allow that to happen and live with it for the rest of my life. It was a sad moment for me as I dazed about the possibilities of one day having a family to call my own. I realized I had to put a stop to this before it went any further.

Life never mentioned anything about Christian to me. I was supposed to meet her that same day, but she did not call. It must have not been important.

I was hot and bothered. I needed some bad. I could not call Victor; he was out of my life completely. In addition, he was dickless. The only thing he was good for was his mouthpiece. I decided to call Tray to see if he wanted to have a little fun over the phone.

He answered the phone all sexy and shit. "Hello," he answered.

It made me hot. I moaned. "Are you okay?" he asked.

"I'm hot. What are you doing?"

He told me he is laying down on his bed thinking about me. I smiled and giggled a bit, then spread my legs wide and began to rub my hot, wet, ooh. It felt so nice. I continued moaning, and by this time, he got the picture and went along with me. We had phone sex for about a good hour. I climaxed three times and loved every bit of it. I told him I would call him tomorrow. But before I hung up, he asked me a question I was not quite sure of:

"When will I get a chance to taste you?"

I grinned and told him never.

I woke up at 10:03.

Someone was ringing my doorbell. Whoever it was, was having a bad day, and was about to make mine just as bad. I got up, walked downstairs, and went to the door, but no one was there. I went into my kitchen and got a glass of water to drink.

Something caught my eye. Someone was standing at the side door aiming a pistol at me. I quickly ducked, crawled into the dinning room, and ran upstairs. I heard glass shattering everywhere.

"Come here, Leah."

It was a female. It sounded like Spirit. I got my clothes on and approached the room door, then realized I left my pistol downstairs. But I had a pistol hidden inside my closet in a box.

"Come out wherever you are!" she shouted.

I could hear her coming up the steps. I turned off the bathroom light. I could see her feet from underneath the door. As soon as the door opened, I let off three shots into her chest. The body hit the floor restless. I walked over and removed the mask, and to my surprise, it was Spirit coming for revenge, but failed.

Three minutes later, the police arrived. My neighbor, Mrs. Thomas, heard the shots and called them.

The first person I saw was Lt. Paul.

"Leah, what in the hell you've done?"

"Lt., I did nothing."

"You never do anything. You're good, right?"

I cracked a smile and replied, "No sir, I'm not. But I won't allow any harm done to me."

"Yeah, I see. But I've thought about something for a long time and decided we want you back."

Him wanting me back made me feel needed. He explained he did not want me going to jail for killing people or for taking justice into my own hands. What he said made sense, so I accepted the offer and received my badge back. Before he left, he told me to learn to observe my surroundings and never trust a stranger. Most of all, never give in easily when my enemy has me cornered.

That really gave me a lot to think about, even though I felt I was already doing what he insisted. He was always encouraging, and I respected him for that.

"Thanks a lot, Lt."

"No problem. My kids don't listen. Neither does my stupid ass wife."

"Come on, Lt. You're being rude and cruel," I said laughing at him.

"Well, it's true. Ask them."

"Do you want a cup of coffee?" I asked pouring myself a cup.

"Sure, honey. I'm not keeping you, am I?" Lt. asked, rubbing his stomach.

"No, of course not. Looks to me you're hungry."

He said he was and I made him two sandwiches and fixed him a cup of coffee.

We sat and talked about my first year working for him and Lt. Terry. Somehow, it went from me to him telling me the same stories I have heard a million times before. He talked himself to sleep.

"Lt., it's 12:32. Get up."

I offered him a room to stay the night. However, he refused and said he had to get home to his wife.

"Remember one thing, Leah. Put God first and family second," he laughed giving me a kiss on the forehead and telling me goodnight.

On the way out, his pager go off. It was his wife paging him.

"Oh boy, my wife needs me. I'll see you Friday."

I said goodbye and went to bed. All I could think about was what he said about putting God first and family second. I did not want that woman in my life, but knew I could not run from her any long.

My phone rang, taking my mind off that matter and putting it on something even more shocking,

It was Lt. Paul. Someone murdered his wife and kidnapped his grandchild.

TWENTY

Along Came a Rat

I arrived on the scene at 1:19 Cops were everywhere. I got out and ran over to Lt. Paul. He stood motionless over his wife's deceased body. I felt so sorry for Lt., and at that moment, my heart became weak and very sad. It was a very emotional moment for all of us. I walked over to him, placed my hand upon his shoulder, and told him I was there for him.

His daughter arrived seconds later. "Mother!" she screamed running to her side.

"What happened? Who did this?" I asked Paul.

He handed me a letter, and I begin to read. Son of a bitch; it was from Sammy.

Lt. Paul's daughter, Kayla, was devastated when she got the news about her son.

"Why my family?" she asked me.

I told her not to worry. I would get justice for her family. She insisted on helping me catch Sammy. I refused and did not want her involved with Sammy. He was a dangerous man.

"With or without you, Leah," she cried out to me. If she was going after him, I did not want her to do it alone. Therefore, I agreed she could come and help me take down Dresser.

"Just don't get in my way," I told her.

"Don't tell my father about this."

I gave her my word I wouldn't, and we left it at that. Lt. Paul walked over and gave Kayla a hug.

"Leah, that's why I say put family first," he said, reaching out to me.

He wanted me to work the case on his wife and grandson. I knew I had to get down to business and solve this case, along with my own, finally.

I did not go home that night. Kayla and I stayed with her father. I stayed up and watched the house. I didn't get any sleep until 4:00 I was so tired.

The next morning, I woke up in a cold sweat. I had another bad dream. I got up and walked downstairs into the kitchen, where Kayla was making breakfast.

"Good morning, Leah."

"Good morning."

Kayla smiled, but it quickly faded away.

"You know, mornings aren't going to be the same without mother around," she said, wiping tears from her light blue eyes.

"Why hasn't he called?" she cried out.

"Don't worry. He'll call," I said gazing out of the window.

I knew that soon, Sammy would. He wanted something, and I was the one to give it to him.

"How are you so sure?" she asked.

"Because he wants something,"

"Yeah, well all sick dogs like him want something."

"Where is Paul?" I asked. I noticed he was not around.

"He left early this morning to make arrangements for you know what."

It was a depressing moment. I had to leave. Kayla came along with me. I did not want to leave her all alone in that house.

"What if he calls while we're away?" Kayla asked.

I had all calls forwarded to my cell phone before we left the house.

When I researched Sammy's files, I discovered he still had siblings alive. I had to find out where and how I could connect with him. And they would know how.

I also discovered Sammy's mother lived in San Diego, along with his three brothers and sister. I gathered information on them and paid each one a visit, starting with his mother.

Kayla was starting to get on my nerves, nagging me about Sammy.

It was already bad enough I thought about him 24/7. I did not need this shit at all. I told her to shut the fuck up, sit back, and enjoy the ride or I was going to put her ass out of my car.

On the way to San Diego, I let Kayla take the wheel. I was sick and tired of driving. I needed a break to relax from all that tension I was feeling.

We arrived in San Diego at 10:01 finally. I could not wait to stretch my legs.

"Okay, pull over at the store. I'll take it from here."

I got out and went inside. I had pictures of Sammy's family, so I asked the cashier had he seen any of them around.

He said the last time he saw them was about 7:00 today to buy food and gas. He said he hadn't seen the wife, or at least not yet. I asked his name, and he said it was Andrew. I asked him if I could take a walk around the store and asked if I could use the employee restroom since there didn't seem to be one for customers. He gave me permission, and I looked around to see if the coast was clear before I went in.

Instead of going in the restroom, I ran into the office next to it. I quickly searched for a video recorder. I looked and looked, but no sign of a VCR.

Then, I noticed wires running to a safe. I had to get inside.

After searching for a key and ransacking everything, I still had no luck in finding it. I could see the screen, and Andrew was walking back towards the restroom. I had no choice but to do it.

"Please don't rob me!" he shouted.

I told him to remain calm and everything would be okay.

"I only want the video recordings. All the tapes," I explained.

"How far back?" he asked.

I did not know how far. I grabbed an empty duffle bag and told him to fill it up with old and new videos. As he did, I watched the monitor. Customers began to arrive.

"Hurry up," I told him.

After he finished, I grabbed the bag and told him to walk out ahead of me. I pulled out a one hundred dollar bill and handed it to him.

"This is between you and me," I said. I paid for gas and took off.

"What took you so long? Don't tell me you robbed the place."

"No, just open the bag."

"Tapes? I would have preferred the money," she laughed. I paid her no attention.

"Where are we going now?"

"To see mama dearest."

"Who?"

"Sammy's mother."

"Good, maybe we can kidnap her old ass."

That was something; I was thinking the same thing and started laughing.

We drove around San Diego for a while until we came across two guys digging a hole in the ground. I told Kayla I was not sure what they were doing and really did not care. I needed to know how to get to France Street. I rolled my window down and called both the guys over.

"What is it, lady? We have a job to do," one of the guys shouted.

"Yeah, what's up?" the other one asked.

"No need to be rude. I only want to know where France Street is located."

The tall, dark skinned brother walked over and asked me for a piece of paper.

"What business you have with France St?"

"Business, that's all," I replied.

He explained to me only one person who lived on France St was Olivia Dresser, Sammy's mother. No one was allowed on her property but family.

"I am family." He looked at me and started laughing.

"Asshole," I said rolling my window back up and pulling off.

"Why don't you use you're navigation system?" asked Kayla.

That was a good question. I never got a chance to use it. I knew where everything was located in San Francisco and LA.

Kayla turned it on and typed in the address to Olivia's residence. The navigation directed me to France Street. Olivia had the whole block on lock. Her home was huge.

I parked at the front gate and got out.

"May I help you?" a man shouts from the other side of the gate.

"Yes, I'm here to see Mrs. Dresser."

He looked at me strange.

"You mean Mrs. Notch?"

"Yes, Mrs. Notch. Sorry." I apologized, not knowing she remarried. He asked me for my name and my reason for arriving. I told him I was married to her son Sammy, and I really needed her help finding him. Boy, was I asking for it; this was plan B with no strings attached.

He told me to go through the gate. I drove up this very long hill -- a mile long.

"That was a long ride," I said looking over at Kayla, who was about half sleep.

"It took long enough to get here."

"Right, so here's the plan. I'm Sammy's estranged wife. You're my sister."

As we exited the car, a male servant walked out and greeted Kayla and me.

"Please come in," he said.

"I hope Sammy don't show up."

"I hope he does. That way, I can kill him in front of his mother," I whispered back to Kayla.

"She will be with you shortly. Please have a seat. Would you two like anything to drink?"

I said no but Kayla asked for tea. I told him we would be fine.

Minutes later, a huge door opened and out came a little woman.

"Welcome," she greeted Kayla and me. She had this mug on her face as if she just stepped in dog shit.

"Thanks for having us," I replied.

"You're Mrs. Dresser?" she asked Kayla.

I quickly said yes. Kayla turned and looked at me crazy.

"I thought you were Mrs. Dresser," Kayla whispers.

"I changed my mind."

Mrs. Olivia walked over towards Kayla and told her to explain why we were there.

Kayla looked at me, and I knew I had to step in.

"Ma'am, you're asking the wrong one. I'm Mrs. Dresser."

"One of you better answer me," said Mrs. Olivia.

I explained to her I was married to her son. She took a good look at me and if I was sure. She then informed me that his wife died over seven year's ago.

"Well, it's funny how it happened. One night in Vegas leads to a lifetime of issues. We also have a child."

"A child?" she asked.

"Yes, a baby boy," I said as tears filled my eyes.

Mrs. Notch was not the only one buying my sad story. But Kayla was feeling the emotion too. I could see it all over her face.

"Where is the child?" Olivia asked.

"Sammy kidnapped him from me," I replied weeping. Olivia got up from her seat.

"I've seen this child. He seemed afraid when I met him. I asked Sammy whom he belong to. He told me a friend's child."

"So, Sammy has been here?" I asked.

"Yes, but he never stays for long."

"Do you know where the child is or where Sammy might be?"

"No!" she shouted shaking her head. "I'll try my best to get your child back. However, Sammy is a grown man. He won't listen to me. We used to be so close, until he started selling drugs and killing innocent people. I never minded the drugs," she said smiling. "It gave me the life I never imagined," she explained.

"I can see that much," I said admiring her fine living.

I explained to Olivia I needed her help, and without a doubt, she agreed to help me.

"I know I'm wrong for saying this. But my son is better off dead or in jail," she said in disappointment.

I agreed with her a hundred percent. He was better off dead and that was the truth. It must really suck when your mother thinks that low of her own child.

"I understand. But it can be fixed?" I said.

She looked at me with a curious smile.

"Oh really?" she asked. "I've tried many times to have him killed. But it never works."

I knew then Sammy must to have done something horrible to his mother, and I wanted to know what.

"Why?" I asked.

"My love. I never got a chance to love or find love after the death of my children's father," she told me putting her hand over her heart. "It's okay;

tell me."

"See, Sammy's father was a wise old man. Always making plans for us to conquer the world. He would always tell the children to be the best that they could be. He was powerful and meek. I loved him so much," she said holding a heart-shaped medallion filled with platinum diamonds tightly in her hand.

"When he passed, Sammy went nuts -- out of control and untamed. Later, I found a new lover. He loved me as Frank did."

"Frank?" I asked unsure of whom she was talking about.

"Sammy's father. He got word I was dating and ruined everything; came to my house and ran Earl out of my life forever, telling him if he ever returned, he would put a bullet in his head."

"Did you believe he would?"

"With all my heart. Yes, he was going crazy. I just knew I would never be happy."

Sammy really scared his mother -- physically and mentally. As she cried, I told her it would be okay. Soon, she would not have to worry about that piece of shit. I was disgusted with all the power people gave him.

She continued,

"We argued that same night and it was bad. I could see the evil in his eyes. He wanted to kill me and he tried. As I turned around to walk away from him, he walked up behind me and pushed me. I fell face first down the stairs." Her head dropped in disbelief.

So sad. I could feel her pain. Only because I knew how it felt to lose a baby. I could see so much rage inside of Olivia. It made me very angry.

She told me all Sammy's personal dilemmas and each story made Olivia more fearful of her oldest child. She wanted him dead, and so did I and everyone else. She informed me about a cat by the name of Richard West, an old friend of Sammy who knew every bit of details I needed to catch this fool.

Before I left, Olivia offered me one hundred thousand dollars to kill her son and promised me she would help get Kayla's child back for me. That really made my day. I now had Sammy's mother on my team.

TWENTY-ONE

Second Chances

After Kayla and I left Olivia's place, we headed back to L.A. I had to find Richard West. Olivia gave me a picture of him. Just what I needed; it would not be hard to identify him. She also assured me he worked at a law firm in downtown L.A.

Soon as I arrived back, I went to check things out. Kayla stayed in the car because I was not sure if the place was safe or not. As I exited the car, checking my surroundings, I noticed the office was private.

Before I made way through the front door, I made sure my heat was off safety.

"Hey, how can I help you?" a secretary asked sitting behind a desk placing paperwork into file cabinets.

"Mr. West, please."

She asked me to have a seat and continued what she was doing. I sat for at least fifth teen minutes. I was starting to get bored and upset.

"I wish he would hurry up!" I shouted.

She looked at me and said, "Be patient; he'll be with you."

"Does he even know I'm here?" I asked.

I never saw her one time buzz him.

"Sure, he does." she said pointing at a camera on the wall.

Before I could ask her another question, Richard came out of his office.

"You can come back, ma'am."

I thought he was rather strange. I got up and followed him into his office.

"So Richard, what's been up with you?"

He grinned and replied, "You ask me that question as if you know me."

I mentioned we are all God's children and connect in some type of way.

He agreed with a smile.

"You're right about that. Now please, take a seat. So, what can I do for you, Miss?"

"It's Miss Starr, and I'm here to speak to you about Sammy Dresser."

He took a deep breath.

"Now that, my dear, is confidential," said Richard.

I explained Olivia sent me and that she was a good friend. "Olivia . . . how is she?" Richard asked.

"She's fine."

"That's good. What all do you need to know about Sammy?" asked Richard.

"First, when was the last time you saw him?" He grabbed his calendar and checked.

"About three days ago. He always comes by unexpectedly."

I grabbed my pen and pinpointed Richard's place as a spot to catch Sammy.

"Why the questions -- you aren't a cop, are you?" Richard asked, rising from his seat.

I told him I was doing an autobiography on Sammy and Olivia was writing it. I also told him I was from a publishing company and needed details on Sammy to write an article.

"Sure. But why would Olivia send you or even write an autobiography on her son?"

"The hell if I know," I replied, raising my shoulders. "I just need details on how you met Sammy and your relationship with him. I know a little bit, but not much," I said, toying with Richards's emotions.

"You know what?" he asked, looking at me with a big smile.

"Come on, tell me." I begged.

"I can't do that. Sammy would kill me. No way," Richard said, shaking his extremely big head.

He reminded me of Prince -- a goofy but educated version. I had a funny feeling Sammy was screwing Richard. Nasty to think Richard would scoop that low and mess with someone like Sammy. He was very attractive and well groomed. However, I think my instincts were right about the two.

I told Richard not to tell anyone, including Sammy, about me showing up or anything about the book. He asked why and I told him it's a part of a surprise his mother had for him. I mentioned I was an old friend of Sammy's, and I wanted to surprise him as well.

"I love surprises. But I'm not sure if Sammy does," said Richard.

Before I left the office, Richard gave me his personal information.

He told me to call him in two days and that he would have something for me. I wondered what it was, but did not ask. I just obliged and left.

"Have a nice day," the secretary said to me on the way out the door.

Kayla was sitting on the hood of my car when I walked out. "What are you doing?" I asked.

"Getting fresh air. You took too long, and by the way, my father called your phone while you were inside."

I began feeling around for my phone, realizing she was holding it. I walked over to her and snatched it from her hand.

"Get in!" I shouted.

"Don't be so aggressive. I'm not Sammy," she said with a very nasty and unacceptable tone. I snapped.

"Bitch, you better shut up. I am not in the mood for your shitty mouth. You better watch it."

She stood at the car door looking stupid. I had to get rid of her.

"Where are we going?" asked Kayla.

"I don't know about you, but I'm going home. I've been up all night and I'm so sick of your face," I said looking directly at Kayla. I was so serious; it made me even madder to look at her face.

When I got on the freeway, I called Lt. and told him I was on my way to the station. I also explained to him the information I received while visiting Sammy's mother in San Diego.

We arrived at the station around 4:25. We spent all day in San Diego getting clues on Sammy from family. Soon as we walked inside, Lt hugged Kayla and me.

"Before you two decide to take off all day, please let me know," Paul said nervously.

Kayla told him she called him earlier to let him know. But he did not answer. Paul denied knowing anything about the call. I thought he was losing every bit of his common sense.

He wanted to talk, but I had to go. I noticed three missed calls on my screen, along with six text messages. Most of them came from Life, and to my surprise, Tray. I called him to see what he wanted.

"Hey, sweetie," answered Tray.

I could not help but smile.

"Hey, Tray. What's up?"

He told me to never ask him that question because the answer would always be me. He then asked me to meet him somewhere quiet and peaceful. I wanted to, but I was very tired. I explained that to him and that I had been busy all day and needed rest. I told him I would meet him later if he was not busy.

"I understand; maybe later. Just call me when you awake, sleeping beauty," he said being a sweetheart.

When I pulled up in my yard, Life sat waiting on my arrival. I did not feel like fussing or talking about anything. I got out and walked passed him without saying a word.

"Leah, you're going to just walk by and not say anything?"

"Life, I don't have time. Please leave me alone."

"Oh, I see -- you don't need me anymore?" he said walking away. I stood there until he got inside his car.

"You're going to need me again. Remember that, Leah Starr." he shouted, burning off in his Chevy.

I just knew those same words I said to Life would hit me in the face one day. However, I had many reasons to be mad at him. First off, getting into my personal business, bringing my mother back into my life, and abandoning his child. I really cannot say that because it is a fifty percent chance the child might not be his. However, my gut tells me that child is his.

When I was settled, I did not go right to bed. I had some research to do. I got my laptop that contained all law enforcement technology and did some background checking.

I really liked Tray and wanted something special to happen between us. Nevertheless, before I took things any further with the man I was falling in love with, I had to know who I was dealing with.

As I begin to search, my fingers were crossed. To my surprise, he had no background. I thought that was a good sign. He completed four years of college for real estate and joined the service with fours years served. I wondered why he never told me. I would soon find out. In addition, we were just newly involved with each other and have not gotten very far yet. However, I figured he had great experience with ammo and weapons. After all my research was done, I went to sleep.

At around seven o'clock, I got up and jumped in the shower. When I got out, I fixed myself a sandwich and watched the news to see if they caught Sammy or any criminals related to Sammy's crew. When I noticed there were no leads, I cut the television off.

I grabbed a book to read by one of my favorite authors, Montice L. Harmon. It was a wonderful book entitled, "Expressions of Poetry," a collection of motivational and inspirational poetry about overcoming obstacles and awkward situations. I read about six chapters and then decided to call Life. Why? I was not sure, but knew for a good enough reason.

"I thought you would change your mind," he said grinning.

"Whatever!"

I made sure I explained to him why I was upset and did not want to be bothered. He told me he knew I was pissed about something, but did not confess his wrongs when I pointed them out. Before I picked up that book and read those words, truly, I would not have called to apologize to Life at all. I was curious to know where Loren was, so I asked.

"She's still here driving me nuts," he laughed.

I was in a daze. I looked up and suddenly felt a change come over me, as if someone switched minds with me. Weird, but that is how I felt. Before I went to sleep, I had no intentions of having a conversation with Life or asking about my mother. It had to be Tray or that book I was reading. I felt the need to forgive.

Life asked me if I wanted to speak with her. I took a long breath and exhaled, saying yes. I was a little nervous and confused, but I kept hold of myself. I guess Life did not tell her who was on the other end.

"Who is this?"

"Leah," she whispered. She almost choked on whatever was in her mouth.

"Baby girl, it's you?" she asked.

"Yes Loren it's me."

"Where are you? I've been so worried."

"I'm okay, I'm at home."

The phone became silent on her end. All I could hear was crying and heavy breathing.

"Loren I have to go. Tell Life I'll call him later." Before I hung up, she stopped me.

"Leah, please forgive; don't hold a grudge against me."

I told her I forgive her; I just didn't think I would ever be able to forget. She just did not understand the hurt this whole situation has causing me. I told her we would have to find away to work through this and take our time rebuilding a relationship. It made her feel a lot better knowing I was giving her a chance to be in my life. Again. I said goodbye and ended the conversation.

Soon as I hung up Tray called me. We arranged at the Golden Gate Vision center. Once again clueless to why he wanted to meet there.

I arrived around 7:58 I sat in the car for a minute and made sure I was on point. Before I left the house I put on shorts, a baby T, and pair of Air Dunks Jordan's #25. I had my hair in a ponytail as usual; I was not comfortable with my hair down just yet. I made sure my lip-gloss on point. I got out and walked towards the center.

"So you beat me here I see." I said with a friendly smile.

"Yes, I'm not that far from here. Come on," he said taking me by the hand, walking me into the center.

"May I ask why we are here?"

"Well, we're here to get to know each other well. I would like to know everything about you. Inside out," Tray said looking into my eyes.

I was blown away. Victor was never this considerate about my feelings inside out. I realized the difference between the two. Victor was more street, and Tray was more educated and respectful.

"And may I say you look wonderful tonight."

"You need to stop." I replied smiling. "What?"

"I see you looking at my ass." by the way was hanging out of my shorts.

"Is that wrong?" he asked.

I replied, "No," and thought it was very attractive to see a man attractive to me at that moment in my life. Not saying I thought I was not attractive, I knew it would be a lie if anyone told me I was not. I cannot deny I loved the attention he was giving me. Something I was not use too, but wanted more and more of.

"Are you hungry?" he asked me. "Sure, I'm starving."

He grabbed my hand and we walked to get a bit to eat. We ordered our food and sat down to eat.

"Isn't that water fall beautiful?" I asked.

"Yes it's amazing, but not as beautiful as you," he said reaching for my hand from across the table. I smiled and placed my hand upon his.

I could not get enough of the compliments he was giving me. It made me feel so special.

"So go ahead and tell me something about yourself?"

"Well, I'm an investigator. I have four years in law enforcement, and that's it."

He began laughing. I had to ask him what was so funny. Then he told me, "That's it? I know there's more to your Law enforcement life."

I could not tell him about my personal life. I was not ready for that part of my life to be told. Not just yet.

"My life isn't a fairy tale. More like a nightmare and at this point and time in my life; I don't want to talk about it." I explained.

He told me okay. He acted as if he understood, but I knew he did not have a clue.

He told me a lot about him and most of it dealt with his time in college and in the Army. I started to get bored and wanted to take a nap.

"You want to come back with me to my place?" I said stopping him from speaking.

On the way home, I wondered if this was the right thing to do. My mind told me no. But my body was screaming yes.

Soon as we pulled into the driveway, I got out and opened the front door, asking Tray to come inside.

I went upstairs to change into something nice and comfortable. Tray walked up the steps behind me. However, before he could enter my bedroom I dimmed the lights and laid on the bed.

"Is this what you want?" I ask him as he entered.

"Hell yeah." he said climbing on top of me.

"Please. Take your time with me."

I did not want him to think it was going to be a quickie.

He kissed me, on my neck, gently rubbing my breast. His tongue blew me away. I tilt my head back, and placed my hands upon his shoulders. He kissed me asking me to trust him. Shit, I was giving him my goodies, talk about trusting. However, I did tell him protection was necessary, Anyways, he licked my nipples softly working his way to my belly button.

"Do me right," I moaned trembling chill bumps.

"I got you, bae." he assured me.

Tray grabbed my thighs, lifting them into the air. Wetness was arising with passion to be touched. I started to shake even more; my legs trembled out of control as he placed his tongue upon my flower of goodness. I began to breath heavy, moving but enjoying every moment of him pleasing me.

For some strange fucking reason I began to think about Victor, then Life. It freaked me out. I ask him to let me get on top. I road him slow. He grabbed my hips; I could feel my love gripping his, looking into his eyes. I could tell he loved it. Why wouldn't he? I got that comeback.

I began to speed up and ride faster. He lifted up and we were chest to chest. I wrapped my arms around him and he did the same. I whispered in his ear asking him, "Do you like it?" he moaned, "Yes."

I slowed down and just sat on his dick. He asked me why did I stop, we had been fucking for about forty five minutes now, and I was somewhat tired.

I asked him to be honest with me and promise me he would always treat me right. He agreed, we kissed and continued fucking.

"Make me cum," Tray whispered in my ear.

I fucked him like a real freak, and he came in forty seconds. I told him to never test my skills. However, I must say he had control. I guess living and taking chances was worth it after all.

TWENTY-TWO

You Reap What You Sow

JUNE 2006.

I sat back pretty much and focused on my life. Trying my best to get things together, I called Richard and he faxed me shocking photos of him and Sammy on vacation. I knew Sammy had an ex-lover, but never imagined it was a man. I later found out Richard had a thing for Sammy's brothers. I never got around to talking with them. However, I heard Sammy's sister was working at a flower shop downtown San Diego. I had to pay her a visit soon.

It was Tuesday afternoon, a little breezy out. Not too hot, just how I liked it. I went back to San Diego and stopped by Jackie's Flower shop.

It was fancy; I knew some of Sammy's drug money paid for it. I looked around at the flowers minding my own business when this young girl walked out and greeted me.

"Can I help you with anything?" she asked.

"Yes, can I speak with Miss Dresser please?" she addressed that she was Miss. Dresser.

"Can I please have a word with you in private?"

"Sure, follow me."

We walked into her office.

"This your shop?" I ask already knowing the answer. She replied yes with a smile admiring her success.

"So, can I call you Jackie?"

"Yes, of course. What can I do for you?"

I pulled out a picture of Kayla's son and showed it to her. "Have you seen him?"

She took a good look at the picture.

"No, I haven't seen him." she said nervously walking away.

"Ma'am, my intuition tell me you have."

"Well you're intuition are wrong. I don't know him or never seen him a day in my life." she stated fidgeting with her plants.

I noticed a little girl sitting alone in the next room in a rocking chair.

"That's your child?" I asked walking over towards the baby.

She smiled and replied, "Yes, she's mine."

Standing there dazed for a second, I thought about Olivia.

"Jackie, why is it that Olivia knows who this child is and you don't." I asked holding the picture up.

Jackie shouted grabbing her baby, "I don't know and I don't have anymore answers to you're questions. Please leave now."

I got so angry. That bitch knew something and knew exactly where the child was but did not want to tell me. I wanted to kidnap her and her baby. She looked just like Sammy.

"Leave now!" Jackie shouted.

When I was walking out of the store, she walked behind me and whispered just so I could hear her say, "You'll never find him." I quickly turned around and asked her what she said. She denied saying anything to me and told me to leave.

I could not take her telling me one more time to leave. I drew back and punched her directly in the face. She fell back and landed on one of her plants. Her daughter was inside the shop watching from behind the glass door.

I walked up to her and grabbed her by the hair, pulling her to her feet. I rushed her against the front door.

"Now bitch, I know you know where the baby is located, and you're going to tell me." I said pushing her to the floor. I dragged her inside, cuffed her, and wrapped cheap scotch tape around her mouth taping it shut.

Plan B was now in motion,

I walked outside and drove both of our cars to the back of the shop. I went back inside and grabbed her and her child, placed the baby in the back seat and Jackie in the trunk. I locked the shop up and took off. However, before I left, I wrote a personal letter to Sammy, hoping he would react to it.

On my way out of San Diego, I called Life and explained to him what I had done. He assured me to bring both Jackie and her baby to his house.

"Where did you get her from?" Life asked.

"Slipping in San Diego; the bitch didn't want to tell me what she knew." I said looking at Jackie as she cried.

I snatched the tape from over her mouth, "Where's my baby?" she screamed.

"Shut the fuck up bitch!" I shouted slapping her in the face. "Why are you doing this to me?" she asked.

"If you make it out alive, why want you ask you're brother Sammy."

"I told you I don't know anything. I've seen him once, but never again," said Jackie.

"Who?" both Life and I asked.

"The baby."

I knew she seen the baby and knew where he was. I had to work on getting that information out of her. I shut my trunk, and she screamed her lungs out for help.

"What's next, partner?" Life asked.

"Take the baby to my mother."

"She's not here."

"Where is she?" I asked, looking around for her as my heart raced.

"She's out with Mike. They went grocery shopping."

I could not believe I was so worried about Loren. I told Life to get Jackie out of the trunk and take her wherever he wanted.

On my way downtown, I called Olivia to check up on things. She was out and about grabbing a bite to eat. She invited me to come along, but I told her maybe next time. I had to go shopping, buy me some new clothes. I had money now, so I could buy whatever I wanted.

I drove down Beverly Hills Boulevard bumping T.I's "Motivation," minding my own business when I noticed Lt. Paul. He was not alone, but with some young girl that looked like she was in her mid-twenties. From the looks of it, they were not friends; more like a couple. I slowed as I came to a stop and watched as the two made contact. Lt. Paul did not waste time giving his mistress a kiss, along with a hug. I knew something was not right with this picture. It had me confused and doubtful. I could not believe my eyes.

I parked and got out and followed them into a Victoria Secrets store. I did not want to interrupt the happy moment they were having. So, I laid low and watched.

I shopped while I was inside Victoria Secrets. I had every right to look good for Tray. Damn, that man made me feel so good inside out. I wanted more and more of his taste. I could feel him all over me. Wow, I never had anyone do it like this.

Back to basics, it had been only six days since Lt. wife's death, and he was already creeping. Looked to me he had been creeping. It made no sense to me. I grabbed my phone and took pictures of their every movement. While doing so, a number flashed across my screen.

"Hello." I answered.

"I got you're letter bitch. You better not hurt a hair on my sister, or..."

I knew he would bite like bait. "Or what Sammy,"

"You'll die for sure. Where is she?" he shouted. "Where's the child?"

"I have no fucking child. What are you talking about?"

"Sammy I know you have Lt. Paul's grandson."

"No I don't, I have no dealings with Paul Griffin. We have not dealt with each other for about six years. I know nothing about a child being missing." Sammy told me, and for some strange reason I felt he was not lying.

"So, you're telling me you know nothing about Paul's grandson being kidnapped or his wife murdered?"

"No, now where is my sister?"

"I don't know, maybe she's left town or in the San Francisco River."

"Oh, you want to play games? Fine, we'll do it the hard way," he shouted full of rage.

"Yes daddy, I like it rough." I said laughing my ass off. It was so funny. He did not realize how bad I wanted him dead. Just about as bad as his mother did. I knew now I could get his ass right where I wanted him.

"Laugh now, Leah, but believe you'll never rest upon the face of this earth. I will hunt you down and kill you myself. And I want my diamond."

I told him whatever and hung up my phone. Dumb fuck, he called unrestricted and all his information came through my radar. I guess he was so mad he forgot to block his number.

"Damn it." I shouted after realizing I had lost Lt. Paul and his lover. I began walking around the store searching for the two. As I did, my attention was taking by a pair of black pumps. In addition, they were my size. I had to have them.

"Ma'am can I help you?" a voice asked behind me.

I turned around to find the same girl Lt. Paul was with, standing in my face.

"Sure!" I said proudly handing her the pair of pumps I chose. Someone shouted her name, "Pam!" we both looked and there stood Lt. Paul.

I quickly turned my head so he would not notice me. I guess he did not because he did not call for me.

"I'll be right back." Pam said running off to Lt. Paul.

They began talking. What about, I had not one clue. I stood there patiently waiting on her to return. Finally, she ran back over to me.

"Will this be all?" asked Pam.

"Yes for now. You know you two look cute together." I said, trying to make conversation, hoping she would tell me something I did not know.

"Yeah we do."

I knew now they were lovers.

"How long have you two been together?" I asked.

"Three years or more. It's been such long time." she grinned.

"He looks married. Are you two married?" I asked looking at her hands. She held her hand up proudly showing me a ring Lt. Paul had given her. This was outrageous and really freaked me out.

"How long," I ask realizing I was asking too many questions when she looked at me strange.

"Long what?" she asked confused and unsure.

I replied, "Married," pointing at her finger.

"Oh, yeah, only a week. See he's been going through tough times. His ex-wife passed about a week ago."

Listening to her talk opened my mind to reality. His wife died; he got married the following week. Sammy claimed to have nothing to do with the death of his wife and grandson disappearance? Something was not right and I felt deep inside Lt. Paul knew as much as I did about his situation.

"That's sad." I said agreeing with Pam. "How much," I asked.

She grabbed the box and showed me the price. "Wow, fifteen hundred?"

"Yup, We don't do layaway," she said smiling.

For a minute, I wanted to reply with something real fucked up to say. But instead, "I'll take them. I have the money." I said with no intentions of being rude. I knew she did not mean any harm. Normally, I would have gone completely off on her ass. But I remained calm and showed common sense. Strange, huh?

"Are you going to try them on?"

I told her later tonight when I meet up with my man. She laughed and told me to have a nice day.

I was lost for words. I did not understand any of this. How was I going to approach Paul about this? I knew soon that Pam and I would see each other again. Moreover, I felt Lt. Paul would be present.

When I decided to call Lt. Paul, he told me he was at the bank cashing in. I thought maybe his wife's insurance money or will? I knew Kayla mentioned something about a will. It was not that important to me. Now it had become a problem I must get to the bottom of.

Soon after telling me this, he rushed off the phone. Lt. Paul rushing me off the phone was some new shit. Usually, I would have to be the one to end the call.

I did not know if Sammy was playing around or telling the truth. It did matter to me because I wanted Kayla's baby back and Sammy dead. I was confused and did not know where to go. Thinking to myself, I realized we all have to pay a price in our lives. I just did not understand why now this matter was happening to Lt. Paul. Why was he seeing other women? Did Kayla and the rest of his family know about it? Was Paul old ass doing the killings?

I was not sure what to think. Sammy knew now the diamond was not real. Nevertheless, why was he just now telling me? Everything was strange; I really did not know whom to trust, knowing now I would have to watch my back.

After leaving downtown, I went by Kayla's house to check on her. I explained to her that Sammy called me and denied having her baby. She freaked, I could see she already had been crying before I arrived. Her face was red and puffy.

I sat comforting her, telling her everything would be all right. I made her a promise I would find her baby if it took me being killed or me killing.

She expected me to do my best at finding her child and I would. I still had to complete plan B. but new shit kept coming up getting stranger and stranger. I had a lot on my hands knowing I was the only person in the entire world that could solve this case. Every issue became apart of my life.

Kayla stopped me before I left and asked me a question that had been bothering me for the last past two hours.

"Do you think my father will be okay?" she asked.

I wanted to tell her he was perfectly find. Then she would ask more questions I did not have time for. Therefore, I explained to her her father was going through some things and that the lost of someone close to you was hard.

"No, Leah, he's been this way before my mother passed."

"How long?"

"For about two years; I always thought he cheated on my mother," said Kayla, wiping tears away from her eyes.

Kayla was not a fool; she knew her father was cheating on her mother.

"Why would you say he was cheating on your mother?"

"This strange woman calls the house asking for him all the time."

"Well, maybe it's a friend." I inquired.

"No she's not a friend. That was the first thing I asked her before hanging up the last time we spoke. She told me I would be her daughter. What does that tell you?"

She was not telling me anything new. I was just glad she had a clue her father was cheating. That way I did not have to tell her.

"Did your mother know about her? And were there any problems with your mother and father in the home?"

"No, you've met my mother."

"Yes of course I did. She was a sweet woman." I replied with a friendly smile.

"That's how she's always been. A good mother and wife. Why would my father cheat on her?"

"So where are your older brothers and sister?" "They'll be here Tuesday to lay my mother to rest." Kayla grabbed her chest, as if someone had hit her. "Are you okay?" I asked Kayla rushing to her side. "I'm fine. Just a little heartburn." she replied.

I told her if she ate some mustard, it would help the heartburn go away.

"Really?" Kayla asked. "Yup, Works every time." "Wow, I never knew that."

"I'll try my best to talk to your father. To see what's going on. Just pray about it Kayla and remember prayers the key to understanding."

"I do pray. Nothing seems to unfold." she sighs, rubbing her chest, pulling strings of her hair out.

I grabbed her and shouted, "Listen to me; your going to have a nervous breakdown if you don't chill out. Your faith in God is gone, and that's something you're going to need in order to help me find your child." I pulled her close to me and hugged her as tight as I could. It'll be alright; cry on my shoulder."

"Please get my baby back, Leah," cried Kayla.

I began to think about my baby and how enraged and devastated I was over the loss of my child. Of course any mother would be.

Kayla complained about being tired and went to bed.

I helped her to bed and got to myself. I called Tray to see how his day was going. He explained he was spending time with his boys. He was such a great father to his kids. I told him to have them ready by eight. I had tickets to see the Lakers in action.

When he told the boys about the tickets I could hear them rejoicing over the news. That made me happy because I wanted them to like me.

After I left Kayla's crib, I went home. I had to get my mind right and off this situation before I went out with Tray and his boys tonight. Life called me soon as I got in. Jackie was giving him a hard time and he was ready to get her the hell out of his house. I told him to hold her down for me a little while longer. I had to know for sure if Sammy had anything to do with Kayla's baby.

Olivia told me she had seen the child, Jackie told me she knew, but would not tell me. So now, where was the child? Somebody had to answer.

After I settled in, I took a shower and put on some clothes. Jazzed up and looking fine in my new heels. My outfit was on point, Gucci tank top with a pair of skintight Baby Phat jeans. I laid my hair down and candy curled it. I knew there would be many celebrities there so I put on my thousand dollar earrings and bracelets.

After I got ready, I sat and watched a little television until 7:30 Then I took off to Tray's house.

It was my first time going, so I was a little nervous. I arrived at his house at 7:58 I sat inside my car a while before going up to his door.

I called him before I arrived. So he knew I was on my way.

"Hey, I'm waiting outside." I said soon as Tray answered the phone. He met me at the door and welcomed me in.

"Come in."

"Damn, baby, you're looking Hollywood."

"Excuse me?" I asked looking over my shoulder.

He just stood there smiling. When I looked into his eyes, I saw love, life, and tragedy?

"You're beautiful." he replied looking passionately into my eyes.

"Really," I asked in disbelief.

A man never told me I was beautiful, besides my father. "Have a seat. We're getting ready."

"The game starts in ten minutes." I said walking behind him.

He turned around and kissed me. "What was that for?" I asked.

"Just something I forgot to do when you arrived." he said smiling. I got weak in the knees. I really wanted this to work.

"Come on, I want you to meet my kids." he took me by the hand and walked me into the dinning room.

"Kids, this is Leah." Tray said introducing me. Both of the boys walked up and greeted me. "Are you guys Lakers fans?" I asked.

Traven Jr. stood afar watching me.

"I love basketball, period. Tray, you do, too," shouted Andrew, Tray's youngest son.

"What about you, Jr.?" I asked.

"I don't talk to strangers," he replied rudely.

I just stared at him for a while. I couldn't say anything.

"What are you looking at?" he asked me.

I quickly shouted for Tray. He came running into the dining room.

"What's the problem?" he asked.

I pulled him off to the side and told him about his boy attitude. The little fucker chomped me off. I did not want to get him into trouble, but it was a little too late for that.

"What's your problem, Jr.?" asked Tray.

He just looked at his father and rolled his eyes. Tray slapped the shit out of him.

"No, Tray!" I shouted. "It's not that serious," I explained to him rubbing his back trying my best to calm him down. He was pissed and ready to beat the shit out of his son.

"It's okay; he doesn't like me right now. It takes time." I whisper to Tray.

"Go get you're things." he shouted. "Where is he going?"

"To his mother."

"So, he's not coming with us?" I asked.

"No Leah, he has to learn not to be disrespectful to me or anyone else."

I told him I understood. I sat patiently waiting on them to get it together. While I waited, little Andrew kept me company.

"Are you going to be our stepmother?" Andrew asked out of nowhere. I told him I did not know, and to be honest, I did not at that time.

We left at 8:09.

I left my car at Tray's and jumped in with him and the boys. We drove to his ex-wife's house.

Tray watched Jr. from his rear view. I wondered what he was thinking. I know he seen himself inside Jr.'s eyes. Hell, they looked just alike.

"Jr., give me a reason to give you another chance."

"I'm sorry, Lisa." Jr. replied.

"It's Leah." I said correcting him.

I convinced Tray he was sorry so we could go see the Lakers in action.

"No, Leah. I'm not going back on my word. I don't need any body telling me how to raise my kids," Tray shouted.

"But you just asked him why you should give him another chance."

"It doesn't matter anymore. My mind is made up."

"Well, we can call it a night. Take me back to get my car," I insisted. He stomped on the breaks, making a u-turn. Jr. and Andrew began yelling for their dad to slow down. I just looked at him. He was mad and so was I. I knew then he was very stubborn.

I never wanted him to think I was trying to tell him how to raise his kids. I only wanted the four of us to go see a damn Lakers game. I know I needed time alone, time to figure out how I was going to get Kayla's son back. I was not the only one worried. Tray had feelings bottled up inside him; it was written all over his face.

I am not going to lie. I would have said I did not care, but I did. I was in love with this stubborn man. I could not deny it. In addition, to say it turned me on, but I was not about to give in.

He offered me money for the tickets. I told him not to worry about it. I got inside my ride and left.

TWENTY-THREE

DéJà VU

DéJà vu hit me hard. On my way home, pictures flashed in and out of my head. Visions of me killing Sammy. All I could see was blood everywhere. I know it had to be me to do it because no one else was brave enough. Not even the law.

I never understood why so many people feared this man. Even his mother.

I received a call from Lt. Paul; he wanted me at the station tomorrow morning. For what, I had not a clue.

When I arrived home, I was surprised to find Christian there waiting for me. First thing came to mind was how did she know where I stay?

"Hey Leah, I hope you don't mind me stopping by unannounced."

"How did you find out where I stay?" I ask suspiciously.

"I asked around you know." she replied.

"What do you want?

"I need your help."

I was not in the mood for doing any favors. However, I knew she would not leave me alone until I accepted. I told her to come inside, but before she did, she returned to her car to get her child.

"I know you might say no. But you're the only person I can trust right now.

I did not have all night to talk to her, so I told her to cut to the chase. "Well, I need you to watch my son for me tonight.

"For what reason Christian?"

"I'm going out of state," she caught herself, "I mean out of town. I'll be back in the morning."

For some reason, I felt she was lying.

As she continued talking, a vision came to me. I was dazed; I could not hear anything Christian was saying. I saw her laying in a pool of blood and her son crying out.

"Leah, are you okay?" Christian asked me.

"Where are you going?

"Out with someone I met recently." she replied.

I had a bad feeling. I did not want to share with her the vision I had. I just knew this guy was going to kill her.

"How long have you known this guy?

"For about three weeks or so. He's wonderful," she smiled.

"Okay, I'll watch him." I said confused and worried

She jumped up and hugged me

"Thanks a lot, Sis, you're the best. And one more thing,"

"What?" I asked

"Please don't tell Life," she begged me.

I explained to her that it was our little secret. She gave me her son and left.

I called Life to talk about the visions I was having. I wanted to know what they meant. He told me that when people have visions of someone dying, it is always the opposite sex that dies. He told me not to worry but that was hard to do. The baby began crying while I was on the phone with Life.

"Who's child?" he asked.

I told him a friend of mine from the neighborhood. "Don't lie to me Leah."

The way he said it made me feel bad, and I did not make any promises to Christian, and probably will never see her again.

"That child sounds like my son." Life said.

When he said that, I remained quiet for a minute. He called my name three times, but I still did not answer. Minutes later the phone hung up.

Damn, I did not want Life thinking he could not trust me. I was the one with the trust issues. It did not need that to be the both of us.

I fed the baby and put him to sleep. He was a good baby. All he needed was a warm bath and something to eat and he was on his way to sleep.

6:09 AM

The next morning was hell. The baby woke me up crying out of control. I did not know what was wrong with him. I picked him up and rocked him in my arms, and he fell back to sleep. I waited on Christian to return or call me to let me know everything was okay. However, no call or show.

I phoned her eight times and got no answer. I had to think fast, I knew I could not take the baby with me to work. I had to find someone to keep him until I returned.

Then I noticed Mrs. Thomas walking out to get her morning newspaper

"Hey, Mrs. Thomas. How are you today?" I ask.

She smiled and replied, "I'm doing fine, sweetie. Wow, he's beautiful. What is his name?"

I felt stupid because I forgot his name. "Hello!" Mrs. Thomas shouted

"It's Life." I replied.

"What a beautiful name."

"Mrs. Thomas I have to be to work at eight, and I have no one to watch him and..." before I could finish, she grabbed Life out of my hands.

"Don't worry about paying me anything. I'll keep him whenever you need me too,"

What a relief. I got my things together. While doing so, another vision came over me. This time it was Lt. Paul covered in blood. Now I thought that maybe it was from his wife's death. Only because it looked so familiar. This was getting out of hand; I wanted to know why I was having these visions.

I got dressed and went to the station to meet Lt. Paul. When I arrived, no one was in sight. I sat inside my car and waited for him to show up. I had a key but thought it would be safe if I waited.

Minutes later, I noticed lights coming into the parking lot. It was another police officer coming to work. He parked next to me, got out, and fired up a cigarette. For some strange reason I started craving for a smoke. I rolled down my window to inhale the second hand smoke that filled the air.

He looked at me, "Have one?" he replied.

I did not know him like that, and was not sure of his actions. "No thank you," I replied.

The clock read 7:10 Lt. Paul had some explaining to do. The officer asked me if I had a key and I told him no. I decided to call Lt. Maybe something was wrong with Kayla.

I could tell he was busy, he answered the phone heavy breathing, "Hello," he sounded.

I remained silent on the phone for a second hearing someone giggling in the background. I knew for sure he was fucking, and this kind of situation was out of my league.

"Paul, what are you doing?" I asked.

He cleared his throat replying, "Leah is that you?

"Yes, you told me to meet you at the station at eight o'clock."

"I'm so sorry, Leah. Hold tight I'll be there.

"Okay, but you need to hurry up. I've been sitting up here for about 45 minutes, and it isn't fun."

He asked me why I had not gone inside yet. I told him I did not feel like messing around with the alarm system.

"There's someone besides you there right?"

"Yes." I replied.

He gave me instructions to give the guy the information to the system and to go inside and wait for his arrival. I okayed him, then realize I never told him it was a guy. Lt. Paul was really becoming a fucking suspect. I was so fucking angry.

What was he trying to do? I quickly snapped "I'm not doing anything until you get here." I shouted hanging up the phone.

If he was about to set me up, at least I wanted to look him in the eyes once I killed his hit man.

This was troubling. I needed answers and knew just where to get them. I phoned the National Investigation Associates to speak to someone who worked there; he put me in on to a lot of shit. In addition, I needed to know something ASAP.

We talked about politics, family, and my future agencies. Ole Alex, he always had a thing for me. I never gave him a chance or the benefit of a doubt. He was much older than I was. He knew how to keep me on point and make me smile. That is what I feared the most about him. I just do not see myself having a man that controls me, or have some type effect on me.

We arranged to meet up later that day, and talk about some more important issues. Whenever I finished my conversation with my friend, Alex, Lt. Paul pulled up.

Him and the guy instantly made eye contact and held a conversation soon as Lt. exited his patrol car. I kept my eyes on the two as they carried on.

Lt. Paul threw up his hands for me to come on; I grabbed both of my pistols making sure both were loaded, ready to take a bitches head off.

At that point and time, I did not even have mercy for Lt. Paul. I would have smoked his ass too. I discriminate against bullshit and was not with it.

As I exited my car, the guy who sat in the parking lot walked behind me as I headed towards the front door. It was strange how he waited until I got out of my car to walk inside. I kept my hands on both sides of my hips where my Glock nines were.

"This thing kills me." Lt. Paul said trying to punch in the code.

"Take your time Lt." I replied.

The guy watched over my shoulders. I turned around and looked directly into his eyes asking, "Who are you? I never seen you around here before."

He began laughing as if something was extremely funny. "I don't see shit funny. Who are you?" I snapped.

"Hold up little lady, no hard feelings. I'm new right Lt?"

Lt. Paul agreed. I had enough, I told Lt. Paul to move out of the way, punched in the security code, and went inside.

"Wow, she's just now knowing the code." the guy replied.

I did not say a thing knowing I would have my time to investigate his ass.

I walked into the kitchen and put on some coffee. As I prepared the coffee, I watched Lt. and the guy talk. By the time the two walked inside the kitchen the coffee was done brewing.

"So new guy, what's your name?" I asked soon as he walked in taking his attention off Lt.

"Steven," he replied.

"Steven…?"

"Sorry, Steven Martin," he said blushing.

Steven was light skin, standing at about 6 feet, very handsome. I may say his eyes were what attracted me to him. However, something threw me off about him also.

Paul called me into his office to have a talk. -- Something I had been waiting to do.

By the time I walked into his office, other officers were arriving. Steven stood in the kitchen window smiling and watching me. I cracked a smile in return.

"Have a seat, Leah," Lt. Paul directed me, closing the door behind him. I was hoping he was about to explain to me why all these strange actions have taken place. It was not only becoming a thing of revenge for my father's death. But also the life of Lt. Terry.

"Do not tell Kayla anything about what I'm about to tell you," he whispered as if we were not the only two present in his office.

I just looked at him for a long time without saying a word. "Promise me, Leah." Lt. begged me.

"Tell what? Something she already knows. Your daughter isn't a fool Lt."

I could not hold back what I felt inside; I could see it was troubling him. Misery was all over his face. I could tell he had many sleepless nights.

"How you figure she knows?

I told him to ask her. I wanted no part in his scandalous betrayal. I was not the one doing the fucking around.

I sat there and wondered why he would do such a thing to his family.

"How do you live with it?" I asked him.

"That's personal, Leah, you wouldn't understand."

I figured he did it only because he could. From that moment, having that conversation with him changed my complete prospective about him. You always think men like Lt. Paul would be the prime example of what you wanted your husband to be like one day. I am sure once his daughters' thought the same thing until his dirty secrets started to unfold.

I didn't see him as my friend anymore. More like an enemy that had no mercy or remorse for his family.

"So, have you found leads on my wife?"

I told him what Sammy told me, and explained it detail to detail. "Sammy denied having anything to do with your wife's death and grandson's abduction."

"That son of a bitch is lying; don't believe a word he tells you. He's nothing but a snake in the grass." Lt. Paul states firmly.

I wanted to tell him he was a snake also. However, I remained quiet and just listened to him tell me what he wanted me to hear.

"You sure are taking your time catching the fuck," he replied.

"When the time is right I will. What are you doing Paul?" I asked him.

"Well you need to get on it. Hurry up!" he shouted.

"Lt. there's a time and season for everything, and believe me when it's all over and done, every dog that has betrayed and lied to me will be hit." I said with an evil grin.

I had to get out of his office before I exploded. I went to the restroom to pull myself together. I sat inside a stall and cried. Lt. Paul did not realize how bad I wanted Sammy dead.

Without realizing I was inside, a female officer walked in having a conversation with someone about Sammy Dresser.

"Yes, girl, I didn't know he was Sammy Dresser and I didn't want him to know I was a cop."

This was interesting. I did not move at all. Just sat there listening. "He's my ex boyfriends best friend." she told her friend on the other end.

This gave me more input on what I needed to know in order to get close enough to Sammy.

She went on about how Sammy would never be captured and how her ex boyfriend guards Sammy with his life. She told her friend she knew all Sammy's whereabouts and how he could be caught.

I flushed the toilet and she quickly ended the call.

"Who's in here?" she asked.

"How long have you been here?" I asked as I walked out.

She told me not very long. I told her if she wanted to keep her job to keep her damn mouth shut. She looked at me strange, then rolled her eyes.

"Is there a problem?" "Should there be?" she asked.

Before I could say anything, a vision came to me. I was choking this bitch to sleep.

"You're nuts. You need to think about early retirement."

"No, it's time for you to find another job." I said walking up in her face.

"Back away from me or you'll regret it," she said with her hand on a can of pepper spray.

"You're going to spray me?" I ask pointing at the can of mace.

It was so funny to me. I could not stop laughing. This bitch was kidding me.

"Dare me. I'll do it and say you attacked me."

I knew I could beat this bitch ass right now if I wanted too. She broke all the rules as a police officer.

I turned around as if I was walking away, but turned back quickly punching her in the face.

"Awe!" she screamed.

She tried getting back to her feet but I pushed her back on the floor. I grabbed her by the hair and went to work on her ass beating the shit out of her. She found away to kick me off of her. When I fell back, I quickly pulled my hoodie over my face. She grabbed the can of mace and ran towards me spraying. "You bitch." she screamed as we both hit the floor.

By this time, people were starting to crowd around watching us go at it. I hit her one good time in the stomach, she folded. Once I got to my feet, I stomped her ass to sleep. Lt. Paul ran over and grabbed me, why did he do that? I pushed him so hard he flew into one of the stalls.

Lt. Paul told the officers to arrest me. They ran over and grabbed both of my hands throwing me to the floor.

"Let go of me." I screamed.

I was so fucking mad. But not as mad as the bitch getting her ass whipped.

"You'll never find him. I hope he kills you all," she shouted.

I turned and looked at Lt. Paul as he looked at me. "Lock both of them up. I have no need for neither of them." said Lt. Paul.

He walked over to me and whispered, "Calm down. You will be out. I do not know who to trust Leah; I have people working for both Sammy and me. I'm putting you off the force for a while. I'll collect your gun and badge."

Before he walked out of my sight, I made sure he knew how I felt.

"I will never work for you again. You are a nasty son of a gun, and soon a later you'll pay for all your dirt."

I was charged with disorderly conduct, and my bail was $1,500. I tried calling Life, but he did not answer the phone. I was left with no choice. I called Tray, and to my surprise, he came through for me.

TWENTY-FOUR

A Low down Dirty Shame

Friday: July 20, 2006

Tray arrived soon as they were releasing me. They also released that bitch. We made eye contact; and I knew we'd meet again soon.

"What's going on Leah?" Tray asked me taking my attention off her.

"Nothing major. I had some business to take care of."

Before I walked out of the station Lt. Paul stopped me. "Leah, I hope you're not mad with me," said Lt. Paul.

For a moment I wanted to punch the shit out of him, but instead I replied,

"Oh no, I'm fine. I am not mad at all. I will say that was the best decision you've ever made."

"Why is that, Leah?" he asked me as I walked towards the front door.

"Things are starting to make sense. And I don't want to work for this investigation company anymore."

I explained to him I would be working with Washington Investigation Unit, and planning towards my own company. He looked at me weird saying, "That's wonderful, but it takes money to do so." he replied with a grin.

"Oh don't worry I have plenty of that, and will have plenty more when I turn in Sammy's dead body."

"Good luck." he replied.

"I'm not the one who needs it Lt."

"See you later, Leah. I have a wake to attend."

"Yeah you'll be seeing me soon." I said walking out.

Tray took me back to the station for my car. While riding, he just kept eyeing me.

"What!" I shouted frustrated and annoyed.

"Oh, nothing, I just wonder about you now and then."

I did not ask why. I just sat there wondering why I was there. When we arrived at the station, I got out and walked to my car. Tray rolled up beside me and asked, when will we see each other again?"

"You're doing that now." I said being funny. He told me to stop playing, and to tell him.

"I'm serious Tray. Thanks once again for coming through for me and helping out."

I told him I would pay him back. But he told me I did not have too. However, I insisted.

"Don't worry about it Leah, it's pay back for the tickets you wasted. So when will I see you again?"

"I'll call you later tonight. I need a little time alone."

"I understand. Think of me while you meditate," he said smiling. Soon as I got inside my ride, Olivia called.

"Where are you?" she asked.

I told her on my way home. She wanted me to come by her place but I did not feel like driving out to San Diego. Therefore, I asked her to meet me in Los Angeles.

We agreed to meet at Coo'Jo's, an urban popular restaurant in downtown LA with some of the best food money can buy. I drove over and waited on Olivia to arrive. I put on my Chanel shades, reclined my seat, watching the scenery.

Something told me to look to my right, and there was Lt. Paul all dressed up in a suit headed towards a white Tahoe. He was carrying a suitcase, and in such a hurry. Once inside he rolled down his window watching suspiciously at every car and person that went by.

Minutes later, someone got in on the passenger side and made an exchange with him. Words were said but I could not make out the conversation. I was too damn far.

Paul threw his hands up handing the suitcase over to the passenger. Next thing I know the passengers exits and a female gets out. Soon as she turns around facing my direction, it shocked the hell out of me when I realized the familiar face. It was the same woman from the station I had problems with earlier that morning. I could not believe my eyes. She walked to the back door and pulled out a car seat with a child inside it. She then handed Lt. Paul a vanilla envelope. He got out of the Tahoe and walked back to his patrol car placing the car seat inside.

I truly believed that was Kayla's baby. However, why would Paul have the child? Right than and there I knew he had something to do with his wife's death. Fishy and strange, Minutes into my investigation Olivia popped up. I got out and walked over towards her car.

"Mrs. Dresser," she addressed me.

I told her to call me Asia. That was the fake name I used.

"So have you seen my son since the last time we met?"

"No ma'am. Not yet." She grabbed the menu and browsed through it.

"Would you like anything to eat or to drink?" she asked me.

"No thank you."

My mind was on Lt. Paul and that white Tahoe.

"What's on your mind dear?" asked Olivia reaching into her purse pulling out a thick envelope, sliding it across the table towards me.

"What's this?"

"A down payment; you'll get the rest when the job is done." I opened the envelope and it was full of hundred dollar bills. "How much is this?" I asked while she sipped on a glass of water.

"It's ten grand. I will pay you the rest later. What, it's not enough?" she asked.

"No, it's fine."

"Good, because I have ninety thousand put aside for you when you complete the task. So, when will you be able to do this?"

"Whenever I find him. It's been hard keeping up with him."

The waiter brought a basket of bread to the table.

"Have some." Olivia said offering me a piece of bread. "No, thank you, I'm on a diet."

"Ha, are you serious? Your figure is amazing." she said looking at me smiling, and to say I was flattered by her compliment.

"Oh, I get it. Eating problem?"

"No, I just have to watch my weight."

"Yeah, right." she said grinning.

I told her I was sorry, but there was something I had to do. She told me to go ahead and handle my business, but make sure I handle what we planned.

"Oh I will," I replied getting up to leave.

"Take care and keep in touch," said Olivia.

Soon as I left the restaurant, I called Kayla. She was leaving the house with one of her brothers. I explained to her that we needed to talk about something important. She told me she had something very important to tell me about her father, but needed to explain in person.

The funeral was held at the old Baptist church in San Francisco. I assured her I would meet her there but I needed to change into something casual.

The funeral started at 11:00 I was there and ready for whatever. You know they say the killer always show up at the funerals to prove some type of point. Or to watch the family grieve in pain. What a shame, but I wanted to be the first to know and see them face-to-face.

I was not seeking justice for Paul anymore; it was for his wife and kids. I did not fall in with the rest; I laid low in the back of the church and watched the family view her body. I could tell Paul was putting on, acting as if he missed his wife when he knew I knew the truth, and so did Kayla. Moreover, what made the situation even worse is that he brought his mistress along with him. To comfort him and be that shoulder he could cry on. Sick son of bitches.

She sat in the front with the rest of the family as if she belonged. How scandalous the two looked. I knew this was the wrong place to pull out a gun but I was ready.

While standing in the back, my phone went off. Everyone turned and looked at me.

"What!" I whispered to those that looked my way.

It was Christian, still alive. It brought a smile to my face hearing from her.

"I'm at your place. Where's my child?" It sounded like she was upset.

"He's next door at my neighbor's house. Go over across the street to Mrs. Thomas house and get him."

"Okay, thanks." Christian said hanging up.

Kayla was about to begin her speech. I walked over to the last row and took a seat.

She was full of tears. It was so sad, I felt sorry for her and her family. I had never met Kayla's brothers and sister before. They did not care too much for San Francisco, nor stayed near it. All of them looked just like Paul in some way.

After Kayla finished, Paul walked up to speak. I could not wait to see what he had to say. Lies, lies, lies, and more lies. Every word he spoke was full of bullshit and his kids knew it too.

One of his sons was missing. In addition, his oldest daughter was upset and walked out of the sanctuary. It must have been something Paul said that ticked her off. She stormed outside and I got up behind her and followed.

"Hey you," I shouted getting her attention.

She turned around and asked me what did I want. "I just want to talk, that's all." I said friendly. I am sure she did not want any problems.

"About what?"

I asked her to take a walk with me. I knew Paul would come for her soon as he finished telling his lies. So, we walked down the street to the nearest corner and talked.

"First of all I want to say I'm sorry for your lost. And I'm trying my best to find you and your family justice."

She reached into her coat and pulled out a box of New Ports 100's. "Have one?"

I grabbed one and fired it up. "So, you're Leah?" she asked.

"Yeah. That's me."

"So, what have you found so far?"

"Well, my interests are on your father right now," I said throwing hints.

She smiled.

"Yeah, that's where my interests are also. I truly believe he had something to do with my mother's death," she explained smoking her cigarette as if it was her last.

"I don't think he killed her. I do believe he had someone else to do it." I explained.

"Was it worth it? That is all I want to ask him. But I don't know how.," she sobbed.

"He will never tell you the truth."

"He's a fucking loser. I hate him," she shouted.

"I miss my mother so much. I wish she wouldn't have married his bitch ass."

I had many questions to ask. However, had only a little time to do so. In addition, that moment was not a good time.

Once we finished our cigarettes, they were carrying the casket out of the church.

"Let me go pay my last respect to my mother. Leah, I hope you get to the bottom of this."

Before she walked away, I asked for her name.

"Just call me Angie." she replied.

She around twenty-seven, had long curly hair. Looked a lot like her mother than the others; Kayla explained to me she was a very successful lawyer. One of the best in New York City.

We headed to the graveyard to lay Paul's late wife to rest. The preacher said his final words as the family stood there mourning over her casket. I kept my eyes on Paul the whole time.

As I began walking around the gravesite, I noticed that white Tahoe again. I had both of my pistols on my hips and two around my ankles.

Later another Tahoe pulled up. I looked back at Paul as he witnessed these actions taking place. I called Life and told him to meet me at the old Baptist church gravesite. He assured me he was already there. I looked around noticing his Chevy. I walked slowly over towards his car keeping my eyes on those vehicles.

"What's going on?" Life asked.

"I'm not sure. Those white Tahoe's been sitting there for awhile watching everyone."

"Who are they?" Life asked pulling out a bottle of Gin.

"I don't know. Why are you drinking?" I asked pulling the bottle down away from his mouth.

"Thirsty," he said smiling.

I didn't ask any more questions.

"What do you think is about to go down?" asked Life as we watched the trucks move in closer, picking up speed.

"I don't know. Are you ready?" I asked pulling out my pistols.

They drew Tech 9's at the crowed and started shooting. Life and I got out of the car and hit the ground letting lose at the trucks.

Everyone hid behind the casket for protection. The body fell out and Kayla rushed to her mother's side and tried to place her back inside the coffin.

Life took out the driver in one of the trucks; it crashed into a tree, instantly killing the passenger. A female exited the rear end of the truck and ran towards Life and me. I rolled underneath the car just in time as she began shooting. I got a good aim at her and before I could take her out, Angie ran out of nowhere and football tackled her to the ground. They began to struggle with each other but Angie hit her with one hard blow to the head, knocking her out.

"Damn bitch." Angie shouted standing to her feet.

Unexpectedly, Angie screamed, "No!" turning to see dead bodies laying everywhere,

Paul stood to his feet in shock observing his surroundings. Angie ran over to Kayla who was lying over her mother's body. Angie shook Kayla repeatedly but she did not respond.

Tears filled my eyes, I knew right then Kayla was dead. I walked over to Angie and hugged her tight, "Don't do it." I said as she slowly reached for one of my pistols. I knew she wanted to kill Paul. She gave him such an evil look only one could give their worst enemy.

He walked over where we were and looked down at Kayla's lifeless body dropping to his knees in tears.

His two sons tried to comfort him, but he was out of control.

Angie snatched away from me walking up to Paul slapping the spit out of his mouth. "This is all your fault," she shouted in tears. Raged and highly upset with her father.

"Why did you do that?" one of the brothers asks Angie.

"He's the reason mother is dead, and now Kayla. How could you?" Angie shouted wanting answers.

Paul turned and looked at me. "This is all your fault," he shouted.

Before I could say anything, Angie slapped him once again.

"Stop lying. You know who is doing all the murdering. You plotted all this."

I told her to fallback; it was not worth it, and was not going to solve nothing. The police showed up minutes later.

Loretta Gains, she was convicted of robbery and now first-degree murder. She was only twenty-four.

She explained she would work for everyone. Anyone that would put money into her pockets; this chick was ugly as fuck, and I did not see how any man could sleep with her. Unless he was desperate for ass. However, I guess it is true what they say. Pussy do not have a face just a set of lips.

Life disappeared. I did not even notice him leaving. I am glad he got away safe. I did not tell the cops Loretta was involve with the shooting because I had use for her outside of jail.

Angie and I drove to Life's crib with Loretta tied up in the back seat.

I snatched Loretta out of the back seat, throwing her to the ground. Angie ran around the car full speed kicking Loretta in the face. She looked up at Angie and me and began laughing.

"What's so funny, bitch?" I asked.

She told Angie and me justice would never be served. I grabbed her by the hair dragging her inside the house.

"What's going on Loretta?" Loren shouted.

I looked at my mother asking, "You know her?" Loren dropped her head.

"Answer me mother!" I shouted.

She shook her head affirming that she knew Loretta Gains.

"No way," Loretta replies looking at both Loren and me laughing.

"Loren's my mother, too. If she's your mother, shit, you put it together, Leah." said Loretta.

This shit was crazy and freaked me out. What the fuck? I have a sister?

TWENTY-FIVE

Flash Back

I was lost and needed answers. How could this be? "Mother, why you haven't told her," Loretta asked Loren.

"Loretta is not my child. Sammy adopted and abandoned her. She needed someone, so I stepped in and loved her like a mother," Loren explained.

I was relieved. However, I could see Loretta did not take kindly to what Loren was saying.

"Leah, I'm ready to question her," whispered Angie.

I asked Loretta to come with me to the basement. She acted foolish, as if she did not comprehend what I was asking her. I grabbed her by the hair, dragging her down twenty-five steps, and throwing her to the cement floor. I looked to my left and saw Jackie rocking her child to sleep.

"I brought you a friend," I said, given Jackie the look.

"You can't do this to us. Let my baby go. And me," begged Jackie. "Who is she?" asked Angie, referring to Jackie.

"Sammy's sister."

"I see you've been busy," Angie replied.

Once we placed Loretta into a chair all tied up tight, we began asking questions. At first, she refused to answer any of our questions until I pulled out a knife and began poking the shit out of her with it.

"Okay bitch, I'll talk. Just stop with the poking," Loretta shouted. Angie walked up to her and punched the shit out of her, busting her bottom lip.

"Watch your mouth," said Angie.

"Now what business do you have with Paul Griffin?" I asked.

"He's my boss." Angie started crying. "That bastard. I knew it. I was right," she said looking in my direction, then at me.

"What type of business you two have going on?"

"I was hired to kill his daughter Kayla," she explained.

"Why?" Angie asked Loretta.

"Well, he promised me a meal ticket if I killed her."

As I figured, Paul was behind the death of both his wife and daughter.

"How much is he paying you?" asked Angie.

Loretta did not hesitate at explaining that thirty thousand dollars was involved in the murder of Kayla and Mrs. Griffin.

"Did you kill my mother?"

"No," Loretta denied.

I had a plan but Angie thought different.

"I know you want away with your father. But I have an idea."

"What is it?" Angie asked in doubt of agreeing before hearing what I had to say.

At this point, we could not trust Paul Griffin, and knew he felt the same way about us. So why not use Loretta to do our dirty work.

"If she doesn't kill him, at least he'll be put away for life if we set him up and get him to confess the murders."

"That sounds good, but I want him to suffer as we have. As my mother suffered before her final breath."

I explained to Angie that suffering had already begun for him. In addition, there was more to come when everyone knew the truth about his disloyalty to the community, his career, and family. With these actions, Paul Griffin will be put to death right along with Sammy Dresser.

While talking to Angie, a question came to my existence. I turned to Loretta and asked if she knew Nicole Loston.

"The name sounds familiar," said Loretta.

"What about Lt. Terry?" I asked.

"Oh yeah, a woman name Susan killed him."

Susan? I was confused now. I went upstairs to grab a photo of Nicole Loston. I wanted to make sure Loretta knew what she was talking about and had the right person.

When I returned, Angie was choking the shit out of Loretta. "Angie, no," I shouted grabbing her off Loretta.

"Why not? We know who's behind the murders."

"Damn it, Angie. Remember our plan? You will have the opportunity to do that later. Don't kill our only witness."

She agreed, firing up a Newport.

I showed Loretta the photo of Loston. "That's her," she shouted.

"Are you sure?"

Loretta told me, without a doubt, it was her.

"That's the woman that killed him."

My heart dropped in my lap. I knew then and there Paul had something to do with Lt. Terry's death. Sick son of a bitch . . . but why? I thought the two were close. I crushed the photo in my hand. I felt torn apart and betrayed. I trusted him with my life once upon a time.

I needed air. I ran upstairs and out the door. Damn, Paul Griffin was not who I thought he was, or honest at all. That son of a bitch was becoming another Sammy Dresser.

Standing outside instantly brought back memories. A part of my past I never wanted to remember. I needed a cigarette, and it was perfect timing. Life walked up with a pack in his hand.

"Can I please have one of those?" I asked.

He reached into his pack and pulled out two cigarettes. One for me and for himself.

"Thanks, I really needed one of these," I replied. He lit his, then mine, and we smoked.

"What's on your mind?" Life asked me.

"Nothing much. Just all the information I've come across."

He asked me what I was going to do about Jackie and her child. I was not sure what I wanted to do. However, I did want Sammy Dresser to make a move and come out of hiding. Therefore, I decided to keep her around a little bit longer.

"Where's Mike? I haven't seen him."

"He's on a date," Life said grinning.

"With who?"

"Some friend from out of state. She attends school in San Francisco."

Mike never leaves without his car. In addition, if he left with her, she would have had to be driving something better in order for Mike to leave his behind. I walked up to his car and jumped in looking around. He kept it so clean, it looked as if it just came off the car lot.

Something told me to feel underneath the seat, and to my surprise, I found a pistol along with a black bag. I did not think much about it, but the pistol caught my eye. It was a new gloc nine. The black bag on the other hand got my attention also.

"Beautiful!" I said, admiring the gloc.

Life must have heard me. He walked over and saw the gun.

"Yeah, I bought that for him," he replied.

"Why?" I asked.

"Protection -- he needs it being around you and I. Now put it back," Life said inhaling his cigarette. "Mike's going to kill you if he finds out you've been through his things."

I was not worried about that. Mike knew not to try me. I slid the gun back underneath the seat, feeling that black bag again. I pulled it out and placed it in my lap.

"What are you doing?"

"What do it look like?" I said, unzipping the bag.

"Oh my goodness, what do we have here?" I whispered.

My mind went blank. What was Mike thinking? The black bag contained weed, cocaine, and a second pistol. Life claimed to have had nothing to do with it or knowing Mike was carrying all that weight on him. I grabbed the bag and took it with me.

I called his cell phone but he did not answer. I wanted to ruin his date by telling him I had found his dope. I was not worried; he had to come home.

While thinking of my next move, Tray came to mind. I called him to touch bases. He was getting ready to go out.

"So, where are you going, and who are you taking?" I asked. He thought it was hilarious how I asked him.

"That's funny you asked. I am going to a cocktail party. I was about to call you and ask you if you wanted to come along with me," he explained.

I could tell he was smiling from the way he talked. "Why are you laughing?" I asked.

"No reason. I'm sorry, baby."

He asked me to come with him and was not going to take no for an answer. He did not understand I did not want to go out feeling the way I did. However, I also needed to get out and do something.

It was 12:30 when I got off the phone with Tray. Before I left, I told Life to keep an eye on Angie. I did not want her around her father, and did not want her killing Loretta while I was away.

Soon as I got home, I jumped in the shower. Minutes after I got out, my phone rang; it was Tray. He was parked outside waiting for me. I wrapped myself up and went downstairs to let him inside.

"Come in. I'll be ready in a second."

"Take your time, bae," he replied admiring my figure. The party did not start until one, and just about everyone there would be late showing up.

As I got dressed, minding my own business, Tray walked inside my bedroom and walked up behind me, holding me tight.

"Damn, your ass is Phat," he whispered in my ear.

He squeezed and rubbed my ass in motion. I bent over in front of him and shook my ass on his manhood. It began to rise, standing tall in his pants.

"Looks to me your ready," I whispered.

He grabbed my hips and pulled me closer with his wood pressed against my wet warm womb. He pulled his wood out and rubbed it in motion around my lips.

"Put it in, papa," I begged.

He slowly removed my Vickie's, pulling them down to my ankles, kissing on my thighs. He asked me to get on top of the bed and to bend over. He removed his pants and shirt, leaving his boxers on. He took one finger and put it inside my womb. I squeezed his finger with my muscles, gripping every inch.

"Baby, please let go," Tray asked me kindly.

While he played with my ocean of love, he stuck his tongue inside of me. It felt so amazing as he blew, kissed, and licked me. I instantly came on his finger. He told me he wanted to taste my love, so he licked his tongue inside. I guess it was good because all of a sudden, he became aggressive, pushing me onto my stomach getting behind me and fucking me. He held both of my hands down on the bed, kissing me and telling me that it was the best. As I enjoyed each moment, a flashback came of Victor fucking me. I got so lost in the vision, I called Tray Victor.

Tray realized I called him another name because he slowed down, then asked me what I said. I told him I said 'victory'. The sex was amazing, I came five times.

We both got into the shower together and went at it again. The love was irresistible. After we finished fucking a second time and showered, I put on my freak'em dress, something sexy for Tray.

I did not realize until we made it inside that Tray was being nominated for Broker of the Year. I was hoping he would win and knew inside he wanted it, too.

He introduced me to his coworkers and friends. Across the room sat Lance all alone by himself. Until this female walked over where he was sitting and kissed him. She noticed me looking and gave me a look. I just smiled at her; if only she knew. Lance waved for us to come and join them. We walked over to their table and sat. Lance's wife just stared at me.

"Girl, what are you looking at?" I asked her. Both Tray and Lance looked at me.

"I'm watching you," she replied.

I told her she better watch her man. He was the one watching me.

"Come on, you two; be nice," Lance said.

"We're going to another table. Come on, Leah." Tray insisted.

"Bitches like her get dealt with on the streets," she said looking at me crazy.

"Is that a threat?" I asked standing up from the table.

She got up as if she was ready to fight. Tray had to grab my arm to keep me from walking over to that bitch and knocking her ass out in front of everyone.

"Follow me," Tray asked leading me out of the ballroom.

We walked into the hallway into another room, which had guests and more tables.

"Tray, I apologize."

"Don't. You did nothing wrong. She's crazy and don't like the fact me and Lance hang."

He later told me she was the reason him and his wife divorced. "Why would she think I want Lance?"

"She thinks everyone wants him. I met Lance through her friendship with my ex-wife."

Tray and I walked back into the ballroom to eat. Minutes later, they called to announce the winner. While I was eating, I noticed Lance's wife staring at me while on the phone with someone. I got up and turned my back to her so I would not be able to see her ugly ass face.

Tray and Lance had to stand once their names were called. Their company won an award for best sales of the year. I was not into real estate, so I did not find it interesting. Moreover, from the looks of it, Tray looked as if he was not interested either. I was of course happy for him and his success.

After all was done, the music began. Tray walked up to me and asked me to dance. I reached out for his hand and we slow danced to the sound of Marvin Gaye's, "Let's Get It On." He stared into my eyes as we moved to the music.

"You're so beautiful," he said.

I smiled with a thank you, laid my head upon his chest, and closed my eyes. I could hear his heart beat to the rhythm of mine. It seemed as if no one was else was in that ballroom but him and me.

I was in the zone. For once in my life, I felt appreciated and loved. What set the mood was when Luther Vandross and Cheryl Lynn's "If This World Were Mine" came on. Tray kissed me passionately.

"I think I'm falling in love with you, Leah," he whispered in my ear.

At that moment, I felt the same way. I knew he wasn't lying when he told me he was falling for me.

The strange thing about it was I thought of Victor every time I felt this way. Only because he was the man I wanted to be with, not Tray.

The memories were killing me softly. I knew I had to get a hold of myself because those flashbacks were going to get me into trouble.

When the song ended, Lance's wife, Lucy, walked over and told Tray his ex-wife said not to forget the kids. Tray picked his boys up everyday from school.

Before we left I told Lucy her man was staring at me like he wanted me. She looked back and caught him giving me the eye. I smiled and walked away.

We arrived at school at 3:15. School was just releasing. While Tray exited to get his boys, I stayed inside and waited.

As I sat patiently waiting, I noticed a Tahoe like the one I saw at the gravesite. A oversized woman got out and opened the back door for three children. I am sure they were her children because all three of them were fat as hell like her. She had a mug on her face, but carried herself in fine clothing. If I had had my own car, I would have followed her. I did get the license plate, which read, "Money is power, power is respect." Sounds like the intentions a mafia would have.

After I got all the information down, I called a friend of mine at the station. Henry Donald was a techie that worked in the technician department. He gave me information on the '99 Tahoe. The plates came back to be Pam Bernard. She lived at 306 Patterson Dr, L.A. Henry also gave me information on her background and the only thing that came up was her husband, Tom Bernard, my father's best friend.

TWENTY-SIX

Over My Dead Body

As soon as Tray got the kids inside, we left. I told him to drop me off at home. I had something to do. Plus, my friend from Washington was here visiting me.

I kissed Tray goodbye and told him I would call him later. I went inside to change clothes, then called Jojo, my friend from Washington. We made plans to meet at Fisher's Crab House, a seafood place.

By the time I got there, he was already eating.

"You couldn't wait, huh?" I asked Jojo walking up behind him.

He got up from his seat and hugged me, giving me a friendly kiss on the cheek.

"It's been a long time, Leah," he said, looking into my eyes. I agreed.

"It's been over four years since I've seen you."

"So, what's been going on here in San Francisco?" I cleared my throat and took a sip of water.

"Excuse me. A lot of bullshit, lies, and betrayal," I explained. "So, your company -- are they helping?"

"I wished like hell they would've. I'm the only one doing the work."

"From my understanding, you don't work with San Francisco police department anymore."

"Lt. Paul fired me. He's now a suspect in three cases, two are murders that have been committed, and one's kidnapping."

Jojo looked at me strange, as if he had seen a ghost.

"First off, why would he be a suspect?"

"His wife is dead, his grandson gets kidnapped. This week, his daughter is murdered at her mother's funeral. You put two and two together."

"Wow, but still -- how does that make him a suspect?"

"I got the information from someone who was hired to kill his daughter. This same person also told me he hired someone else to kill his wife. Therefore, that makes him a suspect. Plus, before all this information came about, he was acting really funny."

I went on to explain my reasons, and how I just found out who was behind Lt. Terry's death.

"Lt. Terry is dead?" Jojo asked in shock.

"Yes, it's been over a year now since his departure."

"Sorry to hear that. I know you and Terry were close."

"He was not only my friend. But a father figure to me also."

"What can I do to help you?"

I explained to him that I needed a job, not for money, but to cover my tracks. I did not need charges for murdering these punks.

"Do you want to work with me?" asked Jojo. I could not turn down this opportunity.

"Me working for you?" I asked.

"No, not for me, but yourself. I see you have unfinished business to handle and I want to help you achieve that," Jojo said smiling, biting into his blueberry muffin.

He was very handsome and only twenty-three. We have known each other since high school, and he was the only guy I've known to be a friend and not try to get at me. Therefore, I had much respect for him.

I sat behind him in math class each day and became obsessed with his black, long, curly hair. Yes, he's African American, but with good genes. That was what attracted me to him, besides his sense of humor. Otherwise, he was the big brother I never had.

After we came to an understanding, we chopped it up, talking about old times and plans. I explained to him I wanted my own business, which he knew already. However, I wanted to be my own boss and run things the way I wanted to -- solving cases for those who are in need of justice.

"So, I'll see you later?" Jojo asked.

"Sure. I'll hit you up when I'm done handling business."

On my way back to Life's place, I got a call from Sammy. He offered me information on Paul Griffin. However, he would not give it without an agreement. I had to let his baby sister go along with her child. I told him to keep the information to himself. At that moment, I did not need his help. I already had enough information on Paul Griffin; all I needed was for him to own up to it. I told Sammy the only thing he could offer me was his life.

"Over my dead body," Sammy shouted, cursing me out and calling me every name but the child of God.

While riding, I noticed a car trailing behind me. It began to rain lightly, but traffic became heavy. I had to slow down or end up crashing behind someone. I watched the car behind me as it picked up speed to catch me. Something was strange about this situation. The wipers on the car were whipping fast and it was not even raining hard.

My cell rang, taking my attention off the vehicle. "Hello?" I answered.

"Where is it? I need it back," Mike shouted.

I told him to hold down his tone. He continued yelling he needed his bag back so I hung up on him.

The car pulled up behind me and the driver cuts on their bright lights shining them at me. I pulled over to the side of the road and soon as the driver pulled in behind me, I grabbed my pistol and got out of my car. The driver backed up into a truck putting the car in drive coming full speed towards me. I quickly jumped out of the way landing on the ground. The driver drove into a BMW damaging the side door. Soon as I jumped to my feet, the driver got out with a mask on, shooting rounds at me.

I fell to the ground rolling underneath a parked car. From below, I could see the person's legs. I aimed and shot them in the leg. After the person hit the ground and their gun slid away from them, I jumped up, ran over, and kicked the gun further.

"Who are you?" I asked aiming my pistol.

"Your worst nightmare," she shouted.

It was a female. I was not sure who, but I knew it was a woman from the way she sobbed when I shot her. I snatched the mask off of her face and to my surprise it was . . .

"Why?" I asked her. She began laughing and spitting up blood as tears filled her eyes.

"I didn't know who to believe. You or my father. Now I guess it does not matter. But if he did, please take care of him for me," she said trying to fight the pain.

My heart dropped. I could not believe what was happening. I wanted to kill her, but my heart would not allow me to.

"Do it, kill me!" she screamed. "That way, I'll be with my mother."

I just walked away, got back inside my car, and drove off. Soon as I pulled off, the cops were coming.

On my way back to Life's place, I thought about the people I have trusted along the way, and how each of them had betrayed me. I was confused once again, thinking about why I cannot trust anyone.

When I arrived, Mike was standing outside waiting for me. Soon as I parked, he ran up to my car.

"Where is it, Leah?" he shouted.

As I tried to open the door, he pushed it back shut, almost closing my leg in the door.

"You son of a bitch. Are you crazy?" I shouted.

He started beating on the top of my car and window. I quickly jumped in the passenger's seat and got out. I ran around where he stood, grabbing his neck and pushing him on the hood of my car.

"Now listen. I'll fucking kill you if you try me like this again," I shouted with my pistol aimed at his head. Life and Loren ran to stop me.

"Please Leah, don't hurt him," Loren shouted. Life told me to let it go.

"Now, are you done?" I asked Mike.

He looked at me and said yes. Soon as I let him up, he kicked me in the stomach. I fell back on my ass and my pistol flew out of my hand. Life and Loren just shook their heads. They knew what was about to go down from there.

Mike ran up on me as I tried standing to my feet and pushed me back on the ground, standing over me.

"Let it go, Mike," Life shouted.

Mike said no and continued standing over me. Soon as he turned around to walk away, he was down on his luck. I looked at Life and Loren and told them not to stop me. I got to my feet and jumped kicked Mike in the chest. He fell back onto the hood of the car. I got on top of him and whispered something in his ear.

"See, we're at ground zero once again. This time, there is no letting up."

I grabbed him up and pushed him down into the same mud puddle he made washing his car. I walked over and placed his face down into the muddy water, drowning him a little. Only enough so he would get the picture that I was not the one. He began begging me to let him up.

"Now you want to sell drugs, huh? Like the punks I saved you from?" I asked holding his head up.

"No, no!" he shouted.

I let him go, kicking him in the ass, telling him next time I'd be putting another hole in it.

After the drama, Loren made Mike and me some soup. I was cold and wet. In addition, like always, Life kept the air going. As I ate, I thought about all was taking place. I called Sammy and told him if he wanted his sister back, he would have to give me him in advance. I told him if he loved his sister just that much, he would do so.

Minutes after I got off the phone with Sammy, Olivia called me crying about her daughter. She told me Sammy had something to do with Jackie's disappearance and to hold off on killing him until further notice.

My next step was finding Pam Bernard. I knew I needed a warrant before approaching her residence. I called Jojo and asked him how long it would take before I was official. He told me twenty-four hours, and that was all I needed.

I explained to Life the ropes to the plan I had in mind and took off to my crib. I had enough in one day. I needed rest and it still was raining when I left Life's place. I figured this would be the perfect time to get some peaceful sleep.

I arrived home at 6:09 I did not have time to do anything but sleep. I was so tired. I had so many voice messages from people calling about doing cases for them. I did not want any more cases until I was done with the ones I was working on and not until I started my own investigation business.

I woke up at 1:05 I had a good dream about Tray and me.

We were on vacation at the Bahamas relaxing, celebrating life. It put a smile on my face. I got up and fixed me a snack to eat.

By the time I finished eating, my phone rang. I looked at the time and my intentions was not to answer. But I did anyway.

"Hello!" I answered.

"Where are you?" a female voice asked me.

"Who is this?"

"Carla . . . where are you?" she asked a second time.

"Living my life," I said, wondering why the hell she was calling me at this time in the morning. "What do you want, Carla? I have nothing for you," I asked walking towards the living room.

She started laughing out of control. I did not feel like playing with her loony ass.

"What's so funny?" I asked her.

"You!" she said laughing.

I hung up the phone on her.

I could still hear her laugh, and it got closer. Something told me to turn around, and as I turned, there she stood in my kitchen.

I walked back into the kitchen and stood looking at her. I brushed my arm against my hip.

"Damn!" I said to myself, noticing I did not have my pistol on me. She had her pistol aimed directly at my chest. She began talking, but I could not make out what she was trying to say.

She pulled out a bar, swinging it back and forth. I thought she was going to break my window for sure. However, she did not; she slipped the bar between the doors.

"Smart, huh?" she said smiling and aiming her pistol in my face. I figured that is how she got inside. "Turn around with your hands behind your back," Carla instructed.

I turned around and did as she told me. She walked behind me and searched me for weapons.

"Now, why couldn't you just follow my demands? You wouldn't have to go through this, Leah," she said, rubbing the gun up and down my spine. She kicked me in the leg and I quickly dropped to my knees.

"Now look what you made me do," she said laughing, as if she did not have any sense. I believed she did not have it all together.

"Get on your feet!" she shouted. "I've been watching you for awhile, miss thing, and you been a poor worker."

"I owe you," I said underneath my breath as I stood.

"What did you say, bitch?"

I cracked a smile when I noticed a rack of knives in front of me.

"Remember what I told you the night when you pulled that same gun out on me?"

She swung back and blindsided me with her pistol. I fell forward towards the knives, knocking them all over on the counter. I grabbed the biggest one, turning as quickly as I could, slicing her wrist. Soon as she dropped the gun, I ran towards her, pushing her into the kitchen table. Blood was everywhere. I grabbed the gun and aimed it at her.

"Who's in charge now, bitch," I shouted.

She looked at me smiling as if something was funny. "You wouldn't dare," she whispered.

I looked her in the eyes and told her I would. "Do it, Leah Starr. Do it!" she shouted.

God knows I wanted to, but -- oh, what the hell. I walked up to her and aimed the pistol at her head.

"Now bitch, I want you to remember my face while you're firing in hell," I told her before shooting her in the head. Did I do something wrong? I still wonder to this day. However, she was in my way, and had to be dealt with. It was better her than me.

It took me an hour and a half to clean up all that disgusting blood. I took her body and placed it inside an old chest I had stored around the house. I had to drag her overweight ass out to my car. As I was trying my best to get the chest inside my trunk, Mrs. Thomas came out of her house.

"Sweetie, is everything okay?" she asked me.

I smiled and told her that everything was okay and walked back inside the house. When I got inside, I called Jojo.

"Hello. Who is this calling me, damn it!" he said, answering the phone.

"Chill out, it's Leah. I need you to get up."

"What's up Leah; what do you need?" he asked, taking a deep breath.

"A huge favor."

I asked him to ride with me to L.A in thirty minutes. "Hell no; it is too early in the morning," he shouted.

"Come on, sleepy head. I really need you, Joey," I begged.

The phone became silent and all I could hear was heavy breathing. "Jojo," I shouted.

"Yes, I'm here," he whispered.

"I'm on my way to get you," I said before hanging up.

I needed Jojo to come along with me to Pam Bernard's house. I knew he had pull and was my only hope. He could go to anyone's house, show him or her his badge, and search wherever he wanted. I could not wait any longer. I felt Pam had all the answers I needed about the death of Lt. Terry, Paul's wife, daughter, and grandson. One thing I have learned about Pam Bernard is that she knew everything about everyone.

I also found out she worked for the Los Angeles Press and had top-notch insight regarding all types of information, including what's taking place in San Francisco. She had valuable insight and I was going to find out every detail. I knew if she was married to the one and only Tom Bernard, she knew street information also. Therefore, I needed to jump on this and make sure I had my shit together, just in case something unexpected went down.

I left the house at 2:25.

TWENTY-SEVEN

Show Time

I arrived at the Hilton Hotel at 2:47 Jojo was already waiting for me in the lobby.

"Hey, Jojo," I spoke walking inside.

"Don't hey me -- this better be good," Jojo said sipping a cup of fresh coffee.

"Mmm, that smells good," I replied with a sense of relief. "And why are we up this early again?"

"Business. I just had to take someone's life in the last thirty minutes."

"Come on. Be serious," Jojo said, shaking his head in disbelief.

"You don't believe me? Check my trunk," I said handing him the keys as we exited the building together. He popped the trunk.

"What the hell!" Jojo shouted.

"Keep your voice down; we don't want nobody else to know." I said, closing the trunk.

"How did this happen?"

"I caught her inside my house. There's no telling how long she was there," I explained to Jojo that it was terrifying finding that crazy bitch standing inside my kitchen.

"She placed a gun to my head and told me she was going to kill me. I do not take kindly to threats, and I told her I was going to get her anyway. And soon as I caught her slipping, I took her out," I said getting inside my car.

Jojo thought it was cool how I defended my life and got a thrill out of knowing I killed someone. She was not the first, and would not be the last.

On our way to L.A, it rained. Not too bad, just too much for me. I was ready for a vacation outside of California.

Jojo slept the entire ride there. All I could think about was Kayla wondering if her son was okay, or still alive, and who would take care of him when he returned. Nobody like his mother.

When we arrived at the Bernard's, it was busy. "Do these people ever rest?" I said thinking aloud. "Where are we?"

"At Tom and Pam Bernard's home."

I did not believe Pam lived inside that house. There was all types of trafficking going on. The neighborhood was peaceful. What surprised me is that no one had called the cops on them.

"So, what now," Jojo asked, fixing his curly hair in the mirror. He was always a pretty boy, keeping his appearance up. There has never been a time I saw him half-stepping on his looks.

"Your favorite question," I joked.

"Well, first we need to wait for things to clear up," I said, watching the commotion continue.

"Why in the hell would Pam and Tom label this as their address if it was a trap house?" asked Jojo.

This made a lot of sense. We did not park at the house, but across the street and watched. Four hours passed and both Jojo and I fell asleep.

"Wake up Leah!" Jojo shouted, shaking me out of my sleep.

I looked up and noticed it was now clear. Damn it, even the Tahoe was gone.

"How long have you been up?" I asked Jojo.

"Not to long. Soon as I awake I woke you up." I needed to get inside that house.

"Okay, Jojo, you stay here and keep watch."

"What are you about to do?" Jojo asked me.

"I'm going around back to find a way inside."

I got out and ran up towards the front door and Jojo followed behind me.

"Wait for me," he shouted.

"Look if you're going to be with me, you must watch my back. Stay here while I go around back."

"Leah, we don't have a warrant. Let's wait until she gets back."

I told him the information I wanted she would not give me. Moreover, she was not going to let us search her house without a warrant.

I ran around the house to the side door. As I began searching for a key, something poked me on my back. I did not think too much of it until I heard a bark. I slowly turned and found a pit bull staring me directly in the face.

My mind went blank. First thing came to my mind was to shoot the shit of that dog. Then again, neighbors would hear the gunshots. Second thought was to run but I knew he would catch me. Third thought was I never backed down or ran from anyone or anything. This dog and I had to duke it out.

The dog stood waiting to attack. I was already down on my knees. It would have been easy access for him to grab my neck and rip my throat out.

When he moved, I moved.

I grabbed his throat as soon as he attacked me. He was so strong, I almost lost grip of him. I struggled as he tried his best to bite me. However, I would not let go for nothing. I made sure I had a good grip on his neck before reaching for my knife, stabbing him five times in the neck, taking him down.

I did not want to kill the dog, and I damn sure did not want him to kill me.

Jojo shouted from the front asking was I okay. By that time, I was inside the house opening the front door for him to come inside.

"You all right?" he asked.

"Why wouldn't I be?" I replied with a friendly smile, closing the door behind him.

"We need to find much as we can. Go search the dinning room. I'm going to check things out upstairs."

The entire house smelled like marijuana. It was very strong, as if someone just put one out. I knew it was not anything regular.

I walked into the bedroom and searched the dresser drawers looking for any clues that would tie me to Paul Griffin or Sammy Dresser.

While I searched, I found a business card with Paul's name on it. All I needed was to find . . .

A baby seat. The same one Paul received from Loretta. Of course she was the girl I saw him talking to that day in the Tahoe. The thing that got me was that none of Pam's children were babies anymore. Why would she have a baby car seat?

I continued searching and came across family photos; Tom, Pam and their three children. Tom never told me he was married with kids. However, the photos had shown me different. I also noticed baby clothing that was all new. I put it together and knew for sure Pam had Kayla's baby. No signs Pam just had a baby, no pictures of this child and no damn baby bed.

"What did you find?" he asked coming up the stairs.

"Lots of information that she wouldn't have told us," I said, showing Jojo the photos and baby clothes.

"Look here," I said, handing him the business card with Paul's name written on it.

"Help me out. I'm lost here," said Jojo.

"You see the baby clothes and other details here relating to an infant, right?"

"Yes."

"Okay, put it together and what do you get?"

I was hoping Jojo did not spend all those years in college for nothing. He took a good look at the baby things. Then at the photo in my hand.

"Okay, I got it now. All things are new, but no sign of a baby in family pictures," said Jojo, figuring it out.

"And what else?" I asked.

"There would be family photos with the baby included," Jojo said, looking around for a baby crib. "Wouldn't there be a crib?"

"Right, that's why I love working with you. We are on the same page," I replied, patting Jojo on the back.

"So, now do we have a lead?" Jojo asked me unsure.

"Hell yeah -- she has Kayla's baby and I'm pretty sure Paul Griffin's behind all of this." It came to me.

"How long does it take for a spouse to receive money for life insurance?"

"About three or four weeks; it all depends on the lawyer. While it's in the making, the will remains on probate," Jojo explained.

"So, we have enough time to stop Paul from getting his wife and daughter's insurance money?"

"Wow, he has one on his daughter also?" asked Jojo.

"Yup, he's taking them out one by one."

"But why Lt. Terry?"

"I'm not sure; it has to be for money reasons," I thought.

"Come on, let's go. We can put a hold on them checks. Plus get a warrant for his house," said Jojo.

As we both walked out of the room, I noticed a stuffed bear lying beside the car seat. I walked over and picked it up. I instantly thought about Kayla. She wanted me to get her child back. That is what I promised, and that is what I was going to do. As I glanced out of the window, a tear rolled down my cheek.

As I dazed out of the window, the Tahoe pulled up. Jojo and I ran downstairs. We exited the side door, and just I as opened it, the front door opened also. I slowly closed the door behind me and we crept around the side of the house, making sure everything was clear and no one saw us leaving. We took off soon as we could towards the car.

"Do you think she knows someone was inside?" asked Jojo.

"I'm not sure, and really don't give a damn. She's behind all this shit that's going on."

Jojo drove us to the nearest police department.

"I need to get some information from you concerning date of birth, social security number, you know, the basics."

I gave him the information he needed to put me in the game. In the next twenty-four hours, I was hired through his agency.

"What do you need now?" I asked Jojo.

"A computer to register you into the system."

I told him I had a laptop in the trunk of my car he could use. It already contained the information he would need to get the job done.

While he did his thing, I sat and waited. It only took twenty minutes to complete.

"Bingo -- you're in," Jojo replied unexpectedly, scaring me out of my thoughts.

"So, what about my badge?"

"You're pretty much a badge. But you'll get one within twenty-four hours."

It did not take any time for him to get a warrant to search the Bernard's home.

Once Jojo printed out the warrant, we went back to their home.

"Hurry -- stop her!" I shouted as Pam was pulling out to leave.

Jojo pulled in front of her truck. I jumped out and told her to exit her vehicle.

"What do you want?" Pam shouted.

"Get out. I'm asking the questions here," I replied.

"We have a warrant to search your home, ma'am," Jojo told Pam.

"Where were you going?" I asked her as she exited her truck.

"On my daily route. Minding my own business, Leah Starr."

"Oh so you know who I am?" I asked, looking at her strange.

"Yeah, I know about you. Your name is all over the streets. Now, what can I do for you?"

"I'm glad you asked. Can we take this conversation inside?"

"So, can I get you anything to drink?" Pam asked smiling at Jojo and me.

"No, thank you, we're here just doing our job," Jojo replied, looking around the room.

"So Pam, do you know Paul Griffin or anything about his grandson?" I asked her. She looked at me strange.

"Don't lie to me, Pam. If you know anything, tell me now."

"What makes you think I know anything about Paul Griffin?"

"Come on, Pam. I already know your vehicle was present the day his daughter was murdered at his wife's funeral. He has a lot to do with his grandson's kidnapping. So, it's no secret to me," I explained as she hesitated while taking a seat on her living room sofa.

"I'm listening," I said.

"I know nothing, Leah. I have my own children to see about," she said.

I was not buying any of it. I already knew she had the information I needed. I just needed her to give me more details.

"I have the funniest feeling you're lying to me. I hate being lied to. It makes me mad. Very mad," I said, giving her a nasty look. I was about to punch her in her shit. However, I remained calm.

"Leah, I think she wants to go to jail for a long time. Conspiracy, right?" said Jojo, looking through Pam's china cabinet.

"I'm not going anywhere. What did I do?" asked Pam. I threw my shoulders up.

"Leave. I got things to do," she replied, jumping up from her sofa chair. I walked over and pushed her back on the sofa.

"Watch it, Leah; you have met your match," she shouted. Jojo started laughing.

"You hear her, right? She ain't crazy," I said laughing along with Jojo.

"She must not know. She says she hears your name throughout the hood, and nobody told her?" Jojo said making Pam even madder.

"Pam, I'm tired of playing games with you. I already know you have the baby."

"Bitch I . . ."

I slapped the shit out of her face. So hard, spit slung out of her mouth across the room.

"Watch your mouth. I can see now we're going to have problems." She did not want to talk. Therefore, I told Jojo to cuff her, both hands and ankles. I told him since she did not want to talk to duct tape her mouth shut. She was saying something, but I did not comprehend. Jojo watched her as I searched downstairs. We searched the entire house for an hour. I gathered as much information as I could. When we were through, I arrested Pam Bernard for failure to cooperate and possession of cocaine and marijuana. I found a half of gram upstairs, along with fake identification cards. I bet she wished she had talked.

We took her to LAPD. It was no reason to take her to SFPD; Paul would only let her go. In addition, the charges took place in L.A. I knew the LAPD was strict about drug charges and Jojo had pull with them. I was supposed to join them back in 2004, but Lt. Terry insisted I join forces with San Francisco.

Pam was booked in on a million dollars bond; it did not take much to get that done. At first, the bond was set at twenty thousand, but I had it increased to hold her, giving me more time to get what I needed.

I could not believe it, but Paul called me while I was getting Pam's bond signed. He asked me to join him for dinner. Something inside told me to accept. However, I told him I had something important to do. Funny thing, he accused me of Kayla's death. Now he wanted me to have brunch with him.

"Jojo, did you do that?"

"Do what?"

"You know, put Paul under investigation for the murder of his wife and daughter?" I said, reminding him while sipping a cup of fresh coffee.

"You're right; time is winding down," he replied, handling the problem.

I called Life and told him to meet me at my place around 3:00. Therefore, I could show him a bit of information I discovered; clues to where Sammy may be hiding and Paul Griffin's connection to Pam Bernard.

After Jojo finished what he had to do, we took off to my crib. I knew soon as the paperwork on Paul Griffin was complete, the community of San Francisco would soon discover their Lieutenant was a cold blooded murderer.

"You've never been to my house?" I asked Jojo knowing the answer. Just being funny.

"No, how many bedrooms do you have?"

"Three and a half."

I got out soon as we pulled in and checked my mail box, which I hardly do. As always, when I do decide to check it, I had tons of bills and letters from high school friends.

"This is nice, Leah. Good choice," Jojo said admiring my home. I thanked him and invited him inside.

"I see you haven't fixed up much," he said looking around the living room.

I asked him to follow me. I wanted to give him a tour around the house.

Last, but not least, my bedroom.

"This here is my room. My resting place," I said exhaling with intentions to lie down and go straight to sleep.

"Hmm, the best spot in the house," he said winking his eye at me.

"Stop it, Joey," I said blushing.

He walked over towards me and kissed me on the cheek.

"Nice work today. You are a great investigator."

Lust began to take control of me. I grabbed his face and kissed him.

"Stop," Jojo shouted.

I quickly pulled away apologizing. He told me not to be sorry, but take it slow.

He took off his clothes and watched as I took off mine. After we got undressed, we got on the bed and fucked. Not once did I think about Tray or Victor. Jojo had me in the zone and I really wanted it from him. He was pulling on my hair and biting on my lips gently. I got so wet, I could have filled a cup. He knew what and how to do it. It was as if he knew my body inside out.

"Let's not rush," I whispered in his ear.

He slowed down, grinding deeper inside my wet womb, whispering my name, telling me he wanted to own my cat. I lost control and climaxed in no time. My juices ran all over his manhood. It felt so strong as he pounded my tight walls. It felt like the first time.

"You liked that, daddy?" I asked him.

He told me it was the best he ever had. Where have I heard that before?

I lay next to him thinking to myself. And while doing so Tray and Victor came to mind. Boy, what did I just do? Jojo was my friend. Would that change because of lust? We were not only friends now, but also lovers. I have always been honest, but now, I was not sure if I could be. Tray was good to me, plus a good lover. Victor, on the other hand, was no good for me, but could fuck.

Jojo lay next to me butt ass naked. There I was, lying next to a guy I thought I would never sleep with. I had to get away.

"Jojo, you're ready to go?" I whispered in his ear. He was sound asleep. Boy, was my womb the bomb or what. Every guy I fucked went straight to sleep afterwards. I let him rest and took a catnap myself.

I awoke at 12:36. Not expecting it, Jojo was up and dressed.

"Wake up, baby," Jojo said standing at my bedside.

"What time is it?" I asked.

"Time for you to get a watch," he replied with that lame ass joke that has been played out. However, it did make me smile.

"We need to talk."

He sat beside me and we talked about what took place earlier that morning. I explained to him I had a man and we had something special. In addition, what we did could never happen again. I do not think he believed me because of the simple fact I slept with him. However, I was not joking.

The worst was yet to come. Minutes later, Tray pulled up outside. I was not sure what he wanted. However, I later realized he called my cell phone three times. Fuck! I was butt ass naked with my friend sitting next to me. That would not look right. I jumped up and got dressed. I still had a funny sex smell on me. I knew I had to stay as far away from Tray as I could. The doorbell rang.

I told Jojo to answer the door. I ran into the bathroom and washed off, combed my hair, and brushed my teeth.

I could hear Jojo and Tray talking to each other. They were laughing and giggling about something. I did not want them becoming friends.

I rushed downstairs and welcomed Tray with a kiss. "Hey, sweetie,"

"Hey, I was trying to reach you," Tray said full of smiles.

I told him I was sound asleep. In addition, Jojo just came over and woke me up. He did not want much, just to tell me he wanted me to go to dinner with him and his boys tonight. I told him that would be great and walked him out of the front door.

After he left, Sammy called me and asked me to meet him face to face. What a great idea, I thought. I told Jojo to lay low while I do this. I took him to the police station to get an unmarked car to stake out in. Leaving the station, I called Life and asked him to meet me at the stadium. I knew Sammy was not showing up alone and neither was I.

I phoned Sammy to see where he was. He informed me he was already there waiting on me to arrive. I laid low scoping the scene out. Still no sign of Sammy Dresser. We had walkie-talkies so we could easily have access to each other. I had the strongest feeling it was about to go down. I also had a wire attached to my ear so I could talk to them hands free. In my rearview mirror, I could see Life's car posted up and to my far left sat Jojo.

I asked Life to bring Jackie and her child along with him. When I looked ahead of me, four Ford Explorers pulled in front of my car.

"We got company," I buzzed Life and Jojo.

A guy got out of each truck jumped out with huge guns.

"What's going on?" asked Life.

I reached for my tech and prepared for fire. Next thing I know, Sammy jumped out behind the four men. He grabbed his cell phone and called me.

"Where are you?" he shouted. I sat watching him. "Why the guns," I asked.

He panicked looking around the parking lot. His bodyguards closed in on him.

I asked him to tell the guys to put their guns away. "I'm no fool, Leah Starr," he shouted.

I told Life and Jojo to prepare themselves. I was going to close in on Sammy and his men. From a long range, Life scoped in, trying to shoot Sammy but missed and shot one of his guards.

I jumped out quickly and shot two of his men. I run up to Sammy and stared him in the eyes.

"I finally got you," I shouted, smiling at him.

I did not notice one of the guys was hiding behind the car. He ran up and pushed me on the ground and began kicking the shit out of me. Sammy walked over and told him to stop. I looked up and saw a red dot on Sammy's forehead. Life was aiming to shoot him. I whispered to Life not to shoot Sammy, just his bodyguard.

"Where's my sister?" Sammy shouted grabbing a gun from the man's hand, waving it in my face,

"Get that gun out of my face Sammy." I shouted.

One of the men walked up and kicked me in the stomach. Next thing I know, the guy dropped to his knees. I looked up at him and smiled.

"Who's with you?" Sammy asked me.

"My partner in crime," I whispered, almost out of breath.

Sammy grabbed me by the arm and dragged me to his truck. I could hear Life yelling in my ear.

"Leah, what's going on?"

He could not see me because the trucks were in the way. On the other hand, he was too far.

"I'll kill you if you fight back, Leah," Sammy shouted.

People in the park could hear and see the commotion going on. I knew if I tried to escape, he would kill me. Whenever Life decided to come after me, it was too late. Sammy pulled off.

"Where are you taking me?" I screamed.

"Somewhere you've been trying to get," he replied.

Sammy reached back and hit me as hard as he could, knocking me completely out. When I awoke, I was being tied up.

"Wake up, sleepy head," a voice whispered.

I did not know where I was and forgot what had happened.

"You're in my hands now."

I quickly came back to reality, realizing the voice I was hearing was Sammy's. He laughed as evil as anyone could.

"Oh, so you're mad?" he asked.

I just looked at him as evil as I could. I wanted him dead.

"You're one crazy bitch to think I'm going to let you out of here alive. I'm going to kill you, Leah Starr," he said grinning at me.

I faulted myself because I let Sammy slip too many times. Now that he had caught me slipping, I have fallen into the hands of my enemy. What was my next step? Was it too late for me? My mind was empty. I couldn't think straight.

TWENTY-EIGHT

Illusions

My head pounded. My mind was going blank. I needed help. I was bleeding from the head very bad. I could not keep my head up. I sat in a large room that was pitch black. I could hear rats running around the cold floors of the room. I fell asleep again.

"Wake up!" Sammy shouted, slapping me in the face.

"Now, you're going to tell me where my sister is," Sammy demanded me.

He pulled up a chair and sat in front of me, staring me in the eyes. "What are you staring at?" I asked, trying to balance my head.

"Not much. I will say you are beautiful. Even when you are leaking blood. I think you should have picked a better career choice. You know, something like an office job, sitting looking pretty," he said, running his hands through my hair, getting a kick out of the fact I was harmless and could not defend myself.

"Take your hands off of me," I shouted with all my strength. He grabbed my hair, pulling it.

"Listen here, bitch. I'm going to give you . . ." Before he could make out what he was saying, my phone rang.

"Where is it?" he shouted looking around the room.

He reached into my pocket and answered my cell phone. "Hello!"

"Mr. Parker, how are you?"

"Yes, I have your sweet pussy. Let me ask you something. Is it good?" he asked Life, smiling at me.

He disgusted me. He was a real asshole; nothing like the Sammy I met in Los Angeles State Prison years ago. I thought for sure he took drugs. That would explain his incomprehensible behavior. I do not know what Life was saying on the other end. Nevertheless, Sammy ended the conversation with a big smile.

"Deal," he said before hanging up. "See Leah, there's a lot of people who love you and care for your safety. Your friend, Life -- I think you owe him you're life," Sammy said pulling out a bottle of pills and popping a lot of them at once. I knew he was on something.

He left the room without saying a word. I sat thinking to myself, and at the same time having illusions about death. My mind was still out of it and I could not focus. He hit me bad.

Tray's face popped in and out of my head. However, I could not comprehend his purpose in my life. His kids popped in and out of my head, but I did not understand why and do not to this day. I was losing control over myself. I screamed and cried as loud as I could. I was raged.

While Sammy was away, I calmed myself and prayed to God, asking Him to free me from the bonds of my enemies. I repeated Psalms 56:11 in my head when I was not able to speak it.

"Let those be put to shame and brought to dishonor who seek after my life. Let those be turned back and brought to confusion, who plot my hurt."

I stayed in that dark room three days. No food or anything to drink. I was suffering, but stayed prayed up. I truly believed God was with me.

After three days of waiting to see what Sammy was going to do to me, someone paid me a visit. As I sat staring in the dark meditating on those verses, the room became bright.

"Who's there?" I whispered.

The light got even stronger and it weakened my eyes, I could barely see.

"I'm here to feed you, don't be afraid," a soft voice said. "Here, eat," a young girl spoke, handing me a piece of bread. I nearly choked trying to eat it. My mouth was so dry and sour.

"Slow down," she replied, pouring me a glass of water. Once I took a sip of the water I instantly felt relief.

She poured water onto a rag and washed my face, removing the dry blood that was on the side of my head and face. I could not say a word. All I could do was cry.

"What's your name," I asked the girl.

She told me she was my guardian angel. I stared into her eyes and they were pure white as an angel. She looked as if she was not real, but I knew she was there.

"If you're an angel, please free me." I whispered.

She smiled and said, "Only you can free yourself. Be patient and you'll be set free."

As she began to walk away, I asked her what my visions meant. She told me they all should come to the light. Then she vanished before my eyes.

The room became dark again. Then minutes later, the door opened.

"Who is it?" I asked.

The figure walked closer towards me.

"It's Life -- are you okay?" he asked untying me.

"Yes. Now I am," I said reaching for my bruised head soon as he untied my hands.

"Come on. Sammy gave us ten minutes to exit his building." As we rushed towards the door, a bullets fly past our heads.

"Damn it!" Life shouted.

We could not exit that door. If we did, Sammy would kill us. We could hear Sammy and his gang running in the hallway.

My mind went blank once again. I did not know what was going on. I was lost.

"What are we going to do, Life?"

He ran and blocked the door off, then towards one of the windows ripping the board off of it.

"Come on, Leah." he shouted. However, I could not move. My legs locked in on me. I was starting to lose my senses. All the thoughts that were inside my head left me. I passed out.

I woke up in ICU. I jumped up out of my sleep screaming, realizing where I was. Safe. I looked around wondering if I was dreaming.

A nurse rushed in asking me if I was okay.

"I'm fine. How did I get here?" I asked.

"A guy who says he's your brother dropped you off out front of the hospital. What happened to you?" the nurse asked tucking me into bed.

"I'm not sure. I do not know. Is my brother still here?" I said tense and unsure.

"Yes, he's down in the lobby. Please try and get more rest."

I did not understand what she meant until she told me I had been on bed rest for four days. Damn, it was that bad. Sammy really fucked me up.

Minutes after the nurse exited the room, Life walked in.

"Hey Leah, you've finally decided to wake up," he said smiling.

"Mmm, that smells good," I said as he held a tray full of food. "Have some?"

I did not hesitate reaching for something to eat. It felt like I lost fifty pounds.

Soon as I ate, I threw it all back up.

"Slow down, Leah. It's plenty more downstairs," Life said. I was not hearing it. I had to eat. I needed it.

"So, do you remember?"

"Remember what?"

"You know, what happened at Sammy's shed," he whispered.

"No, I don't remember. Who is Sammy?" I asked.

"Damn, Leah. You don't remember who Sammy is?"

I did not know who he was talking about and it became stressful and agitating.

"No, I don't know. Who is he?"

He shook his head and replied, "You don't remember."

"You're crazy, who are you, anyway. My brother?" I asked.

"It's me -- Life. Your partner," he said holding my hand. I snatched away from him.

"I'm sorry. I don't know anyone by the name of Life."

My memory was completely gone. I did not remember Sammy or Life.

When the nurse walked back in, Life spoke with her. I watched, but could not hear a word they were saying. The nurse stood there staring at me while Life walked out of the room, and that was the last I saw of him.

Later that weekend, a vision came to me. I saw this woman in a pair of faded blue jeans with a white blouse walking through the door. At that time, I was sitting by the window watching the cars go by. Next thing I know, a woman in blue jeans with a white blouse walked inside my room.

She stood at the doorway and stared at me. We made eye contact and instantly I shouted to her,

"Mom!"

The vision showed me hugging her, calling her mother. So that was the first thing I said when we made eye contact.

She ran over to me. "You remember me?" she shouted.

"Yes I do," I said reaching out for another hug. "Mother," I whispered.

She asked me to sit down with her and talk. Life walked in and he was not alone. A tall light skinned guy walked in behind him. I stared at him for a while. Soon, another vision came to me. This time this guy and I were making love. All I was saying the entire time was "Tray".

I jumped up running into his arms, kissing and holding him tight. "Baby, you remember me?" he asked.

"Yes, I remember you, Tray. How could I ever forget your touch?" I said smiling.

Life stared at me the entire way home. I still could not make out whom he was. Moreover, I tried my best to recall knowing him.

Tray and Loren stayed close to me. It took time for me to come around. Now and then, I would snap on Tray and Loren, but I would bounce back and come to my senses. Every time I would have a vision, it was a step towards recovery.

I started having visions of this ugly man attacking me. I was not sure who he was, but Life would tell me it was Sammy. I knew there was only one person that would be able to help me remember, and that was Life.

One Sunday afternoon, Tray, Loren and I went to church. A place I have not visited since I was a little girl. It brought back memories. Some very special moments my father and I had in church. He used to tell me in church and out to put God first. In addition, in the past, I refused too. Now it seemed I had no choice. My life was becoming miserable and full of pain. I had to find away out of this confusion.

When we got out of church, I searched through my phone and saw Life's number and called him. I asked him to come over to my place so we could talk. Before we hung up, he asked me if I remembered him. I told him no and he said I would as soon as he got here and hung up the phone.

He arrived around 3:20. He brought a friend along with him.

"Leah, this here is Mike."

"What's up, Leah?" said Mike.

"Hey Mike."

He walked over to me and whispered in my ear. "Close your eyes and remember, Leah. You saved my life," he said.

"Come on -- let's go, Leah," Life shouted, grabbing my hand.

We drove out to my parents' old house where it all began. When we pulled up to the house Life asked me to step out of the car. I got out and walked towards the front steps.

He walked behind me asking me to think very hard. "Do you know where you are?"

"Yes, my parents' house." I replied.

A cool breeze brushed against my face as the sweet smell took me back. This time, the vision that came to me took me back to that moment I found my parents dead. It was as if I was repeating the worst nightmare I ever had all over again

I began to shake and tremble. I could feel Life holding me up from falling.

"Leah, are you okay?" he asked.

However, I could not answer. It was like I was paralyzed. My mother and father lying on the floor covered in blood. I stood in my vision watching it happen before my eyes.

I was running from something or someone. When I looked to my right, I saw Life running behind me.

"No!" I screamed.

I saw myself running very fast.

I screamed to myself, "Look in front of you." It was too late. I tripped over my parents' dead bodies. Life ran up and reached for my hand.

"I'm here to help," he said.

I just sat there in a pool of blood, scared to death. I reached for Life's hand and he pulled me to my feet. My vision ended and I came back to reality.

Life was holding me in his arms.

"Are you okay? Do you need a doctor?" he asked. "You're burning up," Life said, feeling the top of head.

Mr. Ed across the street noticed me lying in Life's arms and ran over.

"Is everything okay? Leah, are you okay?" Ed asked.

I looked into Life's eyes. "Life Parker," I whispered with tears filling my eyes. I grabbed him and hugged him as tight as I could.

"You saved me," I said.

He held me close to his heart and told me he would always be there for me. Mr. Ed walked closer and placed his hand upon my shoulders and told me he was very sorry. I looked at him and told him not to be. However, those who caused this pain should be ones who is sorry.

My memory was beginning to come back rapidly. I walked out back and stared at the water. Life walked up behind me asking if I was okay.

"Sammy -- he's my enemy, isn't he?" I asked Life.

"He's the reason why all this shit is going on. Your father's death, your memory loss. Everything, Leah," he said turning his smile into a frown.

I walked to a flowerbed in front of the house and stared at the beautiful lilies that were there. The only living plant in the flowerbed. I reach down, grabbed the flower, and smelled its fragrance. Then crushed it into my hand, throwing it down.

"I've suffered too long, Life. It's their turn to feel the rage of pain."

I turned and glanced at Life, remembering someone was missing.

"Where's my friend Jojo?"

"He's still around somewhere. He refused seeing you the way you were," Life explained to me.

"Let's go. It's time to put an end to this madness," I said, getting back inside the car.

On the way back to Life's place, he explained to me how he made a deal with Sammy to make an even trade; his sister for me, and what stuck with me was Sammy's hideout spot. If that place he held me at was it, then Life knew where to find him.

However, I knew Sammy wasn't a fool. He would not remain in the same spot for very long. Alternatively, would he?

Sammy taught me a valuable lesson and that's to stay aware and do not slip up. I cannot make that mistake again. I fault myself for every mishap I have encountered thus far. In many ways, I felt I deserved everything that happened to me. *Stupid, stupid,* I thought repeatedly.

My first move was to get Loretta and either kill her or use her. Paul Griffin was my next move. I had to find his ass and make him pay. No more mercy on anyone; when I asked questions, I wanted an answer. No bullshit. I have paid the cost to be the fucking boss, and in the end, I will have much respect.

When we arrived, Loren was sitting outside on the steps.

"What's the matter with her?" I asked Life.

"I'm not sure, Leah. Go and talk to her. She's your mother," Life said laughing.

"Whatever -- my mother is dead," I replied joking around with him. I got out and walked over to her.

"What's the problem?" I asked, sitting next to her.

I saw fear in her eyes. It was strange and so strong I could taste it. "How are you?"

"I'm fine, and now that I'm back to myself, I can take care of Sammy Dresser once and for all."

When I mentioned Sammy's name, Loren became sick on the stomach. Unbelievably, but blood covered my eyes whenever I mentioned his name. I had to have him.

TWENTY-NINE

A Mothers Love

Loren and I walked inside. She prepared a meal for all of us. "Mmm, smells good," I said, walking into the kitchen.

"Yes, I cooked a little something for everyone."

Life and Mike walked in behind us, shouting and raving about nonsense.

Something was wrong with my mother and I wanted to know what. I looked at Life and Mike and asked the two to leave the kitchen for a second. I needed to speak with Loren alone.

"Mother, what's wrong? And don't tell me nothing."

She took a deep breath. "Leah I don't want to lose you. We are all we got. And I don't want what happened to your father to happen to you," she sobbed.

I walked over and reached out for her. "I'm not going anywhere," I said hugging her tight.

She looked into my eyes and told me she would die for me. Moreover, from the look in her eyes, I believed every word she was telling me. I trusted her once again.

She asked me to go away with her. She explained to me that she had already packed her things to leave. I quickly took a step back from her.

"I'm not too sure about leaving, mother. I don't know if I can."

"Child, you're so stupid. Sammy is going to kill you. Leave California while you have the chance," said Loren, shaking her head.

"Loren, I don't understand. Don't you want justice for your father's death?"

She just looked at me. Loren did not understand my goal. That was one of the only reasons I joined the investigation business. To seek revenge for my father's death. Not only that, but to keep punks like Sammy off our streets.

"Let the Lord handle him, Leah. He will pay in the end."

"It's a little too late to be running, don't you think? It is not going to end until one of us is dead. And it's not going to be me."

I told Loren if she felt safe leaving, then go. However, I was staying to finish what Sammy started.

I walked down into the basement to see Loretta.

"Get up!" I shouted.

"What's going on, Leah?" she asked jumping to her feet. I asked her to take a seat and she did as I told her.

"I have two options for you. None of them are safe, and you'll pick the first one if you had any common sense," I explained to her as she stared at me as if she was computerized to obey my every command.

"Okay, what are my options?" asked Loretta.

Anxious to know, I told her to help me take down both Paul Griffin and Sammy Dresser. That was the first option. Option two was to die. She took a long pause. I started counting down from ten, slowly pulling my pistol from my holster. I aimed it at her face as I counted from three, two . . .

"Okay!" Loretta shouted.

"So..."

"I pick one. Just promise me something," she asked.

I looked at her strange and told her I was not sure if I could do favors. She told me it would be better if I just killed her, because Sammy would do it anyway.

She was afraid and wanted protection. I explained to her everyone on my team looked out for one another. However, when it's said and done, we have to protect ourselves. I used my situation as an example. I was not going to protect my enemies anymore. I refused to allow my heart to be weak again. I left her no choice but to look after herself.

We quickly began planning. We sat and talked about personal matters -- family, men, and drama. While we sat and talked my phone rang; it was Jojo.

"Hey, Leah."

"Hey, Joey. Where are you?" I asked excusing myself from Loretta.

"At your place now; are you inside?"

"Not as of this moment."

"So, how are you?"

"I'm fine. Do you know where Life lives?"

"Yes. Your mother had me drop your clothes off there."

I could tell something was on his mind. He was not his usual self. Soon as he arrived, I told him the plan we had come up with. It was risky, but worth a try. The good thing about having Loretta was that she had access to Paul Griffin. She was the only one that could see him face to face and talk about dirty work. I was not sure if she would buck once in Paul's face. But Life came up with a great idea that would secure us. If Loretta tried something funny, she would pay for it.

When Jojo and I walked inside the basement, he and Life made eye contact and they did not remove their eyes off of each other.

"Okay Jojo. We need to put work into progress. First, get Paul to admit his doings in the murders and find out where Sammy's hiding."

I had Life explain to Loretta what would happen if she did not stick to the plan.

"This is only if you get foolish," I said, turning looking at Loretta.

I just knew she would run and switch sides. However, one thing I knew for sure. She was not a friend of mine. Life explain to her her responsibilities.

"Loretta, you will by no means show any signs of betrayal or of you needing help. And don't tell Paul or Sammy our plan," Life explains to Loretta.

"I'm not going in front of Sammy," said Loretta, biting her fingernails, scared as hell.

"Why not, Loretta?" I asked walking over to her.

"He will kill me,"

I told her so would I if she did not do it. I was not joking around with her either.

"Well, will I have a pistol?" asked Loretta.

Both Life and I looked at each other laughing.

"Are you nuts?" I asked her, turning my smile into a mug.

"No, I'm not. However, I want to protect myself. Like you said, look out for me."

"Yeah, I told you that. Not to use it as an excuse to get a gun and use it against us. I don't think so," I replied.

Loren walked down the basement steps.

"What kind of child did I raise?" said Loren walking towards me.

"What do you mean, Loren?" I asked her.

She snapped. "It's mother, and why would you release this girl back to the same people who made her this way?"

Loretta agreed with Loren. I did not think she had the right either.

"Why, Leah?"

"You have nothing to do with this. You said you were leaving. I thought you would be gone by now."

I walked in Life's direction towards the basement window. "You're right. But don't blame me for trying to save your life." I told her not to save something she cannot control.

"Mother, I'm grown. I make the choices in my life. Not you or no one."

I was upset now. I wanted to throw something. However, Life told me to calm down.

"You'll regret turning me away," said Loren.

"You'll regret more than I will. My mother's dead, right?" I asked her.

Loren smiled and said, "Thanks for letting me know that's how you really feel. Bye, darling."

As she walked away, my heart wanted to stop her. Nevertheless, my mind told me to let her go.

"What now?" I asked Life.

As he continued explaining to Loretta what her mission was. I had another vision. This time, Sammy, Jojo and Loren were present. Sammy stood in front of me with a pistol aimed at my face. Then, all of a sudden, blood splashed all over me.

"Leah, are you okay?" asked Jojo.

"Yes. I am fine. I think Sammy is going to kill me if I don't kill him first," I said, confused from the vision I just had.

Jojo walked over and hugged me tight. "Leah, we're not going to let anything happen to you again," he assured me.

I had something to do, so I left Life's place. I needed a little comfort from Tray, so I called him. He told me he was handling business, but to come over.

When I arrived to his house, his ex-wife was leaving. She was dropping his boys off. As she passed me, she looked at me strange, and I reflected the same expression. She did not want to take it there. I would have beaten the living shit out of her.

I got out and knocked on the door.

"Come in!" shouted Tray from the inside.

I walked inside and there sat Tray and his handsome sons on the sofa.

"Hey guys," I said soon as I laid eyes on them. Tray stood up and gave me a hug.

"It's sure nice to see you," he replied. He kissed me and sat back down. "Have a seat."

"So, how's school, guys?" I asked.

The both of them screamed they could not wait to get out. "Great! I can't wait, either." I shouted.

Little Andrew asked me why I was excited? I told him it would be many basketball games going on and we could see them all.

"And I would love to take you guys to one of the Lakers games," I said smiling at Andrew and Tray, Jr.

Tray asked me to go somewhere quiet with him to talk. We walked upstairs to his bedroom and made ourselves comfortable.

"Leah, I'm concerned about you. Talk to me," said Tray.

"Well, my only problem now is that me and my mother aren't speaking. And I had this crazy . . ." I stopped.

I did not want to tell Tray I was having visions of being murdered. I just knew he would not understand. "Bad what, baby?"

"Bad dreams about Sammy," I explained.

He did not ask what about. Therefore, I did not go into details. He told me to relax and take a deep breath. I closed my eyes and imagined myself far away on vacation with him alone. A great idea, I thought. It felt good to actually take a deep breath and meditate.

He began rubbing my back and shoulders, whispering sweet nothings in my ear. I was truly relaxed and free. All the tension I had just left my body. I began to fantasize about Tray in my mind. It was more than a feeling. It felt so good. More than a dream. It was extraordinary.

After the comforting was done, I lay next to Tray and thought about my life and all it had become. I thought about Loren also. This would be the second time she had walked out of my life. Rejection hurted like hell and I know I hurt her feelings when I refused to leave with her. However, she must understand I have choices to make on my own. Why would I want to walk away now?

Tray and I talked about real estate. I wanted a building to start my own business. He told me about a spot that was less than thirty thousand to settle. We arranged to see the building Monday morning.

When I left Tray's, I did not expect to have company when I arrived home. However, I did.

As I parked, Loren stood on my front porch waiting for me to get out. I sat for a second. I was about to cut my car back on and leave. Nevertheless, I just sat inside and watched her as she watched me. She stormed off the porch towards her rental car. I got out and followed behind her.

"Mother!" I shouted.

She kept walking as if she did not hear me. I walked up and grabbed the door before she could close it.

"Wait!" I shouted.

She looked at me and shook her head.

"Talk to me. Get out of the car," I asked.

She explained she did not have time to waste. In addition, she had to leave soon as possible. I walked around to the passenger's side and got in. She took a deep breath and exhaled, "I've come to ask you once again to leave behind this lifestyle and come with me while you still have time."

I dropped my head. She still did not comprehend my purpose. She looked at me and pulled my hair back behind my ear.

"I love you so much, Leah, and don't want you to die. I raised you to be a woman. Not a killer."

"I only want justice for what's taken place in my life. It has nothing to do with you anymore. And my intentions are not to hurt you," I explained.

"Then why wont you come with me?" she asked.

"I can't. I'm sorry, mother."

"I want to see you soon, Leah. Very soon. I know you are grown and have a life to live of your own. Just be careful, and remember I love you, my angel,"

We hugged each other and parted ways. It hit me hard because those were the last words she told me the night my father was killed. My love for her grew even stronger at that moment in time. My heart and mind told me I would never see her again.

A mother's love is strong. A relationship I once had with her I will never forget, or the look on her face when we said goodbye.

THIRTY

Payback's A Bitch

The rest of that day was hard for me. Loren left me with a lot to think about. When I got in, I took a hot bath, soaked for about twenty minutes, and relaxed. I had too much shit on my mind and needed time alone.

It was only after 5:15 Time was winding down. I had to make a move quick. Soon as I stepped out of the tub, my phone rang. It was Olivia. She wanted me to meet her later tonight around 8:30 or 9:00 She gave me insight on where Sammy might be hiding. She was so excited she found her daughter and I was hoping Jackie would not be around to identify me as her kidnapper. However, Olivia claimed to not know who committed the act.

After talking to Olivia, I called Life and Jojo. I informed them about the meeting. In addition, told them to stay posted on where we would be gathering. I did not trust anyone, and did not want to get caught slipping again like before.

I got dressed in one of my best outfits. All black everything. Black jumper, black high top Air force Ones -- I was ready to go. I jumped inside my Mustang and took off to San Diego.

When I got into town, I stopped by the same store. The kid I jacked for the videotapes was standing outside pumping gas. He looked over at my car and held up a finger telling me to wait.

"Hey, how are you? How much gas do you need?"

I told him to fill it up. As he pumped the gas, I noticed a women standing at the register ringing up customers. She looked strange and quite familiar. After the kid was finished filling my tank, I gave him a fifty-dollar bill. As he ran back inside, I watched and slowly drove around towards the front of the store. I parked and instantly made eye contact with the woman at the register.

I jumped out and ran inside the store, aiming my pistol at her face, and pulled the trigger.

The young guy ran as fast as he could towards the back room. Before he could close the door behind him, I jump kicked it wide open, knocking him on his ass.

"What do you want?" he shouted.

"I want Sammy. Where is he?"

"I don't know. I swear I don't," the boy shouted.

He sat there pleading for me not to kill him. I told him he was not worth it, but me hurting him was another story. The bitch at the register was the same trick I fought at the station; the same chick Paul had working for him. I told her I would get her back and I did.

I truly believed Sammy ran half of San Diego. I later realized this was where he had to be hiding. However, everyone was connected to him somehow and would not tell me anything.

I told the young guy, whose name was Jonathan Westbrook, I would come back for him if anyone knew about what happened. I also told him to give Sammy Dresser a little message.

"Tell him I'm back, and I'm scraped," I said walking out of the office. I wanted to blow the place up, but decided not too.

I jumped inside my ride and took off. I drove through all the hoods of San Diego searching for Sammy. However, no signs of him or his crew.

Jojo called to inform me Pam Bernard was free on a twenty thousand dollar bond. I was not worried about it; she better not get caught slipping. That was all I had to say about her; just another victim I had to take out. I told Jojo to keep a close eye on her movement, and to make sure he captured any odd activities coming from the Bernards' home. Most importantly, watch for the baby.

I was overexcited, smiling to myself thinking about killing Sammy Dresser. I drove around to kill a little time. Soon as eight hit, I called Olivia.

"I see you made it here safe and sound," said Olivia.

"Yes, ready to take your son out." I said taking a seat.

"What's the 411 on Sammy?"

"He's doing a trade later tonight. This trade involves two other mob bosses besides Sammy. I do not know who all Sammy will bring with him. But I do know if you get your hands on whatever they're trading, you'll be one rich woman."

That made me wonder what it could be.

"So, Olivia, do you know what's being traded?"

I was suspicious about the device Olivia told me they were trading. She said it was worth a fortune. I asked her how she knew all this information, and she told me she overheard Sammy talking to some guy on the phone.

"How are you sure it was a guy?" I asked Olivia.

"I picked up the phone and heard the guy. He wasn't in his prime unless he just had an older guy voice," explained Olivia.

First person came to mind was Paul Griffin. I wondered what that son of a bitch was up too. What did he have that Sammy wanted? Olivia told me to go on the east coast and lay low until she let me know where and when Sammy would arrive.

She phoned me and told me to head towards an old paper company, located by a land field. I drove to the plant and waited. Minutes later, Jojo and Life arrived, along with Mike and Loretta.

I exited my car and walked over to Jojo's patrol car. "What's up, Leah? Where these assholes at?"

I walked around to the passenger's side and got in.

"So, you ready?" I asked Jojo as I pulled out a cigarette to smoke.

"Sure. I just hope we make it out of here safe," said Jojo, looking around without giving me eye contact.

Something inside told me Jojo was about to do something stupid that would make me very angry. He started asking questions about Life.

"You did a background check on him?" I asked Jojo.

"Sure, why not. He looked familiar. So I did a little research."

"A little research, huh?"

"Yes," he replied.

"Come on, Jojo. We don't do little researches. We research the whole nine yards," I said looking at him, shaking my head in disgust.

"I'm sorry, but he's wanted. And that's not a good look for you Leah," said Jojo.

He stared at me for a while, giving me a serious look. I stepped out of the car and walked over towards Life's vehicle, giving him a funny expression. He looked at me, throwing up his hands and raising his shoulders.

"I think you should leave," I whispered to him. He looked at me crazy.

"Why?" he asked.

I looked over at Jojo's patrol car and noticed him on the phone. I was not sure who he might have been talking too. I just told Life to leave now. He kept asking me why. But I did not want to tell him. I asked him to follow my order and leave.

Life jumped out and ran towards Jojo's patrol car.

"Life," I shouted, unsure what he was about to do.

He grabbed Jojo through the window, pulling him onto the ground, punching him repeatedly in the face. I screamed for Life to stop, but he would not.

"Son of a bitch," Life shouted beating the shit out of Jojo.

When I reached for Jojo's cell phone, it was a cop on the other end. I quickly ended the call and hoped the police was not on their way. Mike jumped out and broke the two up. I was so angry with the both of them.

Minutes after everything calmed down, three cars pulled up and parked. I told Life and Jojo I would kill them if they blew this chance for me.

When the cars parked, we had Loretta call Paul to see if he was in one of those cars, and as I thought, he was present. Son of a bitch still had dealings with Sammy Dresser after all. I knew I could not trust either of them.

"Who is this?" Paul asked Loretta.

"This is Loretta. Where are you?"

He stepped out of the car looking around the area as he talked to Loretta on the phone.

"Where are you?" Paula asked Loretta. "I've been looking for you."

"I've been hiding. Trying to plan a move."

"Well, I'm taking care of some business right now at the land site. I'll call you back."

He did not realize Loretta called him private and would not be able to call her back.

"When will I see you again? I need my money for killing your wife and daughter. Plus, for kidnapping your grandson."

Damn, Loretta had me bent. I did not know she killed Mrs. Griffin or was involved in the kidnapping of Kayla's son. I was a little confused because when I asked her about his wife's murder and the kidnapping, she told me someone else did it.

"You heard me, Paul?"

"Yes I heard you -- you know I got you," he replied.

I needed him to admit to the murders. I whispered in Loretta's ear and told her to mention the baby.

"Paul, where's the baby?" asked Loretta.

The phone became quiet. Watching from afar, a car was flashing lights at Paul, taking his attention off the question Loretta was asking him. Loretta called him a couple of times before he answered. He asked for a number to reach her at.

"I don't have a phone that you can reach me at. I'm using someone else's," said Loretta.

The phone hung up.

"Damn it!" I shouted.

"Why are you shaking? I thought you were tough," I asked Loretta, snatching the phone from her hand.

Everyone exited the cars carrying black bags in their hands. I also noticed a young girl, but could not see her face. I stood for a second wondering who she could be. She came with Paul, but I had never saw her before.

Sammy had four bodyguards along with him. All carrying big boy guns. If I wanted, I could have killed all of them on the spot, but stuck to the plan.

After we got Loretta together, we put her into Life's old Chevy and told her to drive down where Sammy and Paul were.

We attached a time grenade to her waist. Just in case she tried anything funny, we would blow her ass up, along with Sammy and Paul. I thought about doing it like that. That way, I would not have to worry about her, Sammy, or Paul Griffin.

When Loretta pulled up, they all turned and stared at the car strange. I could hear their conversation, only because Loretta wore a wire. She parked next to Paul's patrol car.

"What's this Paul; why is she here?" asked Sammy.

"I'm not sure," Paul said, walking over to Loretta.

"Hey Paul. When you mentioned land site, I knew just where you were," said Loretta exiting the car.

I could see the look on Paul's face from the small camera we placed in Loretta's bra, and he was scared as shit.

"How did you get here so fast?" asked Paul.

"What's going on here, Paul Griffin?" shouted Sammy.

Once Loretta turned in the direction Sammy stood, I quickly identified the girl that arrived with Paul. It was Christian.

"Oh my goodness," I said looking at the computer scream. Life sat beside me in shock himself.

"What is she doing here?" he whispered.

"The hell if I know."

"I really need to talk to Mr. Paul," Loretta told Sammy.

Sammy walked up to Loretta and slapped the shit out of her.

"Bitch, don't ever in your dirty little useless life interfere with my business. You hear me?" he shouted.

"I'm sorry," said Loretta falling to her knees.

I watched as Loretta feared that Sammy would kill her. However, before he could do anything else, Paul pulled her off to the side.

"What is it, Loretta? You're going to get the both of us killed."

"Hurry up, Griffin. I don't have all day," Sammy shouted.

"I need my money, Paul," said Loretta.

"I told you I'll pay you. Matter of fact, I will pay you in a second. Okay?" Paul shouted.

As Paul walked away from her, she ran behind him and asked him the question I have been waiting for him to answer.

"Paul!"

"What, Loretta?" he asked turning back around.

Christian walked over to Paul and asked him to hurry. From the look on her face, I could see she was ready to go. It all made sense. He was the guy she met and went out of town with. That is why she wanted me to watch her son. Therefore, she could party and lay up with no-good Paul Griffin. That pissed me the fuck off.

"Why did you have me kill your family?" asked Loretta. Paul stared at her, laughing.

"Why? Because you were the only one I knew that was stupid enough to do it."

"But why your own family?" she asked.

"They became useless. My wife was not worth the fuck anymore. My kids would get the money, and my grandson is worth millions. So, I had you kill them."

He had no sympathy. As he turned from Loretta, I asked her to ask him why he killed Lt. Terry.

"Why did you kill Terry?" Loretta shouted.

Paul stopped and stood there for a second. "What did you say?" he asked Loretta.

"Why did you kill Lt. Terry?" she repeated.

"Because he was useless, too; plus, I wanted the unit for myself. You happy now?" Paul asked.

After he said that, I stopped recording. At that moment, everything around me went blank.

We went in and sniped each of Sammy's bodyguards. All six of them hit the ground. I aimed my rifle at Sammy's pistol, shooting it out of his hand. Paul grabbed Loretta, holding a pistol to her head.

"Come any closer, Leah, I'll shoot her," Paul shouted.

I looked at him and smiled. Life and Jojo were at my side and could handle Paul. So, I turned my attention towards Sammy. I pointed my pistol at his face and walked closer towards him. Life and Jojo had their pistol drawn on Paul.

This moment was a dream come true for me. I finally had Sammy where I wanted him.

"Look at me, Sammy."

He looked at his hand and me at the same time, trying to stop the bleeding,

"What do you want, Leah?" he asked.

I stared at him for a while, before telling him he caused so much pain in my life. Now he was going to pay.

"Then what are you waiting for? Kill me," said Sammy.

I asked myself the same question. Before I could pull the trigger, someone called out my name. "Leah!"

"Mother!" I shouted. Loren ran over towards me, taking my attention off Sammy.

"Mom, you're still here?" I asked.

We both hugged each other. Suddenly, two shots were fired. It happened so fast. Loren placed herself behind me. I quickly turned and shot Sammy three times in the chest. Blood covered my face and clothes. He fell backwards on the ground, bleeding badly. However, he was not dead.

"You can't kill me, Leah. I am God," said Sammy, laughing as if this was a joke. I walked over to him and aimed my gun in his face.

"You're funny. Now its time to end the jokes."

I shot him twice in the head, taking him out instantly. I was always told if a man dies with his eyes open, then he deserved to die.

A big relief came across me. Seeing Sammy dead right in front of me made me feel safe and free from what kept me captured all those years. However, my heart broke all over again when I turned and saw Loren lying on the ground, covered in blood. I ran to her side to comforted her.

"Mom, I'm here. Please hold on," I whispered to her as I cried.

She looked at me without responding to anything I was saying. Her eyes closed, she slipped into a coma...

"Mom . . . Mom . . ."

THIRTY-ONE

Sleeping With The Enemy

We arrived at the hospital at 9:02 Loren was rushed to Intensive Care. The doctor told me they would have to perform surgery on my mother.

At 9:05, the cops arrived and arrested Life. I tried my best to clear his name but it was too late.

Jojo walked up to me and told me that would be the last time I'd see Life Parker alive. I slapped him in the face. I just never knew he would do something like this. Now Life could be facing hard time in prison, or maybe even death. I paced back and forth, wondering if Loren would make it out of surgery.

At 9:12, I called Tray. He dropped what he was doing and rushed to the hospital. We cried and prayed together for Loren.

I was asleep by 9:30 when the doctor walked out to speak with me.

"I'm sorry, ma'am. We tried all we could."

The doctor told me Loren passed at 9:20 I dropped to my knees, crying like a baby. My heart was broken badly. Just when I had another chance to know my mother again, now she was gone.

While lying there in Tray's arms, I realized I took her for granted. I asked to see her, and the doctor walked us into the room, which her body laid.

She had two gunshots to her back and was covered in blood. I walked towards her body and kissed her on the forehead, whispering "I love you," into her ear. I took my fingers and rubbed them through her hair. I could not stop crying. That moment was one of the hardest I ever faced.

I spent over an hour talking to Loren, crying and praying. However, with all said and done, she wasn't coming back.

Tray grabbed me by the arm walking me out of the room. The press greeted me soon as I exited. Cameras and news reporters were everywhere. They called me San Diego's hero, along with San Francisco. I was all over television and newspapers throughout California. It was madness; I could not get out of the hospital without being followed.

Paul Griffin was booked in after I gave the police the recordings of his confessions. His bond was set to $2 million dollars, plus a hold. I was so upset, I did not know where to turn. Mike and Loretta went back to Life's place, the same place I later ended up.

I went to sleep soon as I got in. Although I was still tired and sad when I awoke, a lot was still on my mind, but mainly my mother.

Loretta was sitting in the living room when I walked inside. She turned and looked at me pointing at the clock.

"I see you're up early," said Loretta.

I looked around for Mike, but no sign of him. "Where is Mike?" I asked.

Loretta wasn't sure where he was, so went back inside the room which I slept and grabbed my cell phone.

"Why are you still here?" I asked Loretta, walking back into the living room.

"I had no place to go, Leah. No money or anything to eat," she said looking pitiful.

My head was killing me from all the crying I did last night. "Damn it!" I shouted.

Loretta jumped up and walked towards me.

"What?" I asked her as she stared at me. She broke down in tears hugging me.

"Please Loretta. I need room to breath. Fall the fuck back," I said, pushing her away from me.

She was excited Sammy was dead, and thanked me for saving her life. I told her it was no problem and walked away.

"So, why are you sticking around? Besides the fact you need a place to stay?" I asked. She acted as if she did not hear me. "Hello!" I shouted.

"I was wondering if you could let me stay around until I find a job. You know, I never got my share of money from Paul."

It was no way she was ever getting the money Paul promised her. And she could not live with me. A total stranger coming into my home; someone who did favors for my enemies. There was no way I could do it.

I thought about it and decided to give her money to leave. However, before I gave her money out of my pocket, I remembered the black bags I recovered from Sammy and Paul. I went to the trunk of my car and unzipped one of the bags.

"Holy shit," I shouted.

I looked around to see if anyone was watching. I thought my eyes were deceiving me. However, it was what I thought; a bag full of money. Nothing but hundred dollar bills.

I zipped the bag back up and grabbed the next one, unzipping it. I paused awhile before opening. I slowly unzipped the bag, and there laid my mother's pink diamond necklace on top of more money. A smile filled my face. I was in such good luck. I could not believe it. The necklace I thought I lost was right in front of me. The only thing I had left of Loren. That necklace meant the world to me, and to have it meant even more.

Underneath the box that held the necklace were blocks of cocaine. Eight evenly cut bricks. I closed the bag and shut the trunk.

"What is it, Leah?" Loretta asked, scaring the shit out of me.

"Nothing that's important to you. Where's Mike?" I asked her again, trying to change the conversation quickly.

"I told you I don't know," says Loretta.

When I got inside, I called Olivia. She owed me money, and I needed it ASAP. She was so excited when I phoned her. She asked me to turn on the television and watch the news. When I did, my face was all over the TV set. Praises came from everyone within the community of San Francisco and San Diego for busting Sammy Dresser.

Olivia asked me to meet her at Motif's Fashion Boutique at 8:00 to collect my money.

I left and went to my place. On my way there, I got a call from the Los Angeles Police Department. It was my friend Henry Donald, who use to work with San Francisco Police Department before transferring to Los Angeles Department. He asked me to stop by the station; he did not say for what. However, I assured him I will be there and went home to change clothes.

After I got out of the shower, I decided to try something different. I grabbed a pair of scissors and begin cutting my hair. This was the first time I ever cut my hair. I looked like Halle Berry, but cuter.

It was time for a change and that day was the day I made that change. I stared in the mirror for a while and realized how much I looked just like Loren Starr.

On my way out the house to meet Olivia, my cell rang. I answered without looking at the caller ID.

"Hello."

"Where you at, baby,"

"Who is this?" I asked.

"Tray -- who else would be calling you asking you that?"

"Hey. I am on my way to handle business. What's up?"

Tray told me he needed to talk to me about something important. I told him to tell me later when we meet for the game. I had tickets for a Lakers game I promised his boys. However, whatever he needed to talk to me about bothered him a lot. I could tell by the change in his tone. It worried him and me also. But at that moment, it didn't matter as much. He was not the type to worry or get upset about anything. The only time I ever saw him angry was when Jr. got smart with me. That shit really pissed him off. I told him to call me at noon so we could have lunch and talk.

My line stayed blowing up. Jojo called me while on the phone with Tray. He wanted to apologize about the fuck shit he pulled on Life. That really tore me away from him. I told him I will talk to him again later on in life.

Soon as I arrived in San Diego, I called Olivia. She was already waiting on me to arrive.

She sat in her expensive clothing all jazzed up, looking wonderful. She had great taste for a seventy-five year old woman. Olivia noticed me outside the window and waved for me to come inside. I walked in and was seated at a small dinning area the boutique had inside.

"Hey, Olivia," I spoke, taking a seat across from her.

"Hey, sweetie, I want to congratulate you on your success." she said sliding me a suitcase. I peeked inside and It was full of cash.

"It's all there. Fifty thousand in cash; plus here's a bonus," said Olivia passing me a thick envelope, which contained twenty thousand dollars.

"Nice doing business with you, Olivia, have a nice day!" I said shaking her hand.

"Leah Starr!" shouted Olivia as I walked away from the table. I stopped and turned around.

"Nice hair," she replied, winking her eye at me.

I felt she knew who I was the whole time and knew exactly what her son did to my family. That way, she knew I would have killed her son anyways. Nevertheless, I gained not only revenge, but a huge profit also.

On my way out of the boutique, Jackie Dresser walked past me, looking at me strange.

"Hey, don't I know you?" she asked me.

I told her I did not think so and that I had one of those familiar faces. My new hairdo had me looking brand new.

When I arrived at the Los Angeles police station, I saw reporters and cameras everywhere. However, they did not recognize me because of my short hair and sunglasses. I walked inside and the first face I saw was Jojo.

"Hey Leah."

"Jojo," I replied, walking past him.

"Leah, please stop," he shouted grabbing my arm. I quickly pushed him away from me.

"You supposed to be my friend, Jojo. You betrayed me," I whispered.

"By locking a fugitive convict away?"

"Oh, so now you want to get loud. Fuck you, Jojo; you ain't shit."

"You weren't saying that when I was fucking your brains out," screamed Jojo. He got everyone's attention inside the station. I walked up to him and backhanded the shit out of him.

"You'll never find pussy this good ever again," I whispered to him before walking away.

I could not believe Jojo put our personal business out there like that. Everyone in the station was talking. I felt so bad.

The head Lt. called me inside his office to congratulate me on capturing Sammy Dresser. In addition, he passed me a check, but before letting it go, he explained to me Carla Spencer raised money for the capture of Sammy. I knew how much it was, the check it was for one million dollars. I almost fainted when I seen those digits. I was ready to deposit it and start my own business.

Before I could make it out of the office, he offered me a permitted position at his station, along with top pay and good benefits. He also told me I'd be the head chief of investigation. It sounded nice, but now that I had the money, I needed to start my own business. I was not sure if I could take the offer. However, I told him that I would think about it.

I paid off my home and took a long vacation out of the United States. I was rich now and wanted to start my life completely over. However, there was still unfinished business to handle.

He assured me he would stand by my discussions and support me throughout my career. Now Lt. Harmon was the man I needed to stand beside me. He could pull major strings for me in time of need.

After I left the station, I went to the bank and deposited my check, plus the seventy grand Olivia gave me. I still had the money I found inside the black duffle bags. I had plans for that money, so there was no need to deposit it.

I drove back to Life's spot to talk with Loretta. When I arrived, she was gone. She left a letter explaining she hit a lick and now I did not have to worry about her anymore. Damn, I needed to talk to her before she left. No one was there at the house but me. Mike was out registering for college. So I hid the money and drugs in the attic.

I called Tray and asked him to meet me at Jack-in-the-Box. When I spoke with him, he did not seem right. It sounded like he was at a police station and not a real estate office.

Minutes passed and no sign of Tray. I decided to call him back. But No answer.

I got out and placed an order to eat to kill a little time. I was thinking he would show up with flowers and candy at the last minute, saying he was sorry and would never be late again. However, it did not happen that way.

After my food was ready, I decided to leave. As I drove towards the exit, a car with tinted windows drove next to me. I had my pistol lying on my lap just in case they acted stupid. The windows rolled down, and to my surprise, it was Christian.

"Hey, Leah," she said smiling.

I mugged her and asked her what she wanted.

"What's with the attitude? I swear I didn't know you were beefing with Paul Griffin," she explained.

I threw my hands up at her and told her to stay the fuck out of my way or get dealt with. She smiled and drove into Jack N the Box.

As I reached three blocks, he called me.

"Where the hell are you? I waited for you to arrive and you didn't show up," I shouted.

He told me things were backed up at the office and said he was on his way. At that moment, I did not want to see him. I told him I was on my way home.

Somehow, he beat me there. He sat inside his F-150 waiting on me to arrive. Soon as I got out of my car, he jumped out.

"Come here. Damn, what did you do to your hair?" he asked, grabbing my arm.

I did not say anything. Just stared at him funny.

"Baby, you look amazing. Beautiful," he said kissing my neck.

"Whatever. What was so important you had to tell me?" I asked. His smile turned into a frown.

"Are you going to tell me or what?"

He sighed. Then walked towards his truck.

"Well, Leah. I've been holding back a secret from you."

I did not believe it. I took it as a joke because I knew everything about him.

"Come on Tray, what is it?" I asked him getting impatient.

"Come on, Leah. It is not a fucking joke. This is serious," he shouted.

"I'm listening."

We walked over towards the steps and sat down.

"I haven't been honest with you. It's something I do on the side for a living."

"Like what, Tray?" I asked curious and confused.

"I'm a private spy. I work for an international investigations unit."

When he said that, everything around me just blanked out. I stood up, looked Tray directly in his eyes, and asked him what affect it had on me. He stood up and told me it dealt with Sammy and my father. At the time he told me this, he had both of his hands on my shoulders. I pushed him away.

"What about my father?"

"Trying to see why he was killed and now that I know, I need what allowed this crime to take place," he explained.

"Oh, yeah, and what's that?" I asked backing up a couple of feet away from him.

"You know what, Leah. The necklace."

"So all this time you weren't with me for me, but for my mother's jewel?" I asked as tears filled my eyes.

He walked up to me and wiped my eyes.

"I was only doing my job. No hard feelings. I'm sorry, Leah."

I stared at him for a while as we looked into each other's eyes. I walked up closer to him and whispered,

"Don't ever step foot back into my life again, or I will kill you like I have done the rest. And that's a promise."

I turned away from him and walked inside my home closing the door behind me.

THIRTY-TWO

My Final Victim

After Tray told me the truth about his private life, I broke up with him. I could not believe he lied to me. Why me? I thought he was the one. He made me feel things I had never felt before. I guess I was wrong for believing he was different; the one for me.

My next move was going to the station to speak with Paul Griffin. My mind was on finding Kayla's baby. He was still missing. No lead to where he could be located. If anyone knew anything, it would be Paul Griffin.

Paul was sound asleep when I got to his cell.

"Wake up, bitch!" I shouted beating on the bars.

"Leah Starr! I'm glad to see you," he said jumping up from his bed bunk.

"Oh, why is that?" I asked.

He explained he needed my help getting out, saying that the force was treating him like shit. I wonder why? It was so funny to me. My first question was how he got the necklace. He started pacing back and forth.

"This young girl got it for me," he said.

"What young girl?" I thought.

"The one that was with me last night."

"Christian?" I asked.

He assured me that was her name. I could not believe she stole my necklace. I asked him how she got it, and he explained she stole them out of my car the night Mike was kidnapped. It all came back to me. For sure, I thought Sammy got the necklace the same night my car was stolen. All this time, that bitch Christian stole my shit. She had her day coming to her very soon. I cut to the chase and asked the question I came to ask him.

"Where's Kayla's baby?"

"My grandson?" he replied smiling.

"Where is he?"

"Safe, in good hands,"

"With Pam and Tom Bernard?" I asked.

Paul looked at me strange, as if he wondered how I knew such a thing.

"He's not safe, Paul. She isn't safe!" I shouted.

He looked away in disgrace, eyes filled with tears of regret. "Do you not care enough for your grandson's safety?"

"Sure I do," he replied.

"Then save him. Tell me where I can find him, and I'll go get him."

"I can't. They won't let you get him," he sobbed.

"Who are they? Tell me, Paul. Come on, you are already facing life in prison. Help me help you." I explained.

Paul took a long breath, and sighed around a bit. I asked the officer to open the cell. I walked inside and sat across from him.

"So, are you going to help your grandson?" I asked in a low and humble tone.

He began crying, then laughed in my face.

"Oh, so this is a joke to you now?" I asked him.

"No, it's not. I just remember the first time I saw your face. You were so young and full of fear. You couldn't wait to learn all there was about becoming an investigator," he laughed.

"You're right. Now I have caught two of the biggest crooks in California. Now, cut the bullshit and talk. I am giving you a chance to make things right. For your grandson, for yourself."

"I know you are. But I have no leads on where he could be," he sobbed.

I slammed my hand down on the table hard, scaring the hell out of Paul. "I don't give a damn about you, Paul. I am here to do one thing, and that is find Kayla's baby. And make sure you fry; that's the promise I made to Kayla before you had her killed."

I walked away from him. I knew now I would have to find the child on my own.

As I walked out of the cellblock, his two sons were walking in to see him. Before I got to the end of the hall, I stopped when I heard fussing and shouting coming from Paul's cell.

His sons were very upset with him. I think if he does not die from lethal injection, he will die from a nervous breakdown.

I went up front and got information on Pam's background. She already had to appear in court for her drug charges.

"Hey, friend," a warm voice said. I turned and it was Henry.

"Hey, Henry."

We hugged each other tight as if we have not seen each other in years. For a moment, I became comfortable and laid my head on his shoulder. I looked up and gave him a friendly kiss on the cheek.

"So, what's been going on with you?" I asked Henry.

"Nothing, living the life here. I have all updated tools; plus, great pay. I can't complain," he said smiling.

"That's great. I'm glad you're happy."

"I'll be happier when you get your own business off the ground. So I can come and work for you."

"Cool. I'm supposed to go check out a building today. And when the discussions have been made, I'll let you know."

Tray was supposed to show me. However, that would not be happening ever. I called the head office to see if anyone would be interested in showing me the building. I talked to a young guy name Solomon Petson. He sounded cute, but I wanted to see his ass in person. Therefore, we arranged to meet around 2:00 to view the office space.

After I got off the phone with sexy Solomon, I turned and there stood Henry looking at me.

"Look, Leah. There she goes," he said pointing at the front door.

I turned to see who he was talking about and there stood Pam Bernard and this skinny chocolate female dressed in a business suit. The two walked up to me.

"Pam!" I spoke.

"Leah Starr," she replied.

"What do you want?" I asked.

"Meet my lawyer," Pam said introducing me to the skinny chick. She held her hand out for me to shake, but I declined.

"She's here to help me fight against you," said Pam, walking behind me. I quickly turned around and pushed her away from me.

"Don't walk up on me like that," I said giving her the evil eye. She smiled, and so did I.

"Get ready, Leah Starr. I heard about all the money you have. The million, sixty grand you got from Paul, Sammy, and your parents' death. Or may I say, father's death."

"Yeah, bitch, I'm rich. So what?" I asked walking away.

"Stop. I'm not through talking to you!" Pam shouted.

I continued walking away, only because she would have made me mad and I would have laid her ass out. However, I guess she did not mind that type of treatment because she continued following me, along with her stick figure of a lawyer.

"What do you want?" I turned asking Pam.

"I just wanted you to know, you'll be broke when I'm done with you."

"Here's your papers; you've been served," the skinny bitch said, barley exhaling.

"By the way, I'm Ashley Grayson, Pam's Attorney." she said, smiling.

"Oh, yeah. I think you two may need more pull. I'm a hard pill to swallow."

After I got away from those tricks, I walked over where Henry stood.

"What's going on, Leah?" he asked.

"Those two are trying to take me to court."

"That's what I wanted to talk to you about. Do you know who that woman is?" Henry asked me.

I did not and really did not care. I was not scared of no one. However, he did tell me she was on of the best district attorneys in the state of California. That she would be impossible to beat. That rather worried me, but I had plans to take Pam Bernard down. I told him I was not worried about Miss Thang.

"I'm just letting you know, Leah."

I was not up for anyone killing my spirit. I walked into Lt.'s office and had a chat with him about the issue that was taking place. He told me not to stress about it. Pam Bernard was going down either way for the drugs she was being charged for. In addition, her home showed evidence she was involved with Paul Griffin and possibilities leading to Kayla's baby's kidnapping. That helped me out a lot and give me confidence. Before I left the station, Paul's oldest son called out to me.

"Leah!" I turned and noticed him standing at the end of the hallway.

"Hey, what can I do for you?" I asked.

"I'm sick of my father. I want to thank you for finding justice for my family. Thank you so much," he said grabbing me, hugging me tight.

"Slow your roll, buddy. I'm not finished. I have to find Kayla's child."

He looked at me strange. "What is it?" I asked.

"Kayla told me she gave her son up for adoption. Said she was sick of caring for him," he explained.

"Excuse me, what is your name?" I asked.

"Julian Griffin."

I had to take a seat on this one. "So, Kayla told you this?"

"Yes. As soon as I got to L.A I asked her about the baby, and that is what she told me. "

Something about this story was not right. I did not understand why Kayla would have lied to me. As I begin thinking about the whole situation, it started to make sense. When I saw Paul making exchanges at the park that evening, I realized Paul had his grandson and gave the baby to the driver of the Tahoe, along with a brief case. That's the only thing that threw me off.

"You saw any papers?" I asked Julian.

"No, I got upset. I'm just as confused as you are."

I could tell he was confused, tired, and fed up with his father. Stressed over both his mother and sister's death. I felt sorry for him. But at the end of the day, it is what it is.

The next step was locating the child's new parents, and who Paul paid to get the child back. I told Julian I would find out the truth and bring Kayla's baby back home.

"Please find Adam. We're the only family he has," he said walking away torn and still in shock.

Adam was Kayla's only son. He was only four years old, young, and harmless. I was determined to find him. It would be a shame and hunt me for the rest of my life if I let those bastards ruin his life.

I left the station around 1:34 I needed to change into something casual. I had to meet with a real estate agent and hoped he looked as good as he sounded on the phone.

I figured he may know Tray, but I did not give a damn. I was not going to tell him I knew him. If we vibe, I just might try him. I am only human. I have the right to think nasty.

I fixed my hair up and got pretty, but business material. However, I did have a pair of thongs on for easy access. They felt good to have on underneath my skirt.

I arrived to the building at 1:57 a red Mercedes sat out front. I parked behind it, grabbed my cell, and phoned Solomon.

"Hey, I'm waiting outside."

He asked me to come inside. Said he was warming the place up.

I got out of my car and viewed around the building. It was small, but just how I wanted my building to be. Nice parking area, beautiful view of the city outside the main window.

"I have to get this place," I said to myself.

I walked up towards the front door and walked inside. Looking around. I saw no sign of Solomon.

"Hello, is anyone here?" I asked.

I thought for sure there was someone inside. Solomon asked me to come in. Why wouldn't he be there?

I walked into what would be my office and it was huge. With an upstairs balcony; which I could not wait to walk up. However, my senses told me to walk towards the back where a kitchen sat. I looked to my right and there stood Tray. I quickly reached for my pistol, pointing it directly at him.

"Come on, Leah. I'm not here to hurt you."

From the look on his face, it seemed he was telling me the truth. But my heart would not allow me to believe what he was saying.

"It's a little too late. You've already have hurt me," I said staring at him. He moved closer towards me.

"Get back, Tray," I shouted almost pulling the trigger.

"What's going on, Tray?" Solomon asked walking into the kitchen. I quickly turned and aimed the pistol at him.

"Don't shoot," Solomon screamed. He was terrified and scared out of his mind.

"What type of games are you playing, Tray?" I asked him aiming the pistol back in his direction.

"Look, I'll leave so you two can take care of business. I thought that maybe I could make things right between you and me. I guess my intentions were wrong,"

I was falling once again. Not being the strong and straightforward woman I said I was going to be. Nevertheless, reality strikes again and I am reminded he never wanted me for me. Only my family jewel.

He walked away and out of the building. Solomon was now on the floor on his knees with his hands behind his head.

"Get up fool," I shouted.

I told him I was an investigator. He thought I was crazy, but in some way, it turned him on, because when he got to his feet, I noticed a big knot inside of his pants. I stared for a minute, but had to catch myself. He was very attractive, five-foot-ten, bowlegged, brown skin, and cut with muscles. The perfect package, and he wore glasses also, which did not look bad on him at all.

"You like?" he asked me as I continued staring at the print on his pants.

"Man, please. Let's get this over with." I said avoiding his question. I just did not want to take it there. Especially after running into Tray; he could have still been snooping around.

He walked me around the building showing me all the dining areas, bathrooms, and even overnight stay rooms located in the basement. We talked for about an hour or so before I made my final discussion, but before I could give it to him, I got an unexpected phone call with information concerning Adam, Kayla's son.

I answered the anonymous number and could tell it was a girl trying to disguise her voice.

"Who is this?" I asked.

"Don't worry about that. If you want the boy back, bring your stupid ass to the Players Meet around 3:05," she replied. The bitch called me stupid. I did not get upset, I just followed orders. I felt the biggest part of my troubles were gone. There was nothing that could stop me.

Solomon had the contract for the building with him. So I signed it and took off.

I arrived at the rundown shack at 3:03 It was located in an open area where no one came. I got out and walked to the front door. I saw this junkie come running from behind the building.

"Hey, follow me," he shouted.

I walked over where he stood, looked around the corner. Suddenly, someone called my name.

"Leah!"

I turned around and there stood Tom Bernard. I reached for my pistol, but he beat me and pulled out his.

"Too slow. So, I hear you're messing with my family. That's a bad mistake," he told me, waving his gun back and forth in my face.

Everything happened so fast. We went inside and walked upstairs. When we reached the top, Pam stood at the end of the hallway holding Adam.

"You are so stupid!" Pam shouted.

Minutes later, Christian walked out of one of the rooms.

"Tell her, Tom. Make her mad," said Pam.

"Oh yeah, Leah, I killed your father in cold blood!" shouted Tom. He thought it was funny.

My heart went to racing and blood filled my eyes. All I could do was call him a bastard. My father's best friend took his life.

"I want that necklace, Leah. Now, where is it?" Tom screamed. My mind went blank. Next thing I know, I went nuts. Tears filled my eyes. My nerves were filled with anger. I had to think fast.

I told Tom the jewel were inside my shoes. And soon as he walked over towards me and bent down towards my shoes, I kneed him in the face.

He fell back and the gun slid across the floor. Me, Christian and Pam looked at the gun at the same time. I ran over towards it as fast as I could and jumped for it. Christian and I struggled awhile over the pistol. I finally got the gun in my hands and shot Christian two times in the head. Tom jumped up, grabbed a steel bar, and ran towards me with it. I shot one of his legs taking him to the floor.

"Bitch," Tom shouted holding on to his leg.

Pam tried getting away but I ran in front of her. "You're not going anywhere." I said.

She smiled and replied, "I will kill this baby if you don't let me go."

I stepped back and let her walk out of the room which they brought me too. I was not worried about her getting away because police surrounded the entire club.

I turned towards Tom and stared at him.

"So, who's got the last laugh now, Tom?" I asked pointing my pistol at him.

"It still doesn't matter. I have nothing to live for, kill me Leah," Tom shouted.

I did not have much of a choice. He had to die for making my life a living hell. For all those years of wondering who killed my family, now I knew it was Tom Bernard. It hurt much more to find out someone my father trusted took his life,

"I had no choice, Leah. Either he had to die or I was killed." I took a long look at Tom.

"Yeah, and now I have no choice. Tell Sammy I said hey." I shot him twice in the head and dropped my pistol.

I fell to my knees and began asking God for forgiveness. My whole world changed that moment. My heart cried out for all the murders I had committed. It was a major relief, and right then, I knew what I wanted to do after this storm passed.

THIRTY-THREE

My Life Two Years Later

My life changed in the year of 2006. I got what I wanted. Sammy Dresser and his crew dead.

I finally opened my own business. Henry kept his word and moved to my company to help me. I also hired a mean pair of investigators right out of college and to say they were the best. Penny Ann Thomas and Susann Pater. Both twenty-two years old.

Jerry Smith was my drug investigator. He was nice looking, tall and slender with long plaits. Henson Bryson was also a drug investigator. Both guys had great personalities.

Corey Johnson was the youngest one. He was only nineteen, but had major skills in rifle expertise. He could identify any bullet and trace it to the correct gun. We were like family; everyone enjoyed working with one another.

I did not want too many people working for me. There were only a few I trusted and the ones I had, did not get much. I did in fact save a spot for Life I visited him each weekend and knew he needed someone and I was right there for him, because he was there for me.

The lawsuit Pam Bernard filed against me was later dropped in late March when she was found guilty on three of counts of kidnapping and drugs charges. She was sentenced to twenty years in prison.

Little Adam was taken to his uncle Julian to live with while his grandfather was sentenced to life in prison without possibility of parole, and when it came time for Pam to testify, she did not hold back on Paul. She told everything in every detail. The judge was disgusted.

I worked each day on simple cases. Nothing major.

Jojo and I were still friends. We talked every now and then. But I still was not over his betrayal. However, each day I kept in mind I had to forgive him in order to be forgiven. I wish I would have understood that years before I took matters into my own hands. At least listened to my mother Loren.

The name of my company was Leah Starr's Investigation Unite. (L.S.I.U.) My company got hundreds of customers and clients within a two weeks period.

I flew to Jamaica twice and visited China. It was such an amazing experience. I could not wait to explore new and different cases. Everything seemed to be going great for me.

I continued dating; matter of fact, Solomon and I went out a couple of times. I did it only to make Tray mad. I did miss him and the boys, but could not see myself back with him. Once a liar, always a liar, and I was not about to go back to that again.

My birthday was coming up. Something I have not celebrated in two years. However, this year I had plans.

May 2, 2008.

Susann became my best friend. She understood everything about me. and understood my purpose. The both of us went shopping. I bought a couple of outfits and some shoes. Nothing major, but the price tags.

While we shopped, we saw two guys standing outside of the store watching us.

"Look, Leah," said Susann pointing at the guys. I kept on shopping.

"Leah, come on. You barely date; the guys are flirting with us. Look how cute they are. Give one a chance."

I was not sure about giving any of them a chance.

I looked at Susann and said, "So you're going to convince me to talk to one of those guys?"

"No, we both need lives. I'm lonely, I need a friend," said Susann.

"Well talk to one of them. I'll be over in the jewel section." I said walking away. Susann followed me instead of approaching one of the guys.

"Why are you still following me?"

"I'm scared, Leah -- come with me."

I grabbed her by the hand and pulled her over where the guys stood. "Hey, this here is my friend Susann and she wanted to know if you guys would like to hang out?"

Susann had the biggest smile on her face. I thought it became stuck at one point. She could not stop cheesing.

"Sure, that's fine. I'm Grant and this is my lover, John."

I turned around leaving Susann there alone. I did not want to laugh in her face. However, it was so funny. Susann played it off and carried on as if she really wanted to hang with them.

I wandered off into a shoe store minding my own business when I bumped into an old friend.

"Leah," a voice whispered from behind me.

I turned to see who it was and too my surprise it was Victor.

"Hey, how are you?" he asked.

"I'm doing fine. Yourself," I asked staring at how good he looked. He had nothing for Leah Starr. For goodness sakes, I ruined the man's manhood.

"Great." he replied.

I didn't see how, when his you know what was cut off. While standing in front of him, I could not help but to stare at his crotch. My eyes gazed away, but it was too late. He caught me staring.

"I got that fixed. You're not going to cut it off again, are you?" he asked being silly.

I slightly smiled back. This was an awkward situation.

He stared into my eyes, and suddenly I was mesmerized. That was the effect Victor had on me.

"Congratulations on taking Sammy Dresser down," said Tray. However, I was dazed. "Did you hear me, Leah?" he asked.

He placed his hand upon my shoulder. When I realized what he had done, I looked at his hand and he quickly pulled it away from my shoulder.

"I'm sorry," he whispered.

I thought I was losing my mind. Looking into Victor's eyes brought back memories, very good moments we shared together. I did not see the bad guy who hurt me two years ago. I saw my love.

I told him it was nice seeing him again. As I walked past him leaving the tight area we were standing in, we brushed against each other.

"Excuse me," we both said to one another, looking into each other's eyes. This was crazy. Next thing I know, we kissed. I got weak in the knees, and my heart skipped a beat.

"No!" I shouted.

"What's wrong? Was it something I've done?" asked Victor stepping away from me.

"You, me. We can't do this."

"Why not give love another try? I miss you like crazy, Leah."

I began crying. My heart was racing and my head began to spin. I needed air.

"You hurt me. Betrayed me. And you lied. I cannot do this again. I refuse too," I said walking away.

Victor ran after me.

"Leah, please stop," he shouted.

Susann came running over where I was.

"Are you okay? What's wrong?" asked Susann.

I walked away from her. I was not in the mood to explain past experiences about someone I once loved.

"Leave her alone," Susann shouted at Victor.

He stopped. Stood there watching me walk away. Before he walked away forever, we made one last eye contact. I could see it in his eyes he was hurting inside. The hurt had been there for a while. I was not sure what my present and past visions meant. When all I could see was his face when I was making love to Tray. What did it mean?

When I got to the car, I sat inside thinking about Victor. Until Susann walked up and got inside to comfort me. It instantly took my mind off Victor.

"Damn!" I shouted.

"What is it, Leah?"

"Why did I have to see him?"

"I wasn't going to ask. But who is he anyway?"

"He's one of my ex-boyfriends from the past. The Sammy Dresser days," I said trying to strengthen my character. "He betrayed me, along with my mother," I explained.

Susann was amazed by the story I told her about my past. I had never shared my past events with any of them. I felt I could trust her enough to tell her.

Her advice was to never take Victor back. No matter what, I felt he deserved the chance to be forgiven. As I forgave my mother, I must forgive him.

After we talked, we met up with the rest of the team. Wednesdays were our hangout day.

"Are you okay, Leah?" asked Susann. I had to pull myself together.

"I'm fine, Susann; now let's go eat," I said smiling at her.

I stayed behind and assured her I would be inside, but she waited for me at the front door.

I got out and went inside with Susann to eat.

"Sorry, we're late. We were shopping," I told the guys taking a seat.

"What all did you get, Susann?" asked Jerry.

"A surprise gift for Leah," she replied.

"I want to see. Can I?" asked Penny. "Sure. Soon after Leah sees it first."

I was still thinking about Victor. I did not understand why he was on my mind now. For the past two years, I thought I would have been over him by now. I grabbed my cell phone and went through my contact list and Victor's picture displayed across my screen. I wanted to press call, but something told me to look too my right.

"Susann!" I shouted hiding my phone.

She was looking at my phone and saw Victor's picture.

"I'm sorry. But remember what I told you."

I was sick on the stomach all of a sudden. I needed some type of medication. I had to migrate.

"Hey guys, I got to go. I'll see you all later," I said excusing myself from the table.

I left.

On my way home, all I could think about was Victor. I tried so hard to take my attention off of him and focus on something else. However, his face would not leave my thoughts.

I reached for my phone and dialed his number. I figured we had to talk.

When I called, the answering machine came on saying the number was no longer in service. I ended the call and dialed 411. I needed to locate him. And in no time, the operator was able to gather his current information. The operator forward me to an automatic dialing system.

I waited patiently for him to answer. Nervous and afraid, I felt much relief when the call went to his voice mail.

I left a brief message.

"Hey, Victor, this is Leah. I was calling you to ask if we can talk. Why, I am not sure. However, something inside of me needs to make something clear to you. When you get this message, please give me a call. My number is still the same. Okay, bye."

Soon as I hung up the phone, Henry called me. He asked me if I wanted to do a case for his department. The case takes place in San Francisco. I was not sure if I wanted to work with the San Francisco Police Department.

The department was sending me false statements about cases. Everyone there thought highly of Paul and became angry with me when they found out I was the one who arrested him. Mostly the men that were there; the women hated his guts and wanted him locked away.

Henry told me an old white woman in her late fifties dropped off information dealing with her daughter's husband. The letter contained information about her daughter's husband cheating on her and abusing their six-year-old son. Sounded like an easy case to handle. I told Henry to let my assistant Penny have the case. It would be her first case with my company.

All my cases were easy to solve, but my most difficult and personal case to date was taking down Sammy Dresser.

I drove to West Avenue and watched hookers and drug dealers do their thing. Before I went home, I stopped by an old friend's house; Loretta.

I needed information on a Latoya Pickler. Latoya was known in the streets as a hood rat, drug-dealing prostitute. She was no half-stepping hoe. Word around town was that she murdered every man she slept with. It was out of my league, but a case I had to pick up. My only concern was that San Francisco Police Department had the case. That is what I hated most about this case. Every time something happened in California. San Francisco

Police Department gets first lead. I needed resources.

When I arrived outside Loretta's crib, which was nice and fenced in, I got out, walked to the front door, and knocked.

Her car was parked outside. Therefore, I knew she was home. I looked out for Loretta soon as I got my business together. I still did not trust her, but I did want the best for her. After multiple attempts, I gave up and walked off the porch.

"Hey you!" a guy shouted standing in Loretta's front door.

"Is Loretta here?" I asked.

"Who are you? What do you want?" he asked.

I told him a home girl from around the way. He asked me to come inside. When I reached the top step, I realized he was butt ass naked.

"Please. Don't mind me," he replied smiling.

I got a little sick on the stomach. The same felling I felt back at the restaurant. I hurried and walked past him.

"Where is she?" I asked.

He pointed towards her bedroom. I walked to the back and opened her bedroom door.

"Leah, get out!" she screamed.

"Oh my goodness," I said slamming the door behind me.

I could not believe what I just witness. Loretta was on drugs. She was inside her bedroom shooting up. That scared the shit out of me. She shouted from the room for me to meet her out front. I hurried and exited the house.

I stood on her front steps, watching the cars drive by. Then, I noticed a BMW driving by very slow. The windows came down and a female looked at me and smiled, throwing up the peace sign. I nodded my head keeping a straight face.

When Loretta finally stepped outside, I asked her to take a ride with me.

"So how long, Loretta," I asked shaking my head. She turns and looks at me.

"Not long. I have control over my habits, Leah. I can stop when I want to," she explained.

I got straight to business. I asked her about Latoya Pickler. She told me very little about Pickler. She only knew her for tricking and dating college football players. Finding her location would be totally left up to me to find out.

After talking to Loretta about Latoya Pickler, I tried convincing her to seek help. However, like all junkies, she was in denial.

I dropped her off at home and went home myself. I was ready to take my ass to sleep. I was tired from stressing useless thoughts about Victor.

Before I hit the street I lived on, I could see flashing police lights all over the place. It looked as if they were at my house. However, I knew better than to think that. I sped and parked behind a patrol car. I got out and ran two houses down from mine. Officers told me a man was killed, along with his wife. Something was not right about this situation. The couple was shot at their home. It really bothered me, had me unfocused. This shit was happening in my neighborhood.

THIRTY-FOUR

New Case

I told officers I would handle this case. I could not believe this happened in my neighborhood. I had to find the underlying cause of this.

I walked over and viewed the bodies. The wife lay on her back with three bullets in the forehead. The sun was still out, and no one saw anything. My neighborhood was full of nosey people. I figured someone saw or heard something.

I grabbed a pair of gloves and searched the wife's purse. There was no money inside. The funny thing is that it was stolen. Because before they arrived home, she stopped by a store and purchased something and the receipt showed that she received a large amount of change in return. A hundred dollar bill to be exact. I immediately called my crew to the crime scene.

As I waited, I went inside and looked around their home. An officer told me the body of the husband was upstairs in the couple's bedroom. The Norson family; they were new to the neighborhood. I had never seen them before. I worked 24/7. I barely see any of my neighbors.

I noticed as I was walking around a pair of bloody shoe prints were left on the carpet. I bent down to check them out. The hair on my neck stood up.

"Heels," I whispered to myself. The killer was a woman indeed. "Oh my goodness," I shouted.

Mr. Norson laid off the end of his bed with his penis inside of his mouth. I vomited all over the floor. It was a sick sight to see.

A strong odor lingered the room that made my stomach bubble. I placed my hand over my noise and mouth. Enough to stop that awful smell from entering my nose. I looked around and noticed more heel prints all over the room.

I looked up and saw this crazy writing on the wall of bathroom mirror. The writing read, "All men are mine. I get what I want when I want without problems. If anyone get in my way, I'll kill them." Signed L.P.

That made my head spin. Penny and Susann came running into the room.

"Hey Lt., what's going on?" Penny asked.

"I'm going to need you to type up a case number for this case. Susann take pictures of every detail that may lead to clues. Get all you can and have it on my desk by tomorrow morning."

"Sure thing boss," Susann replied.

I needed background checks on both victims. I wanted to know why anyone would want the Norson's dead. My gut gave me an idea who might've been behind the killings.

Latoya Pickler came to mind. L.P had to stand for her initials. Who else could it be?

In addition, she is the only one around here killing men. I had another fucked up case on my hands. All I needed was a good ole Newport and a shot of gin. I would be good to go.

I went downstairs to speak with police officers. I had to get those bodies inside my lab. After the bodies were exam they were brought to my office. There Henry would do his investigation.

So many questions were asked, and I did not have any answers just yet.

Soon as I got home, my phone constantly rang. I could not rest, think, or do anything. Around 5:12 I went to the gym to release a little stress. I was weighing 165 pounds. I gained a lot in the past two years.

I worked out until it became pitch dark outside. I stood and watched the city live its life. I could only imagine what was going on in the world that night. After I finished, I went and took a shower inside the gym.

My phone rang as I walk out of the building. An unknown number popped up across my screen. I was not going to answer, but I did anyways.

"Hey, Leah."

It was Victor. His call caught me by surprise. I did not think he was going to call back.

"Victor. Glad you called me back. So what's up?" I asked.

"Shit, chilling. What's wrong now Leah?"

He thought I was playing games with him. I told him to meet me at Jack-in-the-Box.

I arrived at 8:15.

I got out and walked over where he sat and gave him a friendly hug. "Hey, I want to start off by saying I'm so fucking sorry, Leah. I never meant to hurt you. I promise I will never do it again. Also I'm sorry to hear about what happened to your mother," he said dropping his head.

I told him it was okay. I felt my mother went out in style. She died for her child.

We walked over to the window and ordered a plate to eat. We talked about old times we spent together. It was memories I would never forget. Victor told me he had changed his life. In addition, wanted a family.

I felt the same way, but also felt it would not be worth the try. Could I love Victor Thomas once more?

"So, what's next, Leah?"

"I don't know. I have a new case to solve. My business is doing great. What more can I ask for?" I said cracking a smile.

"What about love -- do you have that?" he asked.

Before I could answer him, my pager went off. I had a 911 call in Beverly Hills 90210. I called Corey and Susann, who were already at the crime scene.

Two successful and wealthy men were reported dead. Both married with children.

Susann told me the same prints from the Norson murders were there also. The prints matched up with the same pair of high heels.

I had to end my meeting with Victor and get back to work. We had a mad woman on the loose who needed to be tamed or killed. And I was going to do one or the other.

This criminal was after three things: sex, money, and publicity.

When I arrived, patrol cars were everywhere. Neighbors outside their residence wondering what was going on. Parents feared for their family's safety. Nothing like this ever took place in a safe and wealthy suburb area like Beverly Hills.

Both murders took place across the street from each other. I went to the first house and when I walked inside words were all over the walls. The same message left at the last crime scene. Signed "L.P". I knew it was the same killer and she wanted attention. This bitch was raged with issues. I had to stop her and her actions.

Someway, somehow, I had to figure out how I was going to do so. Everyone depended on Leah Starr to get the job done.

This was where my hunt for Latoya Pickler began. A very enraged story about one woman getting what she wanted, when she wanted it; but paying a painful price getting it.

You know me, Leah Starr. I'll do you bad, and this bitch just crossed the wrong line...

To be continued...

About the Author

"IAmBoSsWRiTeR"

"Apart from my self, BoSsWRiTeR brings a darker side to my imagination. Allowing me to think beyond reality and open my mind to create laughter, pain, happiness, and heartache through the hearts and minds of my characters. They're real and speak to my inner thoughts. Allowing me bring them alive in stories such as Leah Starr's Revenge."

~ BoSsWRiTeR

In the year of 2012, BoSsWRiTeR will release his 1st book, a novel that's a detective suspense about a young woman seeking revenge on the killers of her parents' death. Giving readers not only her story, but deeper feelings relating to ambitions, trust, love and betrayal.

Leah Starr's Revenge will have you wanting more of BoSsWRiTeR's edgy ego of story telling. Along with the extreme determination his characters bring forth to readers, will have you thinking they really exist. His experiences in storytelling have proven his title and image as the one and only, BoSsWRiTeR.

For more information about BoSsWRiTeR please visit:
www.MonticeHarmon.com or www.Facebook.com/BoSsWRiTeR

If you enjoyed Leah Starr's Revenge please leave a review at these online retailers:

Amazon.com
BN.com
KoboBooks.com
Apple iBookstore (iPad)
Reader Store (Sony Reader)
Plus Many More...

BossWriterPublishing

"Writing To Make A Difference For Better Understanding"

850-320-7981

@IAmBossWriter
@BossWriterBooks
@MonticeHarmon

~

MonticeHarmon.com
BossWriterPublishing@gmail.com
www.BossWriterPublishingCo.com

~IAmBoSsWRiTeR~

Upcoming Titles From BoSsWRiTeR:

The Kings & Queens of New York
June 2013

The Victoria Kardase Story: The Rise & Fall of a Hollywood Diva.
November 2013

For updates on official release dates and more titles, please visit:
MonticeHarmon.com

www.ingramcontent.com/pod-product-compliance
Lightning Source LLC
Chambersburg PA
CBHW020653030726
47498CB00002B/492